PRAISE FOR ANDREW MAYNE

THE GIRL BENEATH THE SEA

"Distinctive characters and a genuinely thrilling finale . . . Readers will look forward to Sloan's further adventures."

—*Publishers Weekly*

"Mayne writes with a clipped narrative style that gives the story rapid-fire propulsion, and he populates the narrative with a rogue's gallery of engaging characters . . . [A] winning new series with a complicated female protagonist that combines police procedural with adventure story and mixes the styles of Lee Child and Clive Cussler."

—*Library Journal*

"Sloan McPherson is a great, gutsy, and resourceful character."

—*Authorlink*

"Sloan McPherson is one heck of a woman . . . *The Girl Beneath the Sea* is an action-packed mystery that takes you all over Florida in search of answers."

—*Long and Short Reviews*

"The female lead is a resourceful, powerful woman and we're already looking forward to hearing more about her in the future Underwater Investigation Unit novels."

—*Yahoo!*

"*The Girl Beneath the Sea* continuously dives deeper and deeper until you no longer know whom Sloan can trust. This is a terrific entry in a new and unique series."

—*Criminal Element*

THE NATURALIST

"[A] smoothly written suspense novel from Thriller Award finalist Mayne . . . The action builds to [an] . . . exciting confrontation between Cray and his foe, and scientific detail lends verisimilitude."

—*Publishers Weekly*

"With a strong sense of place and palpable suspense that builds to a violent confrontation and resolution, Mayne's (*Angel Killer*) series debut will satisfy devotees of outdoors mysteries and intriguing characters."

—*Library Journal*

"*The Naturalist* is a suspenseful, tense, and wholly entertaining story . . . Compliments to Andrew Mayne for the brilliant first entry in a fascinating new series."

—New York Journal of Books

"An engrossing mix of science, speculation, and suspense, *The Naturalist* will suck you in."

—*Omnivoracious*

"A tour de force of a thriller."

—Gumshoe Review

"Mayne is a natural storyteller, and once you start this one, you may find yourself staying up late to finish it . . . It employs everything that makes good thrillers really good . . . The creep factor is high, and the killer, once revealed, will make your skin crawl."

—Criminal Element

"If you enjoy the TV channel Investigation Discovery or shows like *Forensic Files*, then Andrew Mayne's *The Naturalist* is the perfect read for you!"

—*The Suspense Is Thrilling Me*

MASTER MIND

Other Fiction Titles

Station Breaker
Orbital
Public Enemy Zero
Hollywood Pharaohs
Knight School
The Grendel's Shadow

Nonfiction

The Cure for Writer's Block
How to Write a Novella in 24 Hours

MASTER MIND

A THEO CRAY AND
JESSICA BLACKWOOD THRILLER

ANDREW MAYNE

Published by Thomas & Mercer, Seattle

www.apub.com

Amazon, the Amazon logo, and Thomas & Mercer are trademarks of Amazon.com, Inc., or its affiliates.

ISBN-13: 9781542020398
ISBN-10: 1542020395

Cover design by Shasti O'Leary Soudant

Printed in the United States of America

MASTER MIND

CHAPTER ONE
THE VOID

Kelsi the silver robot girl pushed her bicycle up the Brooklyn Bridge with her back to Manhattan. It had been a rough night. The tourists in Times Square were rowdier than usual as she'd stood on her box and performed her robot-ballerina routine, balancing on her toes and moving from one precise position to the next.

Lots of people stopped to ask for a photo; none of them tipped. They treated her like a public service, posing in front of her for their Instagram stories about their amazing trip to New York. Even the pigeons made out better than she did.

At one point a man asked for a selfie and put his hand on her ass. Enough was enough and she decided to head home, the silver makeup streaking across her face as the tears began to fall.

At the middle of the bridge, a trio of teenage girls stopped her and asked if she'd take their photo.

She wanted to bark at them, but she remembered her first trip to New York and decided to do as they asked and then go home.

The girls stood arm in arm with the city in back of them and giggled as they tried to get the right pose. Kelsi aimed the phone she'd been handed and tapped the screen to maximize the contrast so the girls and the skyline would be visible.

In the distance she heard a popping sound like a firework, followed by another and another.

Suddenly the city vanished from behind the girls on the screen, and then the phone itself went dark. As she lowered the dead phone and stared into the distance, the lights of Wall Street and all the rest of Manhattan blinked out of existence.

There was another rumble, and all the lights on the bridge went out. Then the cars stopped moving and their headlights went dead.

The teenagers were amused, then nervous. They turned around to look at the city, but it was gone.

In its place was a billowing darkness that Kelsi and millions of others were staring into, unable to comprehend what had just happened.

PART ONE

MAGICIAN

PART ONE

CHAPTER TWO

Alpha

Cortland Alva is a six-foot-five former Wyoming state trooper and current FBI academy student who is standing in front of me, extremely pissed. I saw this coming two days ago when I singled him out for a demonstration during my portion of the course that I co-instruct on survival tactics. What he doesn't realize is that he's about to help me with the second part of the lesson while the rest of the students watch.

My goal as an instructor is to help the one agent out of a thousand who may actually find themselves in a life-and-death situation. Most of my students will never even draw their guns in the line of duty. They'll never have to make a split-second decision on whether to take a life to save their own. They won't have the nightmares. They won't have the guilt of wondering, *What if I handled things differently?* They won't have the panic attacks that come from thinking that if they hadn't acted at the right moment, they wouldn't be around to contemplate their stress. Those are the lucky ones. My job is to make sure they never need to rely on luck, because eventually luck runs out. So, I have to illustrate a point for my students. Sometimes that means bruising the ego of a man twice my size who almost became a pro wrestler. Feelings heal with time. Not all scars do.

I picked on Cortland precisely because he was the largest target. He has the bearing of a person who's never lost a fight. He probably hasn't been in many because people give him a wide berth.

There are stories about Cortland disarming suspects without having to draw his gun. He once punched an armed suspect so hard they smashed a plate-glass window with the back of their skull. The FBI hired him because he had been justified in every case. He could have shot the guy he punched through a window. The man isn't a bully, otherwise he wouldn't be here. But he is overconfident. And other students looking at a man like Cortland might take the wrong lesson from him: that size matters. This can lead to self-doubt, which can lead to fatal mistakes.

I asked Cortland to come to the front of the small auditorium and had him stand in front of me. What I did to him was a magic trick disguised as an awareness exercise. I told him it was the slap game, where we try to anticipate when one player is about to slap the back of the other player's hands.

Moments before, I'd finished explaining that you should never let your suspect determine the rules of engagement. They'll never write them in your favor.

As Cortland stood before me, I reached out and pulled him closer by grabbing his wrists. He didn't see the handcuffs. Nobody did. They were up my sleeve until the moment I put them on his wrists. Like I said, it was a magic trick. But to Cortland and the students watching, it was a miracle.

The powerful man stood there, looking down at his wrists as a woman almost a foot shorter than him and half his weight rendered him incapacitated, or at least restricted enough that I could do more harm to him than he to me. It was a humiliating experience. And like every other time I've done that demonstration, I knew the real lesson would happen when he challenged me to do it again.

"Instructor Blackwood," Cortland, now uncuffed, says in a polite yet irritated voice. "I don't suppose you can try that handcuff trick on me again?" He's standing opposite the table from me and from his vantage can see over the top of my open briefcase.

I'm packing up my notes, seemingly caught off guard. In truth, I'm never off guard anymore. I sleep with a loaded gun under my pillow and a shotgun under my bed. The handcuffs from the demonstration lie in my briefcase, gleaming in the overhead lights. Cortland sees this. Everyone sees this.

If I ask for a moment to get ready, it'll look like a sign of weakness. My previous demonstration will seem like a trick, not a real-world lesson. I need to look as if I've thought of everything.

"I'm sorry?" I say as I move to shut my case.

He nods at the closed briefcase. "Can you try that again on me?"

Cortland has been running through the incident over and over in his mind, trying to figure out how I got the better of him. He finally decided he simply wasn't prepared. He was right.

I lean forward on my closed case. I caught him off guard before and was able to bring his wrists together before he realized it. Now he won't let me do that. He's too strong. I have to get him to do it for me.

"Which thing?" I ask with a lighthearted smile, making myself seem unthreatening.

"The handcuff trick," he says, bringing his hands together to show me.

Perfect.

"Oh." I look to the clock on the wall. "I'm not sure if we . . ."

He relaxes, and his eyes flick to the clock.

His hands drop slightly. *Click.*

"WHAT THE FUCK?" Cortland yells as he looks down at his bound wrists.

Everyone explodes with laughter. Tom Simmons and Ned Antonio, my co-instructors, are standing at the back of the classroom near the door, grinning.

This is the crucial moment, the one I want Cortland to learn from, because in some ways he's the most vulnerable. He lifts his hands and stares at the handcuffs. It isn't shock that he feels this time. It's the reality of life setting in.

All the other students are watching him, waiting to see how he'll react. Is he going to get angry? Will he protest that it wasn't fair?

Cortland appraises his situation. He looks at the steel restraints like they're some ancient scripture. A light goes on. His face relaxes. His anger fades. He smiles.

"You understand the secret?" I ask.

Cortland nods. "Never let your guard down."

"Never," I reply. "And *you* write the rules. Your greatest threats aren't always going to be in front of you. Sometimes they're thousands of miles away, plotting your demise."

He drops his hands to his waist, unconcerned with the handcuffs; he's accepted them now. "The stuff they told us about you—the cartel gun battles, the assassination attempts. I thought they hyped it up to make you into some kind of woke female superhero."

I shake my head. "No. I was dumb and put myself into situations you all should be smart enough to avoid. I'm alive because I won a lottery, not because of tricks like this. They only work when I see what's coming. When I don't, I won't survive."

"Is this why you're not in the field anymore?" asks Rhonda Parry, a petite young woman from Phoenix.

"The bureau decided I was better as a cautionary example than a tragic one."

Tom Simmons jokes that I'm like the shop teacher who's missing a few fingers.

Rhonda is sharp. She studied biology in college, then decided on forensics, but her criminal justice classes made her want to become an FBI agent. She sticks around after class and asks me about cases she's researching and about my own history.

With every class, I get a few cadets like her. They see me as a role model and not the cautionary tale I should be viewed as. I do my best while secretly wanting to tell them to find some boring job and spend their evenings watching Netflix with someone they love and not a stack of folders and a pile of photographs of dead people.

"There have been some more miracle-cure 'angel' cases," she says hesitantly. "I'd like to talk to you about them."

"How about tomorrow?" I reply. "My office?"

"Okay." She gives me a nervous smile.

"Ahem," says Cortland, holding up his manacled wrists.

"Here." I hand him a ballpoint pen.

"What am I supposed to do with that?"

"When I was eight, my grandfather put a pair of handcuffs on me, actually child-size ones, and locked me in a closet with just a pen and a notebook," I explain.

"That's horrible," says one of the other cadets, Denise Elliott.

"No, it was fun. I mean, in my house, this is what we did."

My grandfather was a famous stage magician. I followed in his footsteps until I realized that you have to follow your own dreams—especially when the dream that someone else wants you to follow almost leads to you drowning while performing an escape attempt on live television. It took me a long time to realize that my grandfather didn't have a death wish for me, he just saw me as invulnerable because I was usually several steps ahead.

"Lock children in closets?" she replies.

"Think of it as a tiny escape room? Okay. I was a weird kid."

She shakes her head. "That sounds like child abuse."

"It's why I'm alive today. Anyway, this pen's your key," I tell Cortland. "You and your friend Riley can figure it out. Looking on YouTube isn't cheating."

At the rear of the room, Tom Simmons is trying to get my attention, holding up his phone and pointing to it urgently.

"What's up?" I ask.

"Operations is trying to get hold of you," he replies.

"Me? What?"

"Something weird just happened in New York. They want to talk to you."

CHAPTER THREE
EXPERT OPINION

Before I can pull my phone out, two agents wearing FBI windbreakers brush past Simmons and make their way through the class. My right hand goes to my back under my jacket, ready to grab my gun, while my left clenches the underside of the table, ready to flip it over as protection if this is some kind of attack.

I don't think about doing these things—it's all muscle memory, as indelible as the scars on my body. To everyone around me, I hope I look relaxed, but I can see Rhonda's eyes widen as she reads my face. She spins around and puts her body between me and the two men rushing down the aisle. Her arms go out wide, and she suddenly seems larger.

"What's going on?" she asks in a loud voice.

One of the agents stops to address her, not even questioning why a cadet is challenging him. "We need to escort Agent Blackwood to the airfield. There's a plane taking off in ten minutes. We were given instructions to make sure she's on it."

"It's okay, Rhonda. Let the man pass," I say.

The students part, making room for me to follow the agents. For my class, it must look like something they saw in a movie or a TV show, maybe the one that made them want to join the FBI.

A few years ago, this wasn't all that uncommon an occurrence. I was on a task force that handled unusual cases. Then they became a little too usual. Serial killers using deepfakes, assassination attempts with drones . . . things that used to be weird. Now they're the new normal.

I follow the agents down the aisle. "What do you know?" I ask the man to my right.

"New York City vanished an hour ago."

"Vanished?"

"You'll see the news on the plane. We can't get hold of the NYC field office. Jersey is handling this on their side. They asked us to send anyone we thought should be there. Sheppard asked for you."

"Sheppard? Who's that?"

"Supervisor Sheppard? Crisis Response?" asks the agent, expecting me to know what he's talking about.

"I've never heard of them."

We exit the building and get into an SUV with flashing lights. I hop in the back while the agent I've been talking to takes shotgun and the other gets behind the wheel.

My paranoia has increased. I don't know these agents. I've never heard of this Sheppard. If this is a kidnapping, I made it all too easy for them. I take my pistol from my back holster and rest it in my lap, ready to shoot both of them in the back of the head if my fears somehow are real.

I'd be lying if I said I don't calculate the best head shot in just about any situation I'm in these days. My bureau therapist can't decide if this is a healthy response or a bad one. When you're the FBI's most wanted—as in, the FBI agent with the record of most assassination attempts—conventional advice doesn't always apply.

We drive through the parking lot and onto the road that leads to the marine airfield where the FBI keeps one of its several Gulfstream jets. I keep an eye on the agents, trying to decide what I'm going to do if they don't make the right turn to the airport.

I breathe a silent sigh of relief when we take the road leading to the guard gate. A security officer checks their credentials and waves us through. I slide my gun back in my holster.

The SUV comes to a stop past a hangar where a group of people are standing in a cluster close to a jet. A man in the middle is giving some kind of briefing. I exit and walk toward the crowd.

The man in the middle sees me and calls out over the heads of everyone. "Blackwood?"

"Yes," I reply, looking for familiar faces and not seeing any.

"Sheppard," says the short, gray-haired man who reminds me a little of Dustin Hoffman. "This is Jon Vaslov. He's a physicist working at the academy." He points to a tall man in his late thirties with a receding hairline and a hoodie. "Kari Linman, counterterrorism," he continues, indicating a woman with auburn hair and an expression even more serious than my own. "You can find out everyone else's names later. DC already has a team leaving Dulles. So let's get moving."

Sheppard leads us into the plane. I head for the back, but he calls out to me. "Blackwood, Vaslov, up front."

I take a seat opposite Sheppard's as he sets his laptop and files on the table between us.

How does this man have files if this only happened an hour ago?

"Blackwood. You know weird stuff. What's going on? Is this the Red Chain blackouts all over again?"

Red Chain was a cult that wanted to bring about the end times by starting global panic through blackouts and civil unrest. They came pretty damn close. When I finally found out what they were up to, it was too late to stop the final tragedy from taking place—their own mass suicide in a desert bunker.

While that should have put a stop to them, there were other members who weren't part of the bunker deaths. There was also the question of who had been backing them. At least a question for others. I knew who it was: Michael Heywood, known to the world as the Warlock, a serial killer, cult leader, and hacker who almost killed me after I became his personal obsession.

"I think parts of Red Chain are still active—"

"I know. I've been reading your updates," says Sheppard.

I didn't think anyone was reading them anymore. The rumors were that I blamed Heywood for everything from COVID-19 to the Patriots losing Tom Brady. Which, honestly, are not deeds I'd put past him.

The problem is that Heywood had been in custody most of that time, until he managed to escape during a prison transfer that is still under investigation. Nobody could explain why he was being transferred or who ordered it. There's also the fact that I've been told confidentially that while he was making the FBI run in circles, he was also supplying intelligence to the CIA.

Add to that the fact that Heywood is an alias and nobody has any idea who the hell he is.

The best theory I've heard was a joke from my former coworker Gerald. He once wondered out loud whether Heywood was actually just some Russian-intelligence chaos agent assigned to screw with our heads. While that's doubtful, the man does defy explanation.

"I need to know what's going on in New York," I tell Sheppard.

He types away on his laptop and spins it so I can see the screen. "This is live helicopter footage from the Port Authority."

The camera view shows the Brooklyn Bridge over the East River apparently cut off in midair where it reaches New York City. The helicopter travels north, showing the view of what should be Manhattan. It's just a dark void. A bluish spark lights up part of it, revealing that the void is some kind of cloud.

"What's that?" I ask.

"Discharge," says Vaslov. "Kind of like when the power station at the north end went up back in 2019. But bigger."

There had been a fire at a power station on the island, causing a continuous stream of smoke and sparks that looked like something out of a Marvel movie. This is kind of like that, but bigger.

"No cell coverage?" I ask.

"No," says Sheppard. "No radio, no internet. Nothing."

"What about driving onto the island?" I ask.

"The roads are filled with stopped cars, and all the entry and exit points have some kind of toxic smoke."

"EMP," says Vaslov, suggesting that an electromagnetic pulse disabled all electronics.

"That's the first thing the Jersey field office checked. They've got EMF meters that should pick up anything that powerful," replies Sheppard.

"And?"

"Nothing. Across the river, it's business as usual. This is literally localized to Manhattan, and there's been no sign of an EMP. What else could it be? What's a more exotic explanation?"

"Like a mini black hole," says Vaslov. "We might as well be talking about aliens at that point. It could be some kind of weird atmospheric phenomenon we've never seen before." He thinks for a moment. "At really high altitudes, you can get what are called trolls—huge, dark mushroom-shaped clouds that have massive lightning discharges."

"Could we be looking at one of those?" asks Sheppard.

Vaslov shrugs. "Probably not. They appear at high altitude for a reason."

"Could someone cause one at a lower altitude?" Sheppard is desperate for any answer. "Maybe if they used some kind of inert gas to replicate the oxygen density and had a way to start a plasma discharge . . . I don't know."

I point to the top of a building poking out above the Void. "Well, there's something there. Can we send in a drone for a better look?"

"We have a helicopter waiting for us at the airport. How close do you want to get?" he asks.

"As close as possible," Vaslov answers for me.

I silently question the judgment of taking a chopper too close to what may or may not be an EMP capable of taking down an entire city, but Vaslov is the physicist.

"Okay. I'll get you both on it," says Sheppard.

Well, it's too late to point that out now.

CHAPTER FOUR

FLYOVER

Our Black Hawk helicopter skims across Upper Bay, and the void that is New York City looms before us like a frozen tidal wave of darkness against the luminous blue night sky.

Electrical discharges are visible to the naked eye from here. A thermal camera with a monitor in the passenger compartment shows the outline of the skyline under the mysterious cloud.

"Look there," says Sheppard.

To our left is the Statue of Liberty, still illuminated, looking like a miniature against the massive obsidian backdrop surrounding the city.

"What do we know about what happened before . . . *this*?" I ask over the intercom.

"Not much. There's a dispatch call center in Brooklyn that says right before, they were getting reports of possible car bombs and fires."

Car bombs? Interesting.

"Any reports from the island?" I ask.

"Not yet. We're about to send some people over the bridges on foot with face masks and air tanks. It's so thick there, you can't even make it ten feet. There are also lots of car fires." *Car fires . . .*

We fly closer until the Void looms so high above us that it looks like a mountain range. And yet we're still not even close. The most similar sight I can think of is the plume from a volcano. Last I checked there weren't any active volcanos within thousands of miles of here.

"Vaslov?" asks Sheppard.

"It's like nothing I've ever seen." The physicist is leaning against the window, his mouth open.

"Now you've seen it. Explain it."

"It's like the ash cloud of a volcano," he replies.

Great minds . . .

"There aren't any volcanos here. We also checked with the seismologists," says Sheppard.

"Do they have the data available?" I ask.

"I can get it, but why?"

"We can see if there's anything that matches up with car bombings or whatever."

Sheppard nods, then calls into his microphone, asking for the seismic data. "Anything else?"

"What do satellites show?" asks Vaslov.

"Thermal has buildings. Not much else."

"What about before? Any large light spikes?"

"I can ask. What should we be looking for?"

"Maybe a comet of some kind?" answers the physicist.

"It's not a comet," I reply.

"How do you know?"

"The bridges and the tunnels have the most smoke. I get the tunnels, but why the bridges?" I gesture out the window in their direction. "Look at the smoke on the edge of the bridge. It's not stopping. The wind should have blown that away."

"What are you saying?" asks Sheppard.

"Those car fires are the source of the smoke. Or rather, they're not car fires. Whatever created all this, it's doing it right now on the bridges to keep everything shut down."

"This is a hell of a lot of smoke. Just look at it!" Sheppard exclaims, more from shock than anger at my response.

"Vaslov, how much smoke would one tractor trailer filled with powdered charcoal and whatever else you needed produce?" I ask the resident scientist.

His eyes look up as he does the math. "The energy would be substantial, and assuming the rate of expansion . . . a lot of damn smoke."

"But *this* much smoke?" asks Sheppard.

"Give or take a few dozen tractor trailers . . . yes. Possible. That's the thing about smoke—it's a gas. Well, a gas with solid particles. A little bit of solid goes a long way."

"We're going to go up the East River," says Sheppard after he calls in the request to the pilot.

We go up the waterway with the wall of the Void to our left. The smoke has a slight purple hue to it. Occasionally sparks fly and the shadows of buildings flicker through the haze like cosmic rays.

"How bad is this on the lungs?" I ask.

"We don't know. Hopefully people are indoors," says Sheppard.

"Hopefully there still *are* people," Vaslov adds.

"What do you mean?" Sheppard shoots back.

"What Blackwood said has me thinking. If this is some kind of chemical fire, and if they used an explosion to distribute it into a fine mist, igniting it would be like a massive firebomb. Anyone outdoors would be . . . not in a good place."

"Incinerated?" asks Sheppard.

"No. Maybe those close to it. But they'd be breathing in flaming particles. Which would be bad."

"Take us higher," Sheppard calls to the pilot.

Our helicopter begins to ascend, and the wall of the Void moves past until we can see the night sky above. The tallest skyscrapers poke out from certain spots, their aircraft-warning lights dead.

"We're going to take a closer look," says Sheppard.

"Is that wise?" I ask.

"We'll stay above the mist."

I'm not sure how that's possible, since there are two kinds of mist here. There's the one that's shrouding the city and then a finer, thinner one creating a purple haze around everything near the Void.

The helicopter flies into the thinner mist. Below us, the thicker haze swirls and spreads under the pressure of the helicopter blades.

Our pilot keeps a careful watch on his thermal and infrared monitors, which tell him where the hidden buildings are located.

"Look!" says Vaslov, pointing to the silhouette of a tall building. Along the top edge are the outlines of people waving their arms in the air like shadows on an invisible wall.

We fly closer. Hands frantically gesture for us to land, which isn't possible without a proper helipad. I can even see expressions on faces. Some are frightened, others confused, and more than a few amused. At least we know there are survivors.

Our helicopter continues moving through the canyon of buildings. There are more shadows of people on rooftops. Through a gap between two skyscrapers, I see a bright glow.

"There!" I call out.

The helicopter turns and heads toward the source of light. The mist thins, and we can see an entire block that still has electrical power.

"How is this possible?" asks Sheppard.

"They have their own generator, I'd guess," replies Vaslov. He points to more people. "Look over there."

People are on rooftops, not because the air is better out there, but because they don't want to miss the show.

A thought crosses my mind.

"Sheppard? Can you talk to the news choppers?"

"Yeah, why?"

"Look at all these people watching. If you *did* this, wouldn't you want to see it?"

"Okay . . . ," he replies uncertainly.

"We need to record all the faces of people on either side of Manhattan who are out watching this. Some of those faces will belong to whoever did this. There's no way they'd miss it," I explain.

"Okay. On it."

The interior of the helicopter lights up, and the first thing I notice is the smell of ozone in the cabin.

The second thing I realize is that the engine has stopped.

"Buckle up," says the pilot. "We're about to have a hard landing."

CHAPTER FIVE

CRASH

My great-grandfather, the one who started my family's magic dynasty, which I brought to a close with my application to the FBI, once went over a waterfall in a barrel . . . by accident. He'd been a rival of Houdini and was always looking for a way to outshine the great magician. Eventually his interest in magic faded and he took up farming, only to have his son, my grandfather, answer the siren call of show business and revive the family name—and then for me to leave it in the past.

As Grandfather explains it, Great-Grandfather Henry Blackstar thought it would be a marvelous idea to fake going over the less treacherous of the falls at Niagara and present it as an escape. He'd be locked and shackled—as was our family habit—welded into a barrel, and pushed into the river, only to reappear at the bottom on dry land in approximately the amount of time it would take him to crawl from his hiding location under the platform where the barrel was to be sealed, run down the steps in a fake mustache, and reappear in the crowd below.

What he didn't account for was that the newfangled electric welder he was using because the Sparco-Weld company was sponsoring him would also cause the metal lining of the barrel bottom's trapdoor to weld shut when the electrical current passed through the lid. (Years later, this was one of the reasons his son, my grandfather, made it a point to study physics and chemistry in his spare time.) When the barrel was hoisted by the crane and dropped into the water, poor Henry was still inside.

Moments later, his barrel was swept over the falls; as it bounced off the rocks at the bottom, the trapdoor finally dislodged, allowing him to swim free.

Henry, as poor a planner as he was, did have a knack for opportunity.

He surfaced near the *Maid of the Mist*, the sightseeing boat that takes tourists close enough to the falls to get soaked. This time, the passengers were there to watch my fool great-grandfather attempt an escape. Which is why they were all gathered on the falls side of the boat and didn't see him pull himself up on the other side, probably dazed and confused but acting on his show-business instincts.

He made his way to the upper deck, found the captain's long coat and hat, and slipped them on. He then made his way to the top of the pilot house and fired off a flare he'd stolen.

All eyes turned to Henry Blackstar—fully clothed and dry, standing above the hundreds of people who'd come to watch him die.

It was a great moment of magical theater. A newspaper photo of him hangs on the wall of the salon in the family mansion in Los Angeles to this day.

As Grandfather said, "It would have been a career maker, world headlines, if Dad hadn't chosen the same day that Archduke Ferdinand decided to get assassinated and start World War I."

When I asked Grandfather how Henry managed not to die, he said it was one of the rare times that his father—who hated to talk about the business, lest it give his farmer son any ideas—actually explained something to him. Henry said, "I kissed my balls goodbye and pretended I was drunk, because alcoholics seem to survive everything."

While the first part of that advice isn't terribly helpful in my current situation, the second part is. Prepare for impact, but don't tense up so much you break your own arm or neck.

I loosen up and prepare for a hard landing when I notice Vaslov doesn't have his restraints fastened.

"Vaslov!" I yell, grabbing his harness buckles and clicking them together.

The startled scientist looks down and realizes what I'm trying to do. "Sorry—" *Bang.*

Crunch.

My spine feels like it was just used as a pogo stick. Sheppard's slumped over. He snaps his head up, no longer dazed.

Vaslov is muttering, "Oh my god. Oh my god."

"Everybody out! Watch the rotor!" says the pilot.

His copilot has our door open and is directing us away from the helicopter's rear rotor. We unbuckle and follow the pilot toward the other side of the street. It's pitch-black. The only illumination is from the cockpit's emergency lights.

"Everyone okay?" asks the pilot, doing a visual inspection of each of us.

"I think I pissed myself," says Vaslov.

"Perfectly natural," says the pilot. "I did that my first two times."

I'm not sure if the FBI hiring a helicopter pilot who has crashed more than once is any smarter than hiring a woman like me to teach survival skills. On second thought, we're alive. *Great choice.*

He opens up a pocket and pulls out several surgical masks and hands them to us. "This will help you with the smoke. Sometimes I have to fly close to burning things. Hinder, can you take our passengers toward the lit-up section while I keep eyes on our bird?"

"You got it. This way, folks," says the copilot, using a flashlight to point a path through the mist.

"I can take over from here," says Sheppard. He takes two steps, then mutters, "What am I saying? I have no idea where we are. Hinder, back to you."

"Two blocks right, three blocks north," I say out loud.

"*Somebody* was paying attention," Hinder says over her shoulder.

She starts jogging into the mist, and we follow close behind. We don't know what's going on here, but staying in one place is not a good idea. There won't be any help coming, and we're not sure if we want to run into anyone who *wants* to be out on the streets right now.

We keep up with her pace, weaving past hundreds of stalled cars. When her flashlight hits buildings, we see faces looking out from behind glass, watching us, waiting for an explanation. We don't stop, because we don't have one.

We finally reach a block where some of the lights are still on. All the buildings have their security shutters rolled down. Probably to avoid looting or panicked mobs drawn to the light.

Hinder knocks the butt of her flashlight against one of the shuttered doors. "FBI. We need access to your roof!" she shouts.

Nobody answers.

We try two more doors. Nothing.

I can't blame whoever's inside. I wouldn't open up. Anybody can claim they're with the FBI.

"Let me try this," I say as we reach the next security gate. I kneel down and pick the lock with the kit I always have on me. It unlocks, and I raise the gate so everyone can enter the foyer.

I shut the gate, securing it again, and then pick the door locks and let us inside. There's an empty security desk in the lighted lobby. I walk around it and press the button for elevator access.

It arrives quickly and seems to be as functional as the building's lighting.

Two minutes later, we're looking out from the top of the building at the black sea of mist below us. Helicopters fly in the distance. Hinder pulls out a blue flare and sends it into the sky, letting them know we're downed first responders.

At the far end of the Void, I can see other buildings with their lights on. They're like islands in a sea of electric ink. Why weren't they taken out by the pulse?

"What brought us down?" Sheppard finally asks.

"Electrical failure," says Hinder.

"Like an EMP?"

"I don't know."

Vaslov is staring at something as wind brings wisps of mist toward us. He reaches out and grabs into the air. His hand pulls back something, but it looks empty.

I get a closer glance and can see it's not nothing. He's caught a fine tendril of something. Like a . . .

"Black spiderweb," says Vaslov, finishing my thought.

He pulls a plastic bag from a pocket and slides the strand inside.

My nose twitches as I realize I've been smelling something since we crashed.

"What is that? Ozone?" I ask.

"Some kind of discharge. I've smelled it before," he replies. "I just can't place it."

"What have you got?" inquires Sheppard.

Vaslov shows him the bag. "This. The mist is full of it."

"What is it?"

"I don't know. But this was no truck filled with charcoal."

I don't comment. That was never my theory.

"Could it be a weapon of some kind?" asks Sheppard.

"Look around you," I say. "How is something that can do this to an entire city not a weapon?"

CHAPTER SIX
TASK FORCE

I'm lying on the floor of a conference room in the FBI's Newark, New Jersey, office, staring up at the ceiling tiles, trying to make patterns out of the random dots. I think I've had a total of two hours of sleep. Some of us have had none.

A younger me would have stayed up and bothered anyone who knew anything for more details. The older me realizes that a lot of my mistakes were made because I didn't stop and let my body and brain recover.

Some of the Quantico crew flew back on the jet. I decided to stay behind because I wanted to try to catch the briefing that's set to happen in ten minutes two floors down from here. That's where whoever the director put in charge will try to explain what's going on after reading through everyone's reports, following up with phone calls, and figuring out how to do their best impression of someone who has a clue.

Robert Ailes, the man who pulled me from a desk job and into his special unit, tried to talk me into taking a supervisory role after sending me out into the field started to feel like Russian roulette. I didn't have what it takes for management, however. I like people well enough, but not all of them at once. And I totally didn't have the bullshit factor it takes to be a boss and convince a room full of people that you're less clueless than they are.

There's a knock on the door. "Blackwood?" asks Sheppard.

"I'm changing," I reply.

"Oh, sorry."

"I'm kidding," I say as I get up. "I didn't exactly bring a change of clothes. Come in."

Actually, I keep underwear and a T-shirt in my bag, but that's not what I'd call a proper change.

Sheppard enters with two cups of coffee. "It's black. That okay?"

"I'd take crude oil at this point," I reply, accepting the cup from him. "How are you doing?"

I can see the bags under his eyes. It's one of the signs I notice in men as they age: you can tell how much sleep they've had by looking at their eyes.

"Okay. The mist is a lot clearer. They've got the power back up in some places. But a lot of the grid is fried."

"Casualties?" I ask.

"Still figuring that out. Probably in the hundreds, assuming that smoke doesn't cause issues later on."

"Let's hope not," I say as he holds the door open for me and we head to the elevator. "How's Vaslov?"

"I don't think he's fully gotten over the helicopter crash. I don't think I have, either," he says, staring into space.

"Oh yeah. It's a stunner."

"You were in a plane crash, right?"

"A small one. I caused it."

He looks at me in disbelief. "How do you deal with this? We were in a helicopter crash a few hours ago. You . . . Don't you even think about it afterward?"

"Um, no. Not until now."

We make our way downstairs to the conference room.

"How is that kind of recovery even possible?" he asks.

"My therapist says it's a symptom of unresolved PTSD. I think it's because I know I can't think too much about the disaster that just happened because there's always a new one waiting for me."

We take seats in the back as the chiefs up front talk among themselves and go over notes. One of them has his back to us. He seems to be the one they're all coordinating with. *Poor bastard.*

I see him tilt his head to listen closely and recognize the gesture as one I've seen a thousand times in the bullpen.

Gerald?

I knew he'd been reassigned to headquarters and was managing some internal task force, but other than pleasantries on birthdays, we haven't kept in touch. I sent a present when he and Candice had their little girl, but I didn't pay much attention after that.

"Did you work with him?" asks Sheppard. "One of Ailes's other misfits?"

"Yeah. Ailes recruited him, actually. Gerald was about to take a job at Google. Ailes convinced him to take a huge pay cut and have bullets fired in his direction." I shrug.

"Is he any good as a cop?"

"Gerald? You won't find anyone better. Also, he's one of the smartest people you'll ever meet."

Managing people, my blind spot, was never a weakness for Gerald. He's one of the only true multitaskers I've ever met. He can have a detailed discussion with you while filling out field reports. He taught himself to text without looking at his phone so he wouldn't annoy people while carrying on three conversations.

"Hello, everyone. I'm Gerald Voigt. I've been asked by the director to get this task force going. As you know, last night at approximately 8:00 p.m., Manhattan suffered a massive blackout, disabling virtually the entire electrical grid and destroying almost every phone, computer, and electronics system on the island.

"We're unable to discern at this time what the cause was. Our preliminary guess is a number of chemical EMPs. That's to say, a number of devices that caused an electromagnetic pulse strong enough to short-circuit all local electronics. Until this morning, I'd never heard of a chemical EMP, but it was explained to me that it's a device that uses an explosive charge to apply kinetic energy to a material that then converts into an electrical pulse. Later today, I hope to have a report from the Department of Energy, which has apparently done some research into this area. In any event, this pulse was accompanied by a black mist that shrouded the city for almost twelve hours."

Gerald taps his computer, and an image of an orange traffic barrel appears on the screen behind him. The top is burned off, and soot stains the exterior.

"We've found at least forty of these so far, by last count. We estimate there were several hundred placed around the city. The good news is that one of the thousands of cameras in Manhattan was bound to catch someone placing one. The frustrating news is that because of the EMP, many of the data centers where that information would have been stored have been wiped. However, it's likely that some were backed up before the EMP affected them.

"We believe this is an act of terrorism. Nobody has come forward yet, but given the deliberate, destructive nature of the act, there seems to be no other explanation.

"Because this happened unexpectedly and we have no idea if other cities are going to be targeted, the Department of Justice, at the president's urging, has decided to take an extremely proactive approach." Gerald points to several people in the front row. "We'll be working with the CIA, DIA, and IDR."

"IDR?" I whisper to Sheppard.

"New agency. Information Data Retrieval," he whispers back.

"How come I never heard of them?"

"They were a division of the DIA until a few weeks ago." *The Defense Intelligence Agency?*

"What do they do? Fix your hard drive?"

"Not quite. After COVID-19 knocked us on our ass and somebody realized that maybe you shouldn't trust totalitarian regimes that chronically lie about internal matters to give you honest answers, this idea came up," says Sheppard.

"Okay. But what does that mean?"

"The joke goes that they're a SEAL team with a thumb drive. They go in and get data. The not-so-funny part of the joke is that they have virtual free rein in deciding what they want to retrieve. IDR supposedly has a number of former CIA operatives who did renditions."

"Ah, so they don't have to worry about the same laws that we mortals do."

"Basically."

"That surely won't end up in a *New York Times* exposé five years from now."

"Not if they take the reporter's laptop," sighs Sheppard.

An agent hands me a stapled sheaf of papers as she walks down the aisle.

"I'm just an observer," I tell her.

She looks at a list she's carrying. "You're Agent Blackwood? Jessica Blackwood, right?"

"Yes?"

"You're in here."

Sheppard waits for a moment, then makes an audible sigh as she moves to the next row. "Glad I dodged that one," he says, clearly trying to convince himself that he hasn't been slighted.

I flip through and see a list of names. The column on the left has names of agents; the column on the right, people who I assume are suspects. My name is on the last page.

"Some of you have been given names to follow up on," Gerald tells the room. "These were provided to us by IDR. They'd like up-to-date information on each of them. The ones with asterisks by their names . . . ? Contact IDR immediately if you locate them. Don't engage. Just let IDR know."

There's something about Gerald's voice that tells me he's not too happy about that directive. I have a feeling there may have been some loud words exchanged—first, over the FBI having to turn suspects over to this other agency; second, knowing Gerald, about the quasi-legal nature of what he's been asked to do.

He's part of a new breed of FBI agents that Ailes and others have been trying to promote, hoping to put the politically charged past behind us. Which means for many of Gerald's colleagues and supervisors, he's a by-the-book pain in the ass who won't compromise when it comes to ethics.

I read through the list of names again and immediately see two problems with it.

I realize that Gerald has better things to do than deal with me now, but we need to discuss this list.

CHAPTER SEVEN
SUSPECT ZERO

Gerald is talking to the head of IDR, a broad-shouldered woman in a business suit who has the presence of someone who's spent time in war zones carrying a machine gun. From the way she stands firm, like a concrete barricade, to the way she grabs Gerald's elbow—something you pick up on the battlefield to ensure you're hearing everything your troops tell you—clearly, this woman's an ex-soldier.

"Jessica," says Gerald as I approach. "Please meet Vivian Kieren, the director of IDR."

She firmly shakes my hand. "Blackwood. Pleasure."

She's brief and to the point. Why waste time on sentences when a couple of nouns will do?

Gerald sees the list in my hands. "I see you've got your assignment."

"Yes . . . and I'm a little surprised," I reply, not sure how much I want to say in front of Kieren.

"I had you on a short list before this even came down. It was lucky you were in the area. Well, except for the helicopter. Are you okay?"

"Fine. The pilots did a great job." I'm about to ask why Gerald put me back in the field, but I catch a glance, more of a flicker of his eyes, in Kieren's direction. It could be a tic or a symptom of not enough sleep, but I decide to go with my hunch. "I just wanted to say I'm glad to be aboard with you again."

"Me too," says Gerald, and his posture relaxes. I wasn't imagining it. There's tension here, and I almost said the wrong thing.

"Kieren," I say to the woman with a nod, then return up the aisle to where Sheppard is texting.

"Everything okay?"

"Yeah. You?"

"They're sending some barrels back to the lab at Quantico. Also a truck," he replies. "That could be interesting."

"We'll see."

I take my seat next to him and text my co-instructors, Simmons and Antonio, telling them I need them to cover for me until I'm done with this. Also, to check if Cortland got out of the handcuffs. A regulation handcuff key won't work. You really do have to pick them with the pen.

"Jessica, got a second?" Suddenly, Gerald's standing beside me. "Hey, Sheppard, I'm glad you could bring a team out. Vaslov's been very helpful. And even happier you survived the chopper ride."

"Glad to be here, and thanks." Sheppard sounds like he just got a compliment from the pope.

I can't tell if Gerald is becoming a more commanding presence or if Sheppard feels he's been benched too soon. This kind of task force would be under Sheppard's control if he were really running my old division like Robert Ailes did. God knows what politics are going on behind the scenes.

"See you soon," I say to Sheppard as I stand to follow Gerald wherever he's going next.

"Need me to hold the plane?" asks Sheppard.

"She's got other transportation," says Gerald as he walks ahead of me out of the auditorium and into a small side room. Inside, he takes a chair on the other side of the table and motions for me to sit.

I hold up the papers I've been given.

"What's going on here?"

"I'm sorry about pulling you back into the field. The situation is complicated."

"Not that. I don't know how good I'll be for you, but I don't need to see another lesson plan anytime soon." I raise the list again. "I'm talking about this."

"What about it?"

"Specifically, who's not on it."

"Michael Heywood," says Gerald.

"Yeah, Michael Heywood. Last I checked, he's at large and the reason I almost draw my gun every time there's a new Uber Eats delivery person in my building."

Gerald nods. "I know. I know. We're following that lead, too."

"Really? I didn't hear that back in there."

"Things are complicated right now."

"You already said that. So, maybe make them uncomplicated for me while we're alone?"

"Okay. The FBI has a mole. So does the CIA and just about every other intelligence agency. We've seen evidence that a number of investigations have been compromised by the release of internal information."

"A mole or computer espionage?" I ask.

"Maybe hacking but probably human, too," he replies.

"What does that have to do with this?"

"Everything. We don't think it's a state actor."

"What do you mean?"

"Three months ago, we were about to launch an investigation into New Sun Energy, and the day before we served papers, someone took a massive short on their stock. Twenty minutes before the CIA got approval to launch a strike in the Middle East, we saw a huge move on the markets. All of it going to offshore accounts and leading to dead-letter offices."

"Someone's using top secret intel to play the market?"

"That's all we know happened. Then the DEA was about to raid Gulzam Coceto's hideout. But he got tipped, and someone walked away a hundred million dollars richer. The point is that in some of these cases, the suspects only had minutes to use the illicit information. You'd need a thousand people listening to hidden microphones or reading emails." Gerald pauses. "Or . . ."

Now I understand why the FBI's leading technical mind has been put in command. "Some kind of artificial intelligence?"

"Exactly. We don't just use code to spy on people—we use it to figure out what we need to know. Someone's doing that to us."

"Okay. But why are you here? Why this case?"

"Because I pushed for it when I read the briefings late last night. They smelled funny. Not only are we being watched, we're being misdirected."

"Ah," I say. "Meaning . . . ?"

"This has Heywood written all over it. It's one of his Batman villain comic-book plots that he probably paid some minor-league anarchist group to pull off."

"So why me?"

"Like I said, he's misdirecting us. Who understands that better than you? While we're chasing down former Antifa members and whatever lowlifes we can dredge from the depths of the internet, Heywood's doing something else. And if he just made New York City appear to vanish into thin air, then what the hell's his *real* plan? That's what has me scared."

"Okay. And the list of people? Just busywork?"

"Not at all. You know how he operates. He recruits broken minds. He manipulates people. He's undoubtedly got conspirators. Some of them may be on the list. A number of people on it are on internal watch lists, in any case. It's not random. In fact, a couple of them scare me almost as much as the Warlock."

I point to a name on the list. "What about this guy? I thought he and the FBI got along great. Most people think of him as a hero."

"Yes. And some people think he's a little too good at what he does, which makes him seem suspicious. Let me ask you this: Does anyone really know what goes on in the mind of a man like Dr. Theo Cray?"

PART TWO
SCIENTIST

CHAPTER EIGHT
ROGUE PLANET

When I lay in the jungle, bleeding out my side, watching the stars through a tiny break in the canopy, Johnny long gone and my attacker slumped over me, dead, his blood warm on my skin, I thought about the planets drifting between solar systems—rogues that escaped their own stars to wander the cosmos. Mostly they pass by, causing only the mildest of disruptions to debris at the edge of each system's heliosphere, but sometimes a rogue is captured by a star's gravity and it spirals inward, building up velocity until it gets pulled into an orbit and either escapes or collides with some other world, causing havoc and destruction. That would be an astronomically rare event, but in a galaxy with billions of rogues, astronomically rare events happen every day. There could be some rogue planet drifting in our direction right now. The earth and the moon exist because two heavenly bodies in our own solar system collided. Who's to say the next civilization doesn't get its start at the end of our own?

As a centipede crawled across my face, I wondered whether that next civilization would resemble anything like humanity.

Could something like *me* happen again? Would another village like Bo Luc have to deal with the wrath brought upon them when someone such as myself interfered?

Was I an agent for order or a magnet for chaos? The latter seemed more likely, given what damage I'd done both in my personal life and here, ten thousand miles away from home, where a simple and pure gesture on my part ended up causing more bloodshed than I could have imagined.

"Dr. Cray? Are you with me?" asks the woman with the probing eyes sitting in front of me.

"Yes. Always."

"I think you're suffering from a fever," she says.

"I left that in Portland."

Lights spin.

I fall into the dark.

"Shit," she says, keeping me from falling over in my chair. "I need you to hold it together a little while. Okay? We don't have much time before they realize I got you out with fake papers. Drink this."

I gulp down the water from the bottle she hands me. Something tastes off about it. My mouth starts to slacken, and water drips down my chin as I process what's different. My lips close and I swallow as I realize that the water tastes different because it's clean.

Anything I've drunk in the last month that wasn't alcohol-based was filled with bacteria and parasites. Even before they came for our camp, I'd been suffering from a low-grade fever.

I take another sip of the water and try to pull myself together. I'm no longer in the prison cell. I'm outside. Motorcycles and buses run back and forth on the dirty street in front of me as old women on bicycles weave through them. We're sitting under an umbrella near a stand where a man is selling fruit drinks and snack food.

This is the civilized part of Myanmar, not the Rohingya townships where the army has ground everyone under their boot . . . not the remote villages being quietly eliminated while the world looks elsewhere.

I came here to follow up on a promise to a friend. I was with a group that was trying to help vaccinate the Rohingya and other groups the government was trying to kill off. When the soldiers started threatening us, we moved on. When they started killing villagers . . . I started killing the soldiers.

They didn't know who it was at first—even the team I was with had no idea what I was doing when I sneaked out at night and went on my walks.

Only Johnny knew—the thirteen-year-old kid who'd had two older brothers kidnapped by the army. He told me how to find the commanders and the other men behind the atrocities.

Contact poisons, electrocution . . . I even killed a man with his own tire iron as he tried to fix a flat that I caused. I wish I could say I felt remorse, but that emotion could never materialize after I'd heard the cries from the metal shed at the camp where he'd been torturing and indoctrinating the children he'd taken from their families.

I came here to kill parasites. It didn't matter if I didn't need a microscope to kill some of them.

The moral line is clear for me: *If you kill the innocent, prepare to be killed.*

This woman . . . Who is she? And can she be trusted?

She's watching me carefully, but she's also watching the street and studying every face. When someone's head turns, she casually glances to see whether they're looking at us.

She's smart. She knows how to use all the parts of her environment to sense a threat. She doesn't turn around when a motorcycle with a bad muffler drives by, but anything with a large engine that sounds a little more tuned than everything else on the street . . . she pays keen attention to that.

That's how you spot the government vehicles. Bureaucrats and generals are the ones with repair shops and money to keep their fleets running.

"Give me a second," she says, standing up. "I need to check in and then ask for directions."

She walks a few meters from our table to make a call. Her left side is to me, her right to the street. Straight ahead is where we came from, the small prison where they were holding me.

Through the street din, I can make out her words.

"Yes. Everything's good. We're going to wait here a little while until he feels better. Then we're headed to the embassy."

She ends her call and pockets her phone. I watch as she approaches a woman getting onto a rusty bus and asks directions. The woman has her arms full, and my hostess helps her put a suitcase into the compartment below. The local woman thanks her, and the bus heads off in a cloud of dust and exhaust.

She walks back to me. "Are you doing okay?"

"Yes, the water helped."

"Okay. We need to move. Can you walk?"

"I'm good. Just a little dehydrated." I follow her as she walks into a small alley between a stall selling T-shirts and bootleg DVDs and another with barrels filled with brooms.

We walk across plywood covering a trench where sewage filters into a clogged drain. My brain starts calling out all the parasites sloshing around my feet: cholera, listeria, whipworm, *Giardia lamblia*, *Entamoeba coli*, and *Endolimax nana*, to name a few.

"Here," she says, directing me to the passenger seat of a car parked by a pile of rotting boards and broken tiles.

It's an older Toyota with carpet on the dashboard and a small idol dangling from the rearview mirror. In the back seat, there's a crate of Nestlé infant formula.

"That's for you, if you want. Best I could do," she says. "I have some Pedialyte and other stuff back at the hotel."

She planned ahead. She knew what condition I'd be in when she found me.

But *why* did she find me?

"I'm sorry, who are you?" I ask.

"Blackwood. Jessica Blackwood," she replies, her eyes only leaving the road to check the rearview mirror.

Blackwood? I roll the name around in my head until it registers. I've read about her. I think I even watched a TV movie about her. The actress didn't have a fraction of the real woman's presence. The real Jessica Blackwood has a gracile air, not unlike a dancer's, but also the potential for explosive power, like when you watch a ballerina spring into the air impossibly high or balance on her toes in a way that would make a muscular man cry.

Blackwood was the woman who helped bring down Michael Heywood, a.k.a. the Warlock.

She was also involved in stopping a plot against the pope. She was a law enforcement legend, a supercop who hated the limelight and avoided the press. One day she was everywhere, and then her name vanished from headlines.

What I remember most was her snide nickname: the FBI's Witch. Actually, I recall, she came from a family of stage magicians. And from what I've observed, that lineage is not as far behind her as she would let on.

I've watched her lie about three things in front of me. What else is she lying about?

I could grab the door handle and roll out at the next stop, but I have a feeling even in my best condition, she could catch me before I made it a block. She probably has a plan for that.

If I don't cooperate, what's next? Handcuffs? Stuffing me into the trunk?

Does she know how exhausted I am? Does she know there's no point to this charade? There's no need to threaten me; those things don't work on a man who doesn't want to live anymore.

I tried to get my captors to kill me three times back in the prison, but they refused. I even tried to keep my head down in the bucket they wanted to water-torture me with. I breathed in when they expected me to hold my breath. The attending doctor had to pump my lungs while I tried to fight my body's own sense of self-preservation.

"We're almost there," says Blackwood.

Meaning the embassy.

"Great," I reply. "Or you could just ask me what you want to know now, or take me into custody, or shoot me . . . it doesn't really matter."

"Shoot you? That's a little dramatic. I'm not here to kill you, arrest you, *or* take you into custody," she replies.

I nod. "That's the fourth lie you've told me."

CHAPTER NINE
FLOPHOUSE

She doesn't respond to my statement about the four lies. I can't tell if it's because I've trapped her or she doesn't feel the need to answer me. I suspect it's the latter. Watching her check the mirrors with each turn, I consider that she may be on the run, too. Could there be something even more clandestine than a simple rendition going on?

We turn past a soccer field and start up a narrow road lined with shacks and buildings built at odd angles that would be at home in a Dr. Seuss book if they didn't look like they were one heavy rainfall from tragically sliding down the hill.

Blackwood's left hand touches the scarf around her face. It looks like she's trying to adjust it, but I catch her fingertips pushing into her covered ear, as if she's trying to reposition something.

Earpiece . . .

Who or what is she listening to?

She pulls the car onto a small side road and parks at the back of a car-repair shack. "We get out here."

Blackwood is several strides ahead of me, not bothering to check if I'm following. She's got her eyes on the streets and the buildings around us . . . and the skies.

The Myanmar government can be brutal and efficient in a third world kind of way, but they don't have the resources of advanced economies. They use neighborhood spies instead of drones. When they want to get you, they surround you with trucks in every direction and basically fire into the middle, not terribly concerned if stray bullets hit bystanders or even foot soldiers.

I watched a soldier leaning over the body of his dead companion in what I thought was prayer, only to find out he was taking the other man's cash and cigarettes from his pockets. He was back to marching a moment later, laughing with another soldier about how the man took a shot to the head. I felt more sadness for their dead compatriot than they did. I try not to hate them for that—most are children, and life's as cheap as a video game to kids here.

Blackwood weaves through a back alley and takes me through a gap in a fence, clearly knowing the spot in advance.

"Been here before?" I ask.

"Only on Google Maps," she replies. "Just up this road here."

We go through another fence and get buzzed into a courtyard. A grandmotherly woman with a small child clinging to her neck greets us. Blackwood nods to the woman, then leads me up a staircase to the next level.

The building is surrounded by large padauk trees. The windows are open, with clothes and towels hanging over the edges. Floor mats just outside the doors hold hiking boots and sneakers.

If I had to guess by the footwear, this is a hotel that caters to Westerners. It's a dive by any standards but not crawling with sex workers and drug dealers, like you find in other tourist locations—which, generally speaking, are two of the few reasons someone comes to a hellhole like this place.

Blackwood opens the door to a room and motions for me to step inside. The windows are cracked open slightly, but it's barely any cooler in here than outside. But that doesn't bother me. I stopped worrying about the heat a long time ago.

"I've got clothes for you there," she says, pointing to a bag on the floor mat that serves as a bed. "You can clean up there."

In the corner there's a small privacy screen shielding the toilet and a tiled section where one takes a bath by squatting on a stool and washing with a bucket and hose.

I've got weeks of sweat and grime covering my body. The only clean spots are where they tried to drown me. I kick off my broken sandals, step behind the screen, and take off my shirt and pants, hanging them up.

Something about the sight of the rags lying over the clean, white screen takes me aback.

Rags. I've been wearing rags. The white shirt is stained into some color between tea brown and vomit green. My chinos are so torn that Robinson Crusoe would have been embarrassed to wear them. My underwear is a shred of elastic holding up a loincloth.

Blackwood sits at a table, texting on her phone and not paying attention to my sartorial display.

In truth, it's not the condition of the clothing that has me startled—it's the state of the man underneath. I've watched the effects of my deterioration before, but this is something new, even for me. I reach over to the sink and find a small hand mirror.

Sunken eyes, hollow cheeks, sunburn, and a scraggly beard add up to an image that screams malnutrition. It's not a man looking back at me. It's some kind of zombie that keeps moving, not realizing that its body is already dead and the mind not far behind.

"You okay, Dr. Cray?"

"Theo. Yeah, I'm fine," I lie.

"Let me know if you need any help shaving. I've had practice lately."

I'm too focused on my own condition to ask her what she means. What I do notice is that from the moment she stepped into my cell, never once has she given me a reproachful look. No pinching her nose or rolling down her window. Not one time did she let on what a horrifying sight I've become.

I think I've discovered another one of her misdirections. No matter how matter-of-fact or focused or hard-edged she appears, Jessica Blackwood possesses compassion.

An hour ago I was ready to die and couldn't make myself care for anything in this world. The torture, the interrogations, the grinning police captain who liked to humiliate me as I lay on the floor writhing in pain . . . none of them could break me.

But in twenty minutes, this woman, who may be here to ask me questions and then kill me, has broken me.

For the first time since I watched those stars in the jungle and thought about drifting planets, I care about something.

I want to know what happens next.

CHAPTER TEN
TIME LAPSE

I gulp down a Pedialyte and devour a handful of crackers. After plucking the umpteenth louse from my thin beard, I decided to shave everything off, including my hair. Now the jeans and shirt Blackwood brought for me hang loose over my thin frame, accentuating my starving-prisoner look.

"I brought these," she says, setting vials of different medications on the counter. "I was going to call in a doctor but thought you might want to make your own recommendations."

"Thanks," I reply as I start scanning labels and doing math in my head regarding my body weight. There's also the question of what my liver can handle.

"Where have you been for the last five months?" asks Blackwood.

"Here. Well, Myanmar," I reply.

"The whole time?"

"Yeah. Thereabouts. I think we may have been in parts of Thailand at times. The borders get kind of muddled."

"What were you doing?" she asks.

That's a complicated answer. I don't know how much I care to tell her, let alone remember.

"I came here to vaccinate people."

"I see. Without government approval?" she replies.

"Correct. There had been suspicion that their official vaccination program was using diluted or outdated vaccines on groups that they wanted to . . . minimize. In some cases, military personnel used WHO and UN uniforms to earn their trust."

Blackwood thinks this over for a moment. "So, genocide?"

"I wouldn't say that's the wrong word. This is a more subtle way to do it. They have international organizations looking for trenches with bullet-ridden bodies. If a strain of cholera or COVID takes out twenty percent of the people, it's hard to prove it was intentional."

"Why only that many?" she asks.

"Trust me, if they could get away with more, they would. Part of what they're trying to do is to displace people. If you kill off the elderly and wipe away the very young, people lose their roots and move on."

"Move on to where?" she asks.

"Refugee camps on the border. Anywhere that there's land or resources the government isn't trying to sell to the Chinese or one of the proxies the US works with. But you didn't come here to ask me about the human rights situation in this country."

"The officials here say you're the biggest human rights violator in Myanmar," she replies.

"And yet they let you walk me out of there with just a sheet of paper. That seems pretty amazing . . . or unbelievable."

"There's more to it than that. Can anyone vouch for you being here for the last five months?"

"Nobody who's alive."

Her eyes drift to the crack in the window; she watches a car drive up the path and then make a turn. I now understand why she chose this location on the hill. She can see when anyone is approaching.

"What do you know about Michael Heywood?"

"The Warlock?" I reply. "I studied the case. What was public. Not much."

"What was your takeaway?" she asks.

"I've encountered a lot of personality types. Each one is different, but they all share traits in common. Heywood?" I shake my head. "He's an abhorrent personality among abhorrent personalities."

"Some see him as a kind of leader. They look at him as either a messiah or an instrument for change," she says, watching my reaction.

"Hitler had a pretty big fan club, and women sent Ted Bundy their panties. The self-destructive nature of people doesn't surprise me. Back when I bothered to check my email, I'd get ravings from people who either thought one of the assholes I caught was innocent or I was the culprit in all the killings. There was even a podcast that tried to make that case. The troubling part was that even more people followed my Twitter feed when that theory got popular."

"Did you frame those men?" asks Blackwood. I stare at her, not answering.

"It's a simple question," she says.

"It's not. The answer is, but the question is not. You're not a stupid person, so you already know the answer. I'm just curious what you think my reply would tell you. Or perhaps I just did."

"Fair enough," she replies.

"Good, then let's talk about your lies, starting with you saying you're not here to interrogate me. Clearly that's what this is."

She nods. "Correct. That wasn't truthful."

"All right. Why?"

"I can't tell you that yet. What were my other lies?" She leans in, elbows on the table.

"You told me you were going to ask that woman for directions. You didn't need directions."

"That wasn't a lie. I asked her for directions," she replies.

"Fine, it was a misdirection, then. Your phone call was loud enough for me to hear, but you lied to whomever you were talking to, if anyone at all. Was that for my benefit or theirs?"

"Neither. Next question?"

"You helped put her bags onto the bus. I didn't see you do anything, but I'm sure you did something. That was another misdirection, but clearly for my benefit. I'm sure nobody else was paying attention."

"Observant, Dr. Cray. It appears you were a little more lucid than you let on," she replies.

"Trust me, the hallucinations are real. And I know *this* is real. I know we're here in this . . . safe house. But I'm not sure why we're here or what we're trying to keep safe from. You mentioned the embassy, but that's in the other direction."

"The embassy is being watched," she says.

"I would assume. But who's worried about the embassy being watched? Us or them?" I ask.

"Who is us?"

"The United States government," I reply.

"So, you consider yourself on the side of the US government?"

This is an unusual question. Does she need me to explain my loyalty? "Most of it. There are certain elements within it that I might have a conflict with."

Her posture changes slightly, and her right hand drops to her side, where she more than likely carries a sidearm. "What parts?"

"I was ambushed in the jungle. Two nights before, I saw a small speck flying over our camp. It came from and traveled back in the same direction as a US military installation in Thailand," I explain.

"You think you were being spied on by the US government?" she asks.

"Observed. I think that intelligence found its way to Myanmar military officials."

"You think the US gave up your location? Why? Why not just take you out directly?"

"Because I was irrelevant. Whoever told them didn't do it because they wanted me dead. It was something to trade for. This country shares a rather large border with China. While we may not officially approve of China's disregard for human rights, we still need favors from them. A little bit of innocuous intel can go a long way."

"And you think that's how they found you?" she asks.

"It's the most likely scenario. At present, I'm more concerned with why *you* found me and how you managed to get me out of there. It seemed a little . . . easy."

"It was easy. As for the reason, one explains the other. That document I showed them? The one that released you into my custody? It was real. While official relations are tense, Myanmar and the United States have an agreement when it comes to handling terrorists. Basically, they let us handle them. That's why they let me take you."

"Because I'm on a US terrorist list?"

"Because you're on a list. They told Burmese officials they wanted to talk to you."

I scoff. "That's amusing. So, what am I, Al Qaeda's number two?"

"No, Dr. Cray. I'm here to decide if you're Michael Heywood's number two."

"Never met the guy, although I'm sure he's an asshole. Now what? Do you arrest me anyway and take me to the embassy through a back route?"

"No, Dr. Cray. Th—"

"Theo."

"No, Theo. There's another part to this. Someone wanted you dead. That's why they told the Myanmar military your location. The papers I used to take custody of you? I stole them from the men who are now arriving at the detention center. They're about to find out that a woman already picked you up. The phone I planted on the bus will lead them away from here, but it won't last for long." She puts her hand to her ear again. "Damn."

"What?"

"They split into two teams. One's heading this way." She jumps to her feet and shoves all the medicine into a backpack. "Put on your shoes."

I follow her instructions and lace them up over my blistered feet. "Who's coming? Who's after me?"

"They're called IDR. It's a special operations group used to retrieve people and information in crisis situations," she replies as she goes to the door.

"American?"

She nods.

"Then maybe I should talk to them. Why run?"

"Because whoever tried to have you killed in the jungle sent them here. They don't realize it, but someone is pulling their strings. And his goal is to make sure you're dead."

I follow her out the door and down a back hallway leading to the opposite end of the building from where we entered. Overhead there's the *whoosh* sound of a helicopter. I glance back past my shoulder and see a black chopper hovering near where we parked the car. The sound of police sirens rises in the distance.

"Who wants me dead?" I ask as we run down the back alley, ducking under clothes hanging from lines.

"If you're not working with Heywood, then I'm pretty sure he wants you killed."

The heavy footsteps of military-grade boots stomp down the stairwell we just left. Ahead of us I can see the lights of a police car and hear the wail of a siren. Something tells me that the local police and this IDR agency aren't working together.

Blackwood motions for me to put my back to the alley wall. I do as she says and keep silent. If there's a later, I'll ask her why a man I never met would go to all this effort to make sure I was dead.

CHAPTER ELEVEN
MAN DOWN

Blackwood sidles along the alley wall to the corner, peering past the hanging sheets and rugs, trying to see where the police officers are. I stay back and watch a child look out from a window across the alley, waving to me. I'm about to wave back when I feel a tight grip around my wrist, and Blackwood pulls me closer as she steps into the small area beyond the laundry that's shielding us.

I hear an angry voice yell at us in Burmese, and Jessica pushes me back into the alley. "Down," she says, shoving me to the red clay earth.

In my weakened state, it doesn't take much force for her to do so. *Bang. Bang.*

Holes appear in the white sheets where we were standing a moment ago.

There's a ping of a ricochet and the sound of something being hit, followed by an American voice screaming, "Fuck!"

I raise my head. Jessica shoves me back down. *Bapbapbapbapbapbapbap.*

Automatic gunfire tears through the air, followed by the sound of metal being punctured.

There's more Burmese yelling—not yells of pain but anger.

I expect the sound of more machine-gun fire, but instead there's a thud as a body hits the concrete near the stairs we just came down. The cop starts to yell for us to come out, clearly afraid to enter the alley blind.

"Let's go," says Blackwood.

"One second." I hear a low gasping sound.

I pull away from her grip and run back to the stairs. A young man with a dark complexion wearing tactical pants, a T-shirt, and an armored vest is slumped on the ground, trying to keep the blood from gushing out of his leg.

I drop down beside him and press a palm hard against his thigh, trying to stem the flow of blood. He's too shocked to react. "Hold on, friend," I say to calm him.

Blackwood appears next to me and looks down. "Damn."

"Hold his leg here," I instruct her, guiding her hands to seal the wound.

I search the pockets of the man's vest, dumping out two cell phones, wads of cash, magazines, knives, and, finally, medical supplies. Thankfully he's got a bullet kit. I rip open the package and pull out the wadding designed to go into a wound and stop the bleeding. It's a newer design that's supposed to be safer than the ones used in the past.

"Hold him down," I tell Blackwood.

She keeps the man still as I rip open his pant leg and jam the plug into the hole. My fingers find an exit wound on the other side. I tear open another package and seal that one as well.

"Fuck! Fuck! Fuck!" the man yells as the shock wears off and he starts to feel the pain.

"Hold on, man," I tell him. "My name's Theo. Let me wrap your leg."

"His friends will be here any minute," says Blackwood.

"Good."

"No. Not good. Any one of them is ready to put a bullet in you."

I look over and notice she's used her foot to kick the man's machine gun away from us.

I didn't catch when she did that.

"One more second." I make the wrapping as tight as I can without stopping blood flow to the leg entirely. "You're going to be okay."

"Why?" asks the man.

I think he wants to know why I'm doing this.

"What's your name?" asks Blackwood.

"Willets, Jay Willets, ma'am," says the man slowly as he descends back into shock.

"Remember this moment. Never forget it. Got it? We didn't have to come back for you. Next time our paths cross, you should have no trouble understanding who the good guys are."

He gives a feeble nod, more from fear and shock than any logical point she made. "Let's go," she tells me.

"Keep pressure on it," I tell Willets. "Make sure they X-ray it before they seal you up. The bullet may have hit bone, which could leave fragments."

"Uh, okay," he says faintly.

"You want to leave him a meal plan and set a follow-up appointment?" asks Blackwood as she pulls me to the opposite wall.

"I just—"

"I know. I get it. But we've got to get past Captain Trigger Finger ahead. Focus on that. Got it?"

"Yes."

We keep tight to the wall until we come to a spot opposite of where we were shot at before. The shadow of the local cop shows through the linen as the sun sets behind him.

"How do you say 'I surrender'?" whispers Blackwood.

"I don't think we want to do that. They don't treat women very—"

"No kidding. How do I say it?"

"I think it's *komainnko laatnaathkya maal*," I say in rough Burmese.

"Oh jeez. Screw that. I surrender!" she calls out in a voice that sounds more feminine than the commanding one she used to bark orders at me.

The cops yell back in Burmese.

"What are they saying?" she asks.

"Come out."

"Wait here."

Blackwood puts her hands up and steps forward through the linens. I watch her shadow as she approaches the two men.

"There's a man with a gun back there," she tells them.

One cop starts moving toward me while the other one fires his gun straight down the middle of the alley. Which is dumb for a multitude of reasons, but I don't think it's the time to point that out.

I duck and catch out of the corner of my eye a flurry of shadows as Jessica Blackwood's knee connects with the jaw of the man kneeling to pat her down. As he falls, she spins around and kicks the second man so hard in the back of the head he tumbles forward into the linens, pulling them all down and exposing me.

"Help me grab him," says Blackwood as she pulls the unconscious man at her feet away from the police car, then moves to the driver's side door. I start to climb into the other side.

"What are you doing?" she asks.

"Uh, going with you?"

"Then stay put." She reaches down and puts the car into neutral. "Help me push."

I join her at the back as we give the car a shove and send it down the hill, where it coasts along for a half-mile journey to the bottom before crashing into a field.

She looks over her shoulder at the hotel. "The others are here. We gotta run."

Blackwood takes a path between two adjacent buildings and through a narrow gap barely wide enough for our bodies as rats scurry away beneath our feet. As we hustle along, I hear the sound of boots and men whispering commands to one another in American English.

"Viper's down!" someone shouts.

Blackwood motions for me to freeze, which is no problem, because I'm already frozen.

She tilts her ear up so she can listen. I do the same.

"They must have got him when they were leaving," one American says. "What's that down there?"

"Cop car," says his partner. "Looks like they took these assholes' car and bailed. Let's go. Tell Woody to stay with Viper. Check?"

"Affirmative."

Footsteps start jogging down the hill. From the distance comes the sound of more sirens. That would be backup police. I'm not sure what's going to happen when they collide with this group.

"Now." Blackwood motions for me to follow her.

We emerge from the tight alley and onto a street. Two SUVs are parked in front of our hotel, blocking traffic.

Blackwood holds her hand down low, signaling for me to hurry as we cross the street.

I don't hear anything, but suddenly she says, "Damn. We've been spotted. Faster!"

We leap down the broken steps of a staircase and come to another road. Blackwood moves toward a tiny Honda that should be in a children's amusement park, not on the street.

"Get in."

She starts the car with a key from under the floor mat. I don't ask how she knew. She knew because she put this car here. She planned everything, down to this detail.

Tires squeal behind us, and I spin around to see the SUV racing down the street in our direction, ready to ram us.

Blackwood guns the tiny motor of our car, and it leaps forward. We narrowly scoot out of the path of the truck before it can knock us into the nearest building. She moves our little car up the road at top speed, but the truck's engine is too powerful. It's almost on our bumper. In a moment it's going to slam into our rear and drive us into a telephone pole.

"We're not going to—"

"Shut up," she says.

The truck gains and is almost touching our back window when Blackwood jerks the wheel to the left and sends us down an alley. Garbage bags and newspapers go flying as we hurtle downhill.

I turn back and see the SUV trying to figure out how to solve the physics problem of squeezing between concrete pillars spaced too narrowly to accommodate it.

Blackwood catches the action in the rearview mirror. "Good luck with that," she says as we hit a bump and the car goes flying through the air. I smack my head against the roof and see stars for a moment.

"Seat belt," says Blackwood.

I look down at the two pieces of rope on either side of my seat. "Uh, I don't really have a seat belt."

"Then hold on."

We smash through a fence and cross a road before going down another hill, bouncing around like coins in a dryer. We're heading for a soccer field, it seems.

The car hits the grass, and Blackwood doesn't stop accelerating. I'm afraid our car's going to fall apart around us at any moment. The radiator is already sending out steam, and I can smell burned oil.

We reach the end of the field as scattered players watch us in either confusion or delight.

The car stops, and Blackwood bails out. "Move it," she orders.

She runs and I jog across the dirt lot to another car parked at the edge, near the exit to the playing field. She climbs in, picks up another key from under the mat, and pushes open the door for me to get in.

We're on the highway a minute later, weaving between all the other insane drivers.

Even now, Blackwood doesn't relent. She keeps going, coming close to bumpers, getting yelled at by other drivers. Not caring.

"Where are we going?" I ask.

"Airport."

"I don't have a passport to get on the plane."

"We're going to steal one."

"A passport?"

"No. A plane."

CHAPTER TWELVE
FLIGHT PLAN

I've never been in a tornado, but twenty minutes next to Jessica Blackwood is as close as I ever hope to come. I've watched her commandeer three cars, take out two armed police officers, and evade an entire commando squad while dragging my weak-ass self along with her. And I still don't know why.

Blackwood's eyes are on the road, never wavering. "Those men were with Information Data Retrieval," she explains.

"What's the difference between data and information?" I ask.

She blinks and looks at me for the first time since we took this car. "What?"

"Why not call it IR or DR? Never mind . . . I guess they just like the acronym."

"I need you to focus, Dr. Cray."

"Theo. Just Theo."

"Okay, Theo. We need to steal a plane. I need you to go along with what I do. Okay?"

"Why not just grab the key from under the floor mat? That's worked really well so far," I reply.

"I couldn't arrange that."

"Oh. So we didn't steal this car?" I ask.

"What? No. Not quite. Focus, please? We're not technically stealing the airplane, either. We're just re-requisitioning it."

"I'm not sure I understand."

"The details don't matter. But the men who were after us, IDR, they used a government jet to get here. We're using that jet to get out."

"And how do we do that?" I ask. "Superior firepower?"

"No. Paperwork. I filed a maintenance request right after they landed. I then had it rescinded. Their replacement plane is supposed to be in Thailand, but it actually got diverted to the Philippines. Understand?"

"Not really. But I think I get the drift."

Blackwood pulls onto a road that runs along a metal fence separating us from a runway. At the end of it is a small guard gate. A man with a thin mustache and a military uniform steps out and asks for our paperwork.

Blackwood shows him her FBI badge. He makes a gesture that looks like an eye roll, then lifts the gate and lets us pass. We drive through a row of hangars and park the car in a small lot at the edge of the tarmac. A Gulfstream jet is waiting in the otherwise-empty airfield.

"One more thing," says Blackwood. "I need to have you cuffed. At least until we get onto the plane."

"What?" I'm trying to figure out what kind of a trick this is.

Blackwood gently lifts my wrists. "It won't be tight. It's just for show."

"Are you sure?"

Click.

I glance down at the handcuffs now around my wrists. "For crying out loud."

"Sorry. We don't have time to debate this." She gets out of the car and walks around to my side and holds the door open. "Just keep your mouth shut and act like a prisoner. It shouldn't be hard."

She puts a hand on my shoulder and shoves me ahead of her. As we get within a hundred feet of the jet, a man in a pilot's uniform steps down the stairs and watches us approach.

"Where's the rest of the team?" he asks.

"They're taking another way back. We need to get him out of country ASAP before the locals change their mind."

"I need to check with Kieren," he says.

"Check the paperwork," replies Blackwood.

"I know. But I'm still going to check with her. Hold on." The pilot goes back into the plane.

This doesn't look good.

"Now what?" I whisper to Blackwood.

She holds up a finger and turns her back to the jet. A moment later, she speaks in a lower register that doesn't quite sound like her voice.

"Affirmative. We need to get Cray back now . . . Yes. The authorization is correct . . . Understood."

A moment later the pilot emerges from the doorway. "Sorry about that. Just had to check."

"No problem," says Blackwood in a voice much softer and sweeter than the one she just used. She pushes me up the stairs. "Cooperate and I'll take the handcuffs off," she says loudly enough for the pilot to hear. "Understood?"

I nod and let her shove me into a seat in the back, where I sit quietly while she talks to the pilot up front. I can make out the words *security matter* and *not to be disturbed* before he steps back into the cockpit to explain the situation to his copilot.

"What happens once they realize we're not supposed to be on this plane?"

"Technically, Dr. Cray . . . Theo . . . you're supposed to be on this plane. They're not going to risk sending you back and having the Myanmar government try to arrest you again. Fortunately, the people that control where this plane goes aren't the ones that want you killed."

"And where exactly is this plane going?"

"That's what we need to determine right now. First, why did you help that man back there? He was ready to put a bullet in you."

I try to put it into words that make sense to me. "I'm not a monster. A survivor, a killer, yeah, but I'm not a monster—at least, I don't see myself that way."

She undoes my handcuffs and slips them into her pocket. "Fair enough. The problem is that monsters rarely see themselves that way." She reaches into her bag and drops a stack of folders in front of me. "This is all about what happened in New York. The question is: Why would whoever did that be trying to keep you as far away as possible?"

"I'm sorry, but what happened in New York?"

Blackwood sits back in her seat opposite me and buckles her seat belt as we prepare to take off. "Oh, right. You couldn't know . . ."

"Is it something bad?"

"Very. And now we're trying to stop it from happening elsewhere," she explains. "And I'm supposed to figure out how you're connected to all this."

I'm curious to find out what happened in New York and eager to understand my place in everything, but I'm also tired. I try to stifle a yawn but find myself falling asleep before I can ask any more questions.

CHAPTER THIRTEEN
MASTER OF LIES

"So, a group of terrorists set off a series of EMPs around Manhattan, knocking out the electrical grid and destroying most of the microprocessor-based electronics across the city?" I ask, trying to understand if this is a movie plot or a real thing.

"Yes. We have some suspects in custody, but we don't know if they're aware of who actually initiated this, let alone why," she replies.

"What kind of EMPs?" I ask.

"Chemical EMPs is what they're calling them."

"Interesting. I don't think I've heard of that before." I think for a moment. "I guess it makes sense."

"How so?"

"Know anyone who was around when they went off?"

"Yeah. Me. One took out our helicopter. We had to crash-land. Why?"

"Just curious. Was there kind of a burned-ozone smell in the air? Maybe something kind of acrid, too?"

"I'd say that's exactly how I would describe it."

"Hmm." I try to imagine how you'd take the kinetic force of the explosion and convert it into electricity. It wouldn't be terribly efficient, but if I understand it right, once you have the manufacturing down, it would be extremely inexpensive.

"The strands . . . were they toxic?"

"The strands? What are you talking about?" She leans in to study me more closely.

"From the carbon fiber. I assume it was some kind of long-stranded carbon nano sheet rolled into long threads . . . like a microscopic tube?"

"Uh, yeah . . ."

"Wrap that around a cylinder, put an explosive charge in the middle, and when it explodes, they'd create friction rubbing against each other, building up a charge. Hmm. I guess a second wave could act as a kind of compression wave, which would make them all discharge close together. You time that and you control the kind of EMP they generate?" I ask aloud, trying to understand the weapon in my head. Physics was never my strongest subject. I have always preferred biology and computer science, where things were either too complex for me to have to engineer them or else could be reduced to lines of code. I hate that middle area.

She nods. "That's pretty much exactly how it works. So, hypothetically, if someone wanted to make carbon-based EMPs, where would they get the carbon threads?"

"Good question. I know they're trying to manufacture something like that in microgravity."

"Space?"

"Yes," I reply. "But not at scale. These fibers—they weren't much longer than a foot or so, were they?"

"Correct. We figured it was because they broke," she replies.

"Yes. Or it was the maximum size they could manufacture. If you could make them continuously, then that would be something different. This sounds like some kind of failed industrial experiment that they found another use for."

"They? Who would *they* be?"

I shrug. "I don't know. It sounds like some kind of offshoot of government-funded research into a supercapacitor. But that's not my area. Sorry."

"Okay, but, just guessing: Chinese? Russian? Texas A&M?"

"Could be anyone with the resources. I'd focus on research papers. Basically, anyone who was working on manufacturing carbon nanotubes at scale."

"And then tried weapons applications?" she asks.

"Maybe. But I was thinking about someone who couldn't get a job in that field because of a security clearance issue."

"But not someone such as yourself?" she asks.

"Me? Ha, no. Why?"

"Dr. Cray, do you realize that if some of my colleagues heard you say what you just told me, they'd have you locked up on suspicion of being a coconspirator?"

"Huh."

"Is that all you have to say?"

I shrug. "Saying stuff is what got me into trouble in the first place. I didn't know when to shut up. Do you really think I'm a suspect?"

"I think you're suspicious. But I don't think this attack is something you'd do. To be honest, until an hour ago, I didn't think you cared about anything."

"An hour ago? What happened?"

"You were mumbling in your sleep, 'Make sure Johnny's okay.' Who's Johnny?"

"A local kid, very bright. Taught himself English and Chinese by watching YouTube videos. He was our guide and translator."

"And now?" asks Blackwood.

"I don't know. When things got bad, I told him to run. I think he went to his cousins in the hills. To be honest, I tried not to think about him when I was being interrogated." I still pray that I didn't say anything about him. I tried to drown myself when I came close. "Anyway.

I'm sure he's fine." *Keep telling yourself that, Theo.* "So, let's get back to why you don't think I was involved?"

"Well, your alibi's obviously solid. More importantly, your name popped up on a list of potential suspects, which seemed more than suspicious to me, considering who I think is really behind this."

"Heywood."

"Yes. And also, I don't think his ego could handle working with you," Blackwood explains.

"I've heard that before."

"How about you? How does your ego handle working with people smarter than you?"

"I think we're getting along fine."

"Tactful response."

She thinks I'm kidding. In the last few hours, I've gained an understanding of how she thinks. While I'm good at focusing on one problem and seeing all the possible solutions, I've watched her deal with every threat around us while thinking several steps ahead. She was watching the road, conversing with me, and listening in on the radio that we grabbed to keep tabs on the IDR team.

She probably doesn't think she can multitask well, but under pressure her bandwidth is enormous. Her greatest skill is not trying to focus on any one thing, but reading the entire world around her.

If I had that gift, I wouldn't be in a lot of the trouble I've found myself in. I probably wouldn't be who I am, either. But it might not be a bad trade-off.

"Why New York? Why the EMPs?" she asks.

"Was anything missing?"

"Like Rockefeller Center? No. First things we checked were the Fed, the banks, and all the other high-value targets. Ordinary looting was in the hundreds of millions of dollars. But no, there was no heist. At least none we've detected."

"Test run by a foreign power? Maybe they wanted to see what they could pull off?"

"And risk the repercussions? We doubt it. You worked in counter-terrorism, right? You had a whole lab, I understand."

"Yes. Until I went nuts chasing a serial killer and it was taken from me. Oh? Is that one of the reasons I'm a suspect?"

"It's been thrown around."

"They did me a favor. It was too much pressure. The office politics, the meetings, worrying if my lab manager was going to infect me with some kind of rage-inducing virus. I'm better off without it," I say, not exaggerating.

"We have very different workplace experiences," she says. "So, let's talk about Heywood. What else do you know about him?"

"Besides the secret handshake and the nicknames we have for each other when we're playing video games and plotting to take over the world?"

"Funny. A few liters of water and your sense of humor's back in business."

"I bounce back fast." And then hit the ground twice as hard. "Tell me about Heywood. What's his pattern?"

"His pattern?"

"Frogs eat flies, hop around, keep wet. All my killers had patterns. That's how I caught them. After the fact, it seemed obvious. Joe Vik owned a lot of businesses. One of them was a towing company. Sometimes he'd take stranded-motorist calls and kill the motorists. What's Heywood's pattern?"

"He loves spectacle. He loves things that look supernatural. He wants people to think they've seen a miracle."

"But this wasn't a miracle. This was a bunch of EMPs."

"You weren't there. We called it the Void. It looked like Manhattan got sucked into a black hole. It's—I still can't quite process it . . ."

"But you can explain it. Does Heywood like people explaining what he did after the fact?"

"God, no. He tried to kill me for that," she replies.

"Interesting. So he likes to create supernatural-appearing phenomena and hates it when someone explains it?"

"I'd say that's the short form. Are you sure your paths never crossed?"

"Not that I'm aware of."

Blackwood thinks it over. "Putting suspicion on you doesn't make sense. Maybe his real plan is to do something that still hasn't happened yet."

"Interesting. If not disappearing New York, then what?"

"What if it's something else going on in the world? And New York was a distraction?"

"Possibly. Is there something else weird going on in the world I should know about, Agent Blackwood?"

She reaches into her bag and pulls out a second set of folders. "Quite a lot, actually. And call me Jessica."

CHAPTER FOURTEEN
THE WEIRD FILE

"I used to get all the weird stuff," says Jessica.

"Like *The X-Files*," I reply.

"Yeah, but not as cool. Sometimes it was agents who had problems they couldn't solve. Mostly it was people who heard my name and wanted me to tell them why their house creaked or that the light they saw in the sky was a UFO."

"And?"

"People are nuts. There was too much to deal with. And people hated being told they were mistaken. I had a grad student send me death threats because I told him the mysterious light in a photo he took in an Egyptian temple was the streak of an LED made by camera shake.

"I thought I was doing him a favor. Turns out he thought I was denying that he was Anubis reincarnated. They put him in a mental hospital for a few days. I stopped responding after that," she says with a sigh.

"Very understandable. I got cases, too. Sometimes real ones. That was the problem. By ignoring them I knew that might mean a killer was getting away. I couldn't handle it."

"When you're a cop, they teach you that you have to put away the gun and the badge at the end of the day."

"I've heard that. How did that advice work for you?" I ask.

"Ask my therapist."

"And how does that work?" I find it hard to imagine her opening up and being vulnerable to anyone like that, and I'm surprised when she answers my question.

"It gives me outlook. I can stand back and analyze things a little more. I can see my own patterns. You ever tried it?"

"My mom forced me to see one when I was a kid, after my dad died. He didn't know how to handle my personality. It wasn't very productive."

"I can't imagine trying to diagnose a kid that knew my subject better than I did," she replies with a smile.

"It wasn't quite like that. But yes. I told him that I had feelings, but I felt like they were something I visualized existing two feet to the side of me. I could tell what they were experiencing, but I could also decide to ignore them if I wanted."

"Jesus, Theo. It's no wonder our behavioral-science guys have written books about you." She picks up the stack of folders. "Anyway, one of the cadets at the FBI academy has been keeping track of weird stuff for me, filtering out the usual noise." She flips through the pages and hands me a photo. "Cattle mutilation. The bite marks are big and don't match coyotes or wolves."

I glance at the photo. It's not the first time I've been asked to explain cattle mutilations.

She's right, though—the mouth is much wider than a coyote's, yet not a wolf's. I hand her the photo back. "Probably a mastiff/coyote hybrid. The larger jaw and broken bones are the indicator."

"That's it?"

"Well, I knew once you said 'bite' that it was an animal. The fact that it was weird means that it was an animal they hadn't seen before.

Because it was clearly canine, it means there's either an entirely new species out there or some domesticated dog humans hooked up with a coyote and morphed into a pseudospecies."

"Okay. How about strange light formations over Orem, Utah? There's been YouTube videos of them."

"There's a secret testing ground for unmanned aerial vehicles twenty miles from there. Think there might be a connection?"

"Wait, how did you know that?"

"I was looking at internet routing patterns and started noticing regions with unusually high traffic. That area was one that came up. There's also an FCC blackout zone nearby." I don't point out that she asked me how I knew that and not how I could prove it. She's testing me with things she already knows.

"This is a hobby of yours? Looking at internet traffic patterns?"

"I like patterns. What can I say?"

She digs deeper into the folder pile. "How about this? There have been cases of people who have experienced unusual disease remissions who also claim to have had weird visions of angels in their hospitals or their homes."

"Interesting. Does that sound like Heywood to you? Angels? Miracles?"

"He's not exactly the healing type. If they spontaneously combusted or were found to have died years before, that'd be more his style."

"You'd know better than I. But sometimes patterns aren't what we think when we're up close. Joe Vik was loved locally. Even after he went on his rampage, murdering his family and several police officers, he still had defenders. There were many aspects to Joe."

In truth, there are things about him I still don't know . . . unproven suspicions. Part of me wants to go back. Another part of me is afraid.

"I'll keep that in mind." She sifts through the folders. "I've got a weird zombie thing, but it's in Eastern Europe . . . so. And then there's *this* one, which made my Spidey sense tingle."

"You have Spidey sense?"

"I'm sorry, can only boys have it?"

"Uh, no. Just Marvel characters."

Jessica's got a funny edge to her. She's the girl who liked nerdy stuff but someone told her she was too pretty for that kind of thing.

"What is it?"

"In the last two years, the heads of five different cults around the world have gone missing. There was a doomsday group in Belgium. A 'retreat' in Australia. Another in Mexico. And two in the US. One outside Anaheim, another in Michigan."

"When you say 'missing,' what do you mean?"

"One day they're running things, the next, someone else is calling the shots," she replies.

"Someone appointed from within?"

"It appears so."

"What was that cult out in the desert . . . the one that . . ." I stop talking when I realize who I'm talking to. Jessica was the one who found the vault filled with bodies.

"And now you see why I talk to a therapist."

"Who the hell does your therapist talk to after talking to you? That's what I want to know," I joke, perhaps a little too bluntly.

Jessica laughs, the most open expression I've seen from her. "I'll have to ask her that. That's a good one."

"Thanks. So now you trust me?"

"No more than you trust yourself. Part of me is worried that while you're staring at me, you're thinking about how to crack my skull open and have a look."

"An MRI's much better for that. I could poke around and see what happens when I trigger different neurons . . . ," I joke again, probably too graphically.

"Okay, okay," she says. "Let's put a pin in the cult thing."

"I can tell you one thing," I say. "The printout is on different paper than the others. I suspect your student brought it to you and you made notes. But you didn't want me to see them, so you made a new printout. Unfortunately, she used a paper with different brightness. Probably some eco-friendly, recycled paper."

Jessica examines the pages. "Well, that's a tell I need to pay more attention to in the future. Yes. This cult thing does concern me. A lot. Heywood recruits vulnerable people who've already been through or been in cults. So we'll want to circle back to this."

"You said *recruits*, not recruited. Heywood was in custody, last I heard. Did that change recently?"

"Yeah. He managed to forge some transfer documents, and it got more suspicious and/or more stupid from there."

"How much could he arrange from inside prison? I would think a man like that would have limited access."

"In theory. But we found him working his way around that early on. Then he got transferred to a facility where even I had a difficult time finding out what he was up to. Like I said, it's all highly suspicious."

"What else do you have?"

"Thirty chimpanzees vanished from a zoo in Thailand six weeks ago," she replies.

"Vanished?"

"Yes."

"Hmm," I say. "That word again . . ."

The captain's voice comes up over the intercom. "Agent Blackwood, could you secure your passenger and come up here for a moment?"

"Be right back. Uh, don't jump out." She gets up and walks to the cockpit.

I pick up the article on the missing chimps. It's written in a tabloid style and hints that they may have been stolen for some kind of underworld exotic meat trade, which horrifies me to no end . . . but the chimpanzees vanishing in the middle of a city zoo has me intrigued.

Chimps are incredibly strong, dangerous, and difficult to force to do anything. I did some work with them in the past and love them as a species, but I also find them terrifying. I can't imagine any sane person trying to devise a chimpanzee theft at that scale. It had to be an inside job with the handlers participating. But *why*?

Jessica drops back down into her seat. "Seoul, South Korea, is experiencing an event," she says.

"An event?"

"Another void. The entire city."

"Oh." I'm not sure what to think.

"How are you feeling?"

"Better. Less dehydrated. The fever's gone."

"You want to see a void up close and in person?" she asks.

"As long as it's not from a helicopter."

While I try to sleep and get enough nutrients in me that I won't look like the walking dead, Jessica makes arrangements for when we land. I should call Jillian, the woman I left behind in Austin, and tell her I'm okay, but I can't even begin to think of how that conversation should start.

What do you say to the woman who stuck by your side through life-and-death situations, who literally risked her life to save yours, and whom you then walked out on, not once but twice?

She'd already lost a husband to war. Then I came along, bringing who knows how much pain into her life. The guilt I feel can't even be imagined.

Not knowing what to tell Jillian isn't what's holding me back; it's the shame I feel for what I've done to her. When I left for Asia, we'd ended things. At least through words.

I knew Jillian would never be the one to say we should break up because of what I'd gone through, but I also knew it wasn't right to keep torturing her.

She'd been there for me through my downward spiral. She was there when I came back. When I told her it was probably best if we separated, I said it because she couldn't. I wanted an easy, clean break, but that was a fantasy.

I know I love her, because when I found out she was seeing someone else, a military veteran like her, it made me feel good to know that he was a decent man. I couldn't be that man. I'm glad someone else is.

It also made walking into the jungle easier.

Even so, it's never as easy as that. I hadn't realized how much I missed having someone in my heart until I was close to death again.

"Jessica?" I ask, lifting my head from my seat back.

"Yes?" She glances up from her laptop.

"I need to text someone. Or send an email. Do you think you could help me?"

"Sure. Who?"

"Her name is Jillian. I just want her to know I'm okay."

"She knows, Theo. That's who I was talking to back at the snack stand. But I'll give you a burner phone."

"Oh . . . I didn't know."

"I should have told you. She's the reason I was able to find you so quickly. In fact, I think she's the reason you're still alive."

This makes me sit up. "How's that?"

"She'd been keeping track of you when she could. When she heard you'd been arrested, she started sending bribes to the head of the police station. Basically, money to keep you fed. From the looks of things, that never reached you. But Jillian kept sending because she knew they'd rather keep you alive and the money flowing."

"I . . . I never knew."

"I know. She knows. Anyway, she did everything she could. Hired an attorney. Even talked to a kidnap-and-rescue team. It's better that she didn't use them. But, yes, she knows you're okay and with me. She wanted a photo, but I figured we should let you recover a little first. Want to call her?"

I don't have a response, and now Jessica's dialing her phone. She speaks to the voice at the other end, then hands it to me.

"Theo?" says Jillian's voice.

My words seize up in my throat. All I can manage is a weak yes.

"Oh, Theo."

"I'm sorry. I'm so, so sorry." Tears start streaming down my face. "I'm sorry for what I keep doing to you."

"It's what you do to yourself that hurts. I was a soldier. I was a soldier's wife. I got used to this. You need to—"

The line goes dead. "Jillian? Jillian?"

Jessica types into her computer, then glances up. "Oh, damn."

"What is it?"

"Another void. This one in Singapore."

"The call stopped," I say like a confused child.

"Probably a routing center. Or an overload. She's fine. She knows you're fine. I'll send her an email. That's still working, for now. Get some rest."

CHAPTER FIFTEEN
DARKNESS

"Are you sure they want us here?" I ask when I see the massive armored personnel carrier parked at the end of the runway and surrounded by Korean National Police vehicles with flashing lights.

"I think we're good," says Jessica as she grabs her bag. "Hold on." She takes a look at me and makes a concerned face.

"Do I look like the subject of a hostage-rescue video?"

"Not that bad . . . just . . . well, a little on the gaunt side. Let me see if I can borrow a jacket from the pilot."

I glance down at the belt cinched around my waist with the pants fabric bunched up like a cloth sack. It's not the worst I've looked, but not exactly the image of confidence we want to project. I'd offer to stay behind, but I don't want to miss this.

Jessica returns from the front with a black bomber jacket. "Try this."

I put it on. The bottom at least covers my belt and potato-sack pants. "Better?"

"A little. At least they're less likely to charge me with reckless endangerment." She heads toward the open door and stairs. "If anyone asks, you're a consultant for the FBI."

"Technically, I've been just that. So no stretch there." I glance out at the small group of Korean officials waiting for us. "How exactly did you arrange this?"

Jessica points to a tall Korean woman in a suit with blonde streaks in her hair. She's got sharp features, attractive but forceful. She kind of reminds me of Jessica.

"That's Lilith. I did some teaching for the FBI program that works with international agencies. We got along pretty well. She ran an entire unit that went after North Korean saboteurs. She started out by doing undercover operations when she was nineteen. Tough as nails. If she asks you a question, don't lie to her. She'll know."

"Okay. And what is our situation here? Do we have to worry about IDR showing up?"

"We shouldn't. Fingers crossed. I did a little paperwork while you were sleeping," she explains.

"Okay . . ."

"Being the first to file, make requisitions, and tell the chain of command what you're doing is basically the Hogwarts magic of the FBI. If I say that I brought a person of interest in to interview and I ask a supervisor what questions they want answered, it basically commits them to approving the whole endeavor. Anyway, I can give you plenty more tips later. I learned from a master at sailing the seas of bureaucracy: bullshit reports are the wind in your sails."

"That sounds like a horrible way to live."

"You're telling me. Are you good on the stairs?" she asks.

"I'm good. I feel better than I look."

"Let's hope so."

Jessica steps onto the tarmac and greets her friend with a hug, then motions me forward. I reach the circle of officials and keep my appropriate distance. Lilith gives me a nod, and then two others are introduced, an older man named Dr. Gap-Kyum and a younger Korean official whose name is given as Ray.

The Western nicknames some Asian people use have always fascinated me. I've wondered if adopting that name also helps in assuming, at least partially, a Western frame of mind.

"Are you ready, Dr. Cray?" asks Lilith. Her English is perfect. I suspect she probably speaks a number of other dialects and languages with equal ease. Some minds are capable like that. Johnny could do it, and the poor kid never even had a proper tutor. He could even pronounce the complicated names on our medicine bottles after hearing them spoken aloud only once.

In a better world, he wouldn't be sleeping on a piece of cardboard in the back of his grandmother's junk shed. He'd be in high school and on his way to whatever university he chose. I've seen so much untapped potential in the darkest places. Children who could be doctors. Adults fixing bent bicycle rims with a spoon who could be designing Teslas. If you were to ask me what's broken in this world, I'd say it's the amount of talent found in the places we ignore.

"When the event happened, we'd already had personnel outside the major cities prepared," Lilith explains as we walk toward the massive armored vehicle.

"New York was enough for you?" asks Jessica.

"We fared okay after COVID-19 because we took a hard hit on SARS and learned to be proactive. We also decided to prepare for other contingencies. When we heard about the mini-EMPs, our first concern was, what if our friends to the north managed to get their hands on some?" Lilith explains. "Watch your heads."

She holds the side door open so we can climb inside the vehicle. Jessica takes the seat opposite the door facing a large monitor. I sit next to her.

"This is a little intense," says Jessica, looking around at the interior of the vehicle.

"EMP and chemical agent–proof?" I ask.

"Yes," says Lilith. "We haven't gotten our helicopters protected yet."

"Neither have we," says Jessica with a wink at me.

The others get inside, and Lilith seals the door, then gives an order to the driver. The vehicle begins to move forward with our escorts following on either side.

"We'll take the main highway toward the center. If there's anything you want to get a better look at, let me know. We have several drones up in the air and a long-distance camera on the roof." She points to a large monitor.

For the first time, I notice the large black void in the center of the screen. It's a view of Seoul . . . or rather what should be Seoul. Where Manhattan had been a dark pit in the middle of the water, Seoul is a hole in the middle of a megalopolis. There are buildings . . . and then nothing.

"What's the air quality like there?" I ask.

"Similar to New York. The cloud contains carbon soot that's probably not good for long-term exposure. We have respirators on board in case we have to get out."

I turn to Jessica. "Do you have any satellite images or heat maps of the Manhattan event?"

"I've got an iPad full of them. What are you looking for?"

"This is literally a smokescreen. Both visually and electronically," I tell her.

She hands me the device and opens a folder of images. "You think there's something going on right now?"

"Possibly. I'd be curious to take a look at whatever weird stories we have from New York. The things that authorities claimed were just hysteria."

Jessica makes a small nod. "I was wondering if you were going to ask about that."

"You didn't want to tell me?"

"I wanted independent confirmation that there might be something more to it. There should be a folder there with the kind of eyewitness reports you're talking about." She points to an icon on her tablet.

I read the icon's label aloud: "'Demons and Dementors'?"

"Yep," says Jessica. "More than a dozen sightings. The witnesses used various terms. But the gist is that some people claim there were things in the Void."

"Things?"

"Fast-moving objects. Dark blurs, basically."

I go back to the images of the blackout and start zooming in.

"You don't want to read them?"

"Maybe later," I reply. "I think I know what the witnesses said. I just want to make sure I understand what they were doing."

CHAPTER SIXTEEN
BALANCE POINT

I scan the images showing which parts of the city were in total blackness and which were not. Despite the EMPs, certain areas of the city managed to make it through relatively unscathed. At first, I take that to be random luck, but on closer examination of the photos, I notice the time stamps and realize that some of them eventually did experience a total blackout. Was this because of a delay in the EMPs or some other factor? Hiding secrets behind something meant to seem random?

I pull up the current weather reports for Seoul, Singapore, and Manhattan on the night of the events. There's about a twenty-degree temperature variation, but wind speed is about the same, and they all have strong climate differences with their surrounding areas. The urban-island effect at the extreme.

Jessica is watching over my shoulder. I show her the weather reports. "I'm sure this was noted."

"Yes. People talked about how the weather made the situation even worse. There were a lot of comparisons to the New York 1966 smog event and London's killer fog of 1952," she says.

"Killer fog?" asks Lilith.

"Yeah. Prior to air-quality standards in the US and Europe, the smog problem got critically bad when weather kept pollutants trapped in one area. Our void coincided with a similar weather event."

"And yours," I tell Lilith.

"We get those kinds of fogs more frequently now," Lilith replies.

I check my data. "There're a lot of places with similar climates where this could be pulled off. Seoul and Singapore getting hit on the same night may be a matter of convenience."

"They were waiting for the weather?" asks Lilith.

"I assume so. For maximum impact."

"We're getting closer," says Jessica as she looks at the monitor.

The Void takes up the entire screen now. The only indicator that the monitor's not switched off is the highway and the streetlights visible in front of us. They stretch ahead for several miles, then simply end.

"Can we get out and look?" I ask.

Lilith calls to the driver, and the vehicle comes to a stop. Jessica opens up the door, and we step out onto the deserted highway to view the Void with unaided eyes. My first reaction is pure awe.

The mental model that comes to mind is that of a massive glacier made of black ice that has swept across the city. At the outer edges, the lights of emergency vehicles flash as they try to evacuate people from inside the cloud.

Occasionally I catch the glimmering purple flashes that reports have attributed to EMPs being triggered like aftershocks.

"Who were the first into Manhattan?" I ask.

"Firefighters," says Jessica. "They were the ones with the right gear."

"Do you want to get any closer?" asks Lilith.

"Yes," I respond without hesitation.

"Okay, any particular place?"

I read an address from a browser window on Jessica's iPad. "Can we go there?"

"I think so. What's there?"

"That's where the lights are on. Or at least they're on right now," I reply.

"How do you know that?" asks Jessica.

"I pinged a list of Seoul internet addresses. This one answered back. They're still connected to the internet via a fiber-optic cable that wasn't affected."

"And you think that's intentional?"

"Maybe. The fact that not all the EMPs went off at once was either accidental, a way to interfere with first responders—like yourself—or intended for some other purpose," I say as we climb back into the vehicle.

Lilith tells the driver where to go, and we start moving forward again into the maelstrom.

As I speak, all eyes are on the monitor.

"Think of a squid," I explain. "It uses its ink as a means to escape predators, right? Well, it turns out that ink isn't only a defensive weapon like we thought. We've observed Japanese pygmy squid using ink to confuse and distract shrimp. A feeding strategy. Which makes sense. So whenever we find a useful tool with only one application, I assume that we haven't been watching the animal that uses it closely enough."

Ray listens attentively while Dr. Gap-Kyum nods.

I point at the Void on the screen, which has devoured almost all of the highway in front of us. "This isn't just some fireworks display. And to your point, Jessica, I'm not sure I'd call it a distraction or diversion. Whatever it is that they're trying to hide is happening now, right inside here. Our clever squid is swimming around this area, doing something important. Fortunately, like squid, they share the same weakness."

"What's that?" asks Lilith.

For the first time, Dr. Gap-Kyum speaks up. "They're blind, too."

"Exactly," I say. "However, they have the benefit of knowing where they're going and what they're doing." I think for a moment. "Is anyone here a marksman?"

Ray lifts his hand and says in accented English, "Sniper training. Highest score." He opens his jacket and shows a holstered pistol.

"Perfect. We may need to see if you still have the skill."

"Are you expecting to run into them?" asks Lilith.

"Maybe not them, but possibly one of the flying demons from the reports. If so, I'd love to have one to examine."

"You think it's some kind of unmanned aerial vehicle?" asks Jessica.

"It makes sense."

"To observe?"

"Possibly. But it could also be what took out your helicopter. They might even have smaller EMPs on board designed to take out observers and cover their tracks."

"And when they don't need them, they blow them up and destroy the evidence," she says.

"We're entering the Void," says Lilith as the mist gets progressively thicker around the camera feeding our internal monitor.

"Aside from ideal weather conditions, how does it stay in one place so long?" asks Jessica. "It's eerie."

"Static," says Dr. Gap-Kyum. "Like a cloud. This is a highly charged body." He pushes his fists together. "The discharges we see keep adding energy, which helps bind the cloud. When they stop"—he lets his hands spread apart and open—"it all goes away."

The vehicle drives through empty streets, its searchlight cutting through the mist and illuminating shuttered buildings and closed windows. I only see one or two faces peering out from behind windows; other than that, it looks like Seoul has been abandoned.

"Do you have a thermal scope I can use?" I ask.

Ray gets up from his seat and digs around until he finds a small plastic case. He hands it to me. Inside is a handheld viewer that shows hot spots.

I squeeze over to a porthole in the carrier and view the streets and buildings through thermal imaging. I can see more bodies behind windows and what parts of the buildings radiate warmth. Interesting, but not useful at the moment. I put the scope in my pocket.

The driver calls out in Korean and points to something through his window. Lilith adjusts the camera connected to our screen, and we can see a bright glow in the distance.

I check the iPad and the address. The location's still sending internet data . . . until it suddenly stops. The location no longer responds to my pings. I don't even have to look up to see what happened.

The vehicle comes to a stop half a block from where we saw the glowing lights. "It's gone," says Jessica.

"Yes," I say, "and I think that means they're in there."

CHAPTER SEVENTEEN
Data

Lilith lifts up a seat and starts handing out bulletproof vests from a compartment. She says something to Dr. Gap-Kyum in Korean, then turns to me. "I need you two to wait here."

I shake my head. "You need me in there."

"I can't arm you," she tells me.

"I'm not asking you to."

Lilith turns to Jessica. "Your call."

"Theo will stay behind me and duck when I tell him to. Right?"

"Ducking is what I do best. But we should hurry. If I'm right, the evidence is gonna vanish."

"All right," says Lilith, still unsure about having a civilian along for the forced entry.

Ray has his jacket on and is checking his pockets. If I had to guess, his government job probably involves working with one of the intelligence agencies in an active capacity. He seems familiar with all the weapons and tools.

He grabs my shoulder. "If I see something, I shoot, yes?"

"Shoot," I reply. "I'll keep back in case."

"In case *boom*." He nods knowingly.

We put on gas masks before exiting the vehicle. Lilith's out first, followed by Ray, then Jessica. While Ray and Lilith have their guns drawn, Jessica keeps hers in her back holster, her hand close by. I suspect she could draw and fire before the average person could think to pull the trigger.

"Be careful," Jessica whispers to everyone. "Our suspects will probably be disguised as police or first responders. They won't look like bad guys."

That's an excellent point that I should have thought to mention. Lilith translates it for Ray, who nods curtly.

The lights of the vehicle still focus straight ahead on a glass building in an industrial park. The mist is too thick for me to tell how tall it is, but the name is clearly visible in metal letters above the entrance: Southern Star Systems KMP.

In this age of conglomerates and subsidiaries, there could be a robot factory in there or a warehouse filled with toilet paper. I have the iPad in my hand, but it's about to reach the limit of the armored personnel carrier's satellite internet.

Lilith and Ray reach the front door. Jessica waves me to the side by a huge metal column. I'm pretty sure my body count is higher than the rest of the group's combined, but now's not the time to tell a group of cops that I might be the best person at the vanguard. Plus, all three are no doubt better shots than I.

Lilith aims a light into the lobby. There's a security guard sitting behind a desk, looking confused. She taps the glass while Ray yells at the man to come to the door.

The guard walks up to the glass and stops. Lilith shows him a badge. The guard raises his hands and steps back, saying something in Korean.

Perhaps heeding Jessica's advice that anyone could be a bad guy, Ray doesn't waste a moment. He uses the butt of his pistol to smash the glass door, reach through, and open it before the guard can figure out what just happened.

Lilith bursts through, puts her gun to the man's head, and tells him to lie facedown. He starts to comply, then makes a quick grab for something under his vest.

Whack. Lilith pistol-whips the man so hard blood splatters across the floor, and I could swear I hear the sound of a tooth bouncing off the tiles. Ray shouts behind us, and one of the drivers from the vehicle comes running in and handcuffs the guard.

"This way," says Ray, hurrying down the hall toward the elevators.

We follow after, but I'm not sure where we're headed. "How do you know where to go?" I call out.

Ray comes running back toward me and points to the directory next to my shoulder. His finger taps on a row of Korean characters. "Da-ta cen-ter," he says slowly enough for me to understand.

Of course. The people behind the Void aren't stealing a physical thing . . . they're after data.

Jessica and Lilith are already up the stairs by the time I reach the door to the stairwell.

At the top a door has been pried open and the keypad lock ripped off the wall. Jessica takes one side of the door; Lilith takes the other.

Ray enters, and the two other cops follow him in a precision formation. Jessica gives me a hand signal to stay back while they inspect the long rows of servers that make up the bulk of the facility.

I wait by the door, keeping watch. After they step out of view behind a wall lined with cables, there's not a single sound in the entire facility.

Several minutes go by, and I stay put. Partially out of fear of getting shot by one of my teammates. Footsteps approach, and I pull back into the stairwell. Jessica walks around the corner. She's shaking her head.

"Nobody," she says. "Maybe the door guy can tell us something, but I'm not optimistic."

"Ray and Lilith?"

"Checking the back exit. I have a feeling the guy up front was expendable and intended to give whoever was in here time to get out."

I walk back inside, using a light from a pocket in the vest to illuminate the massive data center. There are twenty rows of server cabinets, each a hundred feet deep. I do a quick calculation in my head. If each cabinet holds twenty servers, there's close to ten thousand servers in here.

As I walk down the aisle, I shine my light into each row, looking for a clue, but every row seems the same. I hear the sound of a door closing. Jessica, who had been following behind me, has her gun drawn.

"It's us," says Lilith.

"Anything?" asks Jessica.

"We think they left on foot," she replies. "There's a large apartment complex not too far from here. We'll ask around and see if anybody saw anything, when we have a chance." She looks around with her flashlight, taking in the size of the complex. "Too bad the security cameras are off. I would like to know what they were doing."

"Me too," I reply.

"Aren't all the computers fried?" asks Jessica.

"Probably. But if the hard drives are shielded, there might be some data left," I speculate.

"I'd love to know what they were after," she sighs.

I cross my arms and try to think of what comes next.

"Very warm here," says Ray, holding his hand near a server rack.

"That's because the fans and cooling system are off. Even though the processors don't have power, all the heat's trapped and . . . *damn.* I'm such an idiot. Nobody move."

"What is it?" asks Jessica with her gun at her side.

"Just stand still." I pull the thermal scope from my pocket. "No more footsteps."

I aim the sensor at the room and see the bright glow of the server racks. Jessica's footprints are visible, as are Lilith's and Ray's in the direction from which they came. I spin around and see my own steps.

"Let me see if I can still find out where they went," I say as I start walking past the server aisles.

"Clever man," says Ray.

"Clever would have been doing this ten minutes ago when their footsteps were fresh. This is desperate." I keep walking, scanning each section, looking for any glow that isn't the servers.

I can see faint footprints of someone running, which would probably be my colleagues' from when they were first searching the room.

When I reach a section just past the middle, I catch a hot spot on the tiles. Several people stood here for a while. I get closer and find the footprints concentrated near one server cabinet.

"Over here," I call out to the others.

They join me in the row but keep a few meters away. I pull a pair of gloves from a pocket and open the door to the server rack. Inside, there are forty servers, all stacked on top of each other, each one containing anything from medical records to entire porn empires. There are no empty slots.

"Did they use a hard drive to steal the data?" asks Jessica.

"That would take too long. I think they replaced a server with another. That's what I'd do."

"They all look alike."

"They do . . ." I take out the scope and look at the thermal image. All of them glow a bright white-blue . . . except one toward the top. This would be the server they brought with them. The one that hasn't been running for several years straight. The cold one.

"Now what?" asks Jessica.

"We write down this location, and when the power comes back on, we find out what was supposed to be here. Also, we need to get a warrant to see what's on this replacement they left." I think for a moment.

"We also need to contact every data center in Manhattan and find out if any of them had fire department personnel ask for access right after the blackout; then they need to dust for fingerprints and find the one server that doesn't have any."

"Singapore, too," says Jessica.

"Yeah. Singapore, too. We may have found what they were really after."

Lilith puts her hand to her earpiece and listens to someone for a moment. "Jessica?"

"Yes?"

"May I speak with you?"

"Sure. Excuse me, Theo."

She walks over to another row. I can barely hear the words, but one stands out: *IDR.*

PART THREE
ESCAPE ARTIST

CHAPTER EIGHTEEN
LANE CHANGE

IDR was waiting for us outside. My paperwork stunt didn't impress Vivian Kieren. Before I could explain, Theo was slammed into the ground, his hands bound behind his back, and he was dragged into a truck while the rest of her team kept their guns trained on me.

I was treated with slightly more professional courtesy, although I was disarmed and shoved into the back of another vehicle with her men on either side of me to make sure I didn't try to make a run for it.

Lilith protested and threatened to take this up with her bosses until Kieren pulled her ace card from her sleeve. Two of them, actually: a dusky, mustachioed CIA station chief named O'Donnell and his right-hand man, Shafner, who had the pale skin of an office drone. They worked with Korean intelligence and had major pull here.

I wasn't sure at the time what kind of bullshit story Kieren told them to get their cooperation, but as I sit here in an interrogation room somewhere in Camp Humphreys, a US Army base forty miles south of Seoul, I have a feeling that no matter what I say, it won't make a difference.

I've been locked in this room for two hours. Twice I've been offered coffee and an armed escort to the bathroom, which is more of a way to cover their asses if I complain about mistreatment than any act of kindness on their part.

The waiting irritates me. But what's killing me is that I know that while I'm in here, they're in some other part of the building interrogating Theo without the pseudopoliteness of coffee or bathroom breaks. I pulled him from a wretched prison cell less than twelve hours ago. He's had half a full meal and still looks like walking death.

I could get out of this room. But then what? Rescue Theo and steal a C-141 StarLifter like in a Tom Cruise movie? The real world doesn't work like that. How would I explain it to my bosses? And I'll bet anything that Kieren has already told them where I am. Not Gerald, but whomever she knows at the FBI who's senior and thinks of me more as an embarrassment than an asset.

The only way out of this is *time*. Which isn't something I have right now. Every minute they're in there with Theo increases the likelihood he'll say something to incriminate himself or agree to something he doesn't realize he's admitting to. Kieren and the CIA would love to say they have somebody materially involved in the Void. Even if, later on, it doesn't hold water.

The door opens, and Kieren enters with O'Donnell and Shafner. They take the seats on the other side of the table from me. O'Donnell watches me, waiting to see my reaction. Shafner is texting on his phone. Kieren sits with her arms folded. She's beyond pissed. My airplane stunt probably didn't help.

O'Donnell speaks first. "Blackwood, I'm sure you already know your career is over."

"Do I?"

"You're not a stupid woman. Of course you know you're done. You've misappropriated a government jet. You helped a suspect escape custody. You interfered with a counterterrorism operation. Should I go on?"

"None of that is true, and shouldn't I have someone from the FBI here? Last I checked, it wasn't policy to interrogate personnel from other agencies without someone being present from that agency."

"Would you like me to get the FBI liaison from Seoul here?" asks O'Donnell. "Norm's married to my daughter. I'm sure he'd love to be in this room right now. Actually, I'm doing you a favor by *not* calling him in. In fact, I'm trying to do you a *huge* favor. There's two ways this ends. One is you cooperate fully, and while your career is effectively over, you get to leave with your pension and no black mark that makes you unhirable. The other option is you put up your little fight, irritate us, but we eventually get what we want and not only is your career over, but we destroy you. No pension. Messy stories in the news about you fucking things up. That kind of thing. So, what do you think?"

I glance over at Kieren and the smug look on her face. She's been quiet the whole time. "I take it he was your office husband when you two worked together in the CIA?"

Neither react, but I catch a tiny grin at the edge of Shafner's mouth as he pretends not to be listening intently. It appears I hit the nail on the head.

"Let's just say it's good to have friends," she replies.

"I want to talk to Theo."

"He's not a well man," says O'Donnell. "We have a doctor looking at him right now."

"Was the doctor with him when you started interrogating him?"

"That's not how we operate. Now, let's focus on you and what you know. Did he say anything that could possibly be incriminating or make someone suspect that he was involved in the events in Manhattan or Seoul?"

"No. Absolutely not," I reply, deciding that *incriminating* is a subjective term that I won't interpret to their benefit. "In fact, the suggestion is completely absurd. He's spent the last five months providing medical treatment to refugees in Myanmar."

"Our sources there say he was working with a terrorist faction," says Shafner.

"And as a reasonable person, you know that's complete bullshit. Your *sources* have been shoving people into mass graves for years." I turn to Kieren. "Do you have any reason to believe Cray's involved in this other than his name showing up on a list?"

She doesn't respond.

I push. "We know who's behind this. It's Michael Heywood. I keep saying that, but everybody pretends it can't be him. Why? Instead, you're chasing down a man who was half-dead when this happened, beaten within an inch of his life because he was trying to vaccinate babies so the next epidemic didn't wipe an entire group of people off the face of the planet."

"Is that what you think of Dr. Cray?" asks O'Donnell. "There's a side to him you don't know. I've seen images of the bodies of some of the people he's 'helped.'"

"Were these images taken from the same drone that was used to supply information to the Myanmar military so they could kill him? Which, if I'm not mistaken, might be a breach of our current sanctions on them? Never mind that using such intelligence to target a US citizen without oversight is probably something the FBI could investigate. At the very least, it's a story the *New York Times* would like to hear. How long after I put that out on Twitter before it blows up?"

"Let's just cuff her and put her somewhere until she's ready to talk," says Kieren to the men. She turns to me: "You tipped off Cray. Helped him escape and then stole our plane. That's pretty cut-and-dried. Isn't it?"

"Is it? Last I checked I was assigned to find the whereabouts of Dr. Cray. You were there, remember? My supervisor understood that. You knew that. I then took him into protective custody. I don't recall anyone identifying themselves as IDR. And as far as I can tell, you didn't let the locals know what you were doing. How is Willets's leg?"

O'Donnell glances at Kieren. "Who?"

I interject. "She didn't tell you? One of her men got shot by a Burmese cop in that little screwup. I guess she didn't tell you who bandaged the wound and saved that man's life . . . That would be Dr. Cray."

"For all I know, Cray pulled the trigger," she replies.

"No. I was there. I'll happily go on the record and explain what happened. As far as the plane? When I looked, the three letters of the agency it belongs to are FBI and not IDR."

She smirks. "I don't think you understand the way the game is played out here. Your little paperwork tricks and bureaucratic jujitsu only work to a point. If I say I found text messages on your phone that have you talking to Dr. Cray and giving him information about the case, those text messages appear. If I say there's a hundred thousand dollars in your bank account you can't explain or a Bitcoin wallet on your phone, who are they going to believe?"

I look to O'Donnell. "Is this how it works here? You openly threaten to manufacture evidence? To what end?"

"We want Cray. We have strong intel about him. That's all we can say."

And now you've got him. God, I'm going in circles here. Why can't they see it? Or . . . what can't I see?

Okay . . . Theo's name shows up on a list, and I'm convinced that Heywood had something to do with that. The problem is, I never took that to its logical conclusion.

Heywood gets mysteriously transferred to a different facility.

Then Gerald tells me there's a mole inside the FBI.

Oh jeez.

The whole mole thing that Gerald's concerned about? That was *Heywood*. I have no idea how, but I think I get the big picture.

"Theo Cray's name shows up on a list," I tell my hosts. "You all buy into it because that same source has provided you with other information, right? Names of spies? Counterintel operations? You're so used to working with scumbags, it doesn't bother you that source is Michael Heywood, a.k.a. the Warlock. Right now, he's pulling your strings, and you don't even see it."

Shafner's eyes lift from his phone. He glances at O'Donnell. I might have gotten to him, at least. I don't know what good it will do, though.

"This is how Heywood works," I go on. "He fed you what he did so that when the time came, he could misdirect you."

Kieren slaps a hand on the table. "I've had enough. Can we just stuff her somewhere for now?"

There's a knock at the door, and a soldier comes in and whispers something to O'Donnell.

"The ambassador's here," he says.

Before Kieren can respond, another knock comes at the door, and an elderly man with a dark complexion and silver-tinged temples enters.

"I hope I'm not disturbing anything," he says in his booming voice. "I'd just flown in from Japan to offer to help, and I heard one of my oldest and dearest friends was here."

Robert Ailes, US ambassador to Japan, my former mentor at the FBI, and the man who saved me from a life of boredom and helped me do whatever good acts I've done in this world, looks in my direction. "Ah, Jessica. It's so good to see you."

He walks around the table, and I give him a warm hug. "Dr. Ailes," I say deferentially.

"Listen to her with that. She's like my own daughter. I hope they're treating you well here."

"We were just wrapping up. I was heading over to the infirmary to see Dr. Theo Cray."

"Cray? He's here?" says Ailes, pretending to be surprised. "I'd been meaning to talk to him. His paper on simulating neural network back-propagation using bacterial films was a work of genius." Ailes glances over at O'Donnell. "Are we good here?"

O'Donnell rolls his eyes. Everyone in the room is aware of who just played whom. I should keep my mouth shut, but I look to Kieren and remark, "It's good to have friends."

Ailes and I walk down the hall with his escorts, and he whispers under his breath, "This better be good, Jessica, or I'm putting you in an even worse place than they were planning to."

"Define 'good,'" I reply.

CHAPTER NINETEEN
CHESSBOARD

After checking on Theo, who was moved to the base hospital to get some much-needed rest and medical care, Robert Ailes and I found a nearly empty base coffee shop to talk out of earshot of anyone connected to Kieren.

I spent the first hour explaining everything that had happened up until the moment he walked in, leaving nothing out. That's my relationship with Ailes. He can tell when I'm lying from a mile away. He can even tell when I'm lying to myself. I didn't tell him I was coming to this part of the world, and I didn't ask him how he knew, but Ailes is the kind of man to keep an eye on people, and he must've heard about my whereabouts through diplomatic channels.

Ailes started off as a brilliant mathematician, made a fortune in the private sector, and then let the last president talk him into helping restructure the FBI to better utilize people who have skills that are often overlooked. As part of that project, he created his own little team of misfit toys—Gerald being one and me another. My years working with Robert were the most dangerous, damaging, and rewarding of my life.

When I was moved to a teaching role, Robert left and later accepted the position as US ambassador to Japan. While it was historically a role that dealt with ceremony and trade negotiations, I'd heard whispers that his real mission was to help build a new US/Japanese/Korean intelligence partnership to counteract the threat of China. If any person could pull that off while avoiding knee-jerk xenophobia, it was Ailes.

He listens to the last details of my account, then shakes his head. "So you decided to travel to Myanmar to retrieve Dr. Cray. Did Gerald sign off on that?"

"Technically, yes. I had prior approval to travel overseas to escort material witnesses, provided they were in custody of local authorities," I explain.

"What you did was a jailbreak."

"Assumptions may have been made. But, Robert, they were going to kill him."

"Who? The Burmese or Kieren?"

"Either. Both."

"I don't see it. Kieren is a blunt instrument. But I don't get why she'd want him dead," he replies.

"All I know is this: Cray's name showed up on a list from an intel source that I suspect *is* Heywood—or is at least controlled by him. If you're Kieren and you've been running around acting on this intel, you're better off putting Cray into a deep hole. Plus, it's a big win for the IDR."

"So you don't think Cray is involved?"

"No!" I almost spit out my coffee. "That's absurd."

"Maybe not as absurd as you think. There's some suspicious things about him."

"What? The whole he-framed-the-serial-killers theory? *You?*"

"No. The way he got some of them. Remember the Butcher Creek fiasco, where the FBI thought they had a serial killer and it was some prankster with a bunch of medical body parts?"

"Theo? Why?"

"Forrester, the man who tried to vaccinate half our armed forces with a bad vaccine, was a crime-scene junkie. Speculation is that Cray manufactured that entire scene just to lure him out."

"Clever."

"I won't even get into how many federal laws he may have broken doing that," says Ailes.

"But he caught Forrester. Sometimes the ends justify the means."

"Sometimes the people who are deciding that cross one too many lines. Take Kieren and the others back there. They started off as upstanding enforcers of the Constitution. At some point they decided they needed to push things a little. Then a little more."

"I think Theo knows his boundaries," I reply.

"Maybe he did once. But he's also dived off the deep end more than a few times. That can change you in ways you don't realize. His PTSD has PTSD. Look," Ailes tells me in a confiding manner, "I'm not revealing anything you're not going to find out, but there's an open investigation into Dr. Cray. I don't know what they've found out since I left the FBI, but I know there are people who have it in for him."

"Is this professional or because he's made more than a few of them look like complete idiots?"

"The effect's the same."

"I can't speak to his methods or what's going on upstairs. But I know this world would be a much worse place if he hadn't made the choices he made. I think he lives with that every moment of every day. I know *I* do. But I was lucky to have you watching my back, covering for the stupid stuff I did."

"You're a fan of the guy," Ailes says.

"He's a piece of work, but in the last day, I've seen him at extremes, and I trust him." I shrug. "When he's not thinking, he's trying to fix things."

"But he's also exceptional at breaking them. And that's why everyone's so interested in him," says Ailes.

"They're interested in him because some anonymous source fed them his name. None of this is remotely like anything he's been involved with. It's painfully obvious to me."

"Hmm." Ailes thinks for a moment. "You think Heywood wants Cray out of the equation because he's afraid of him?"

"It's part of his playbook. Remember when you put me on the Warlock case and my face made it into the news? Heywood freaked when he realized the FBI had sicced someone on him who understands magic and illusion methods. So, what did he do? He made highly public threats on my life. He made me part of the story because he knew that the FBI, assuming one agent is the same as another, would pull me from the case. Which they almost did, until you intervened. And after that, with each of his cartoon-villain plots, he got somebody to try to kill me. Red Chain, whatever. But this time we're dealing with something bigger. His biggest deception of all. And he's not worried about me, because it's more than a magic trick. It's Cray he wants off the chessboard."

Ailes thinks this over. "Do you *really* trust him?"

"I do. Do I know what his real motives are? No. Do I think he's a soldier who's been at war too long? Definitely. But we need him right now. We think we know how the Voids happened, but we have no idea why. Heywood's up to something even I can't comprehend."

"Something he doesn't want one of the world's leading computational biologists looking at too closely."

"At least not the one who also happens to have caught more serial killers than half the FBI."

"Fair enough. It's obviously not my call, but I'll vouch for you and talk to some friends. I'll have to explain why turning him over to IDR would be a bad idea. Hopefully they'll listen. What's next?" asks Ailes.

"That's easy. When Theo wakes up, I'm going to ask him to think of the most horrifying plots against the world that he can imagine."

CHAPTER TWENTY

MASTERMIND

Theo is sitting in a chair, staring out the window of his room of the base hotel. My room has a view of the base and the runway; his looks out over the morning fog–covered tracts of farmland south of Camp Humphreys. I can't tell if he's looking inward or outward. He hasn't touched the cup of coffee I brought him. The watch on the table with the timer running and the bottles of water near medicine packages tell me he's been focusing on getting his body back into shape instead of tending to his cravings.

"Want me to order you some breakfast?" I ask.

"No, I'll stick to liquids for a little while longer." He picks up a protein shake. "The key, I think, is to dilute them. My stomach hasn't processed this much nutrient-rich food in a while. That's one of the problems in trying to treat people who are malnourished. Our urge is to force-feed them, but that can make things worse."

"Like with Auschwitz survivors," I muse, thinking back to a documentary I watched on how the Allies had to nurse them back to health.

"Exactly. We know a lot more now. Thankfully. And my situation was nowhere near as bad, but I saw men back in that prison who weren't much better off," he says, still staring out the window.

"Hard to imagine how someone could do that to another person," I reply.

"No, it's not. You just make a person not a person. You start with a label. Maybe it's a different political party or religion from your own. Then you make them that label and everything you hate about it. I watched military commanders do that with young children, getting them to hate people in a different village." He points to the television in the room. "We have our version. We even tell ourselves convincing little fictions that it's okay to hate those other people because they're the ones who are *really* filled with hate. We make ourselves judges." His eyes go down to his hands in his lap. "I made myself a judge. I'm sorry. You have some folders. You want to talk about something?"

"It can wait," I lie.

"No, it can't. I apologize." He turns away from the window and rests his elbows on the table. "What can I do for you?"

I feel awkward saying what I'm about to say after his observations on the nature of good and evil. "Well, this is a bit uncomfortable for me to ask. But I was wondering if you'd be up for a bit of role-playing?"

"Role-playing? What do you mean?"

"I'm convinced that Heywood's at the center of this. The problem is, I can't prove it, much less explain what 'this' really is. Some think the Voids are an end in and of themselves. You and I think otherwise. The data-center heist clearly shows he's up to something."

"But it could be ancillary," says Theo. "That may not be the goal, either. More like stealing the jar of candy on the way out after a bank robbery."

"Fair enough. But whatever it is, I'd rather figure out what he's trying to do before it's revealed. You follow?"

"I think so. So what role do I play?"

"This is the awkward part. I want you to think like a criminal genius who wants to do as much harm as possible."

"Is that what you think he's up to?" asks Theo.

"He's evil. He has no problem with murder. I'm just trying to figure out how you would scale that up. I was hoping you could help. Everyone I've talked to pretty much starts with 'steal a nuclear bomb' or 'get a hold of some kind of bioweapon.' I was wondering if you had something more imaginative."

"Nuclear is hard. A private individual could still pull it off, if they had enough resources."

"Really? Everyone I've talked to says you'd have to be a nation-state, and then we'd still know something was up."

"I think Bill Gates or Elon Musk could pull it off," replies Theo. "Disguise it in plain sight as fusion research. The key would be keeping a lid on the people working for you. But you could have a hundred physicists and engineers working on compartmentalized projects while only a small team really knows what's going on."

"That's scary to think about," I reply.

"Is it? I could have changed the tide of World War II if I brought my laptop back in time. From uranium refinement to code breaking, it would give me godlike powers. Now we all have them. Anyway, I don't think he's going nuclear."

"Why not?"

"Too small-scale. So, you take out a city. Earthquakes do that all the time. The last pandemic hit the major ones. It was painful; we're still recovering, but we're still here. The damage from September 11 wasn't just the people lost, it was the psychological impact and how it changed all our lives. If you want to do real damage, you don't just break a thing, you destroy a system."

"Okay. How do you do that?"

"Lots of ways." Theo looks up for a moment. "It's not just what you do, but how you go about doing it. If you study the strategy of terrorists, you'll notice that they went from focusing on initial damage to creating follow-up attacks that killed first responders. One bomb to hurt the civilians, a second to kill all the people who rushed in to help. This has affected the way we do crisis management and made the first attack even more deadly. We don't rush in to help the wounded as quickly because we need to make sure it's safe to do so. Now, accelerate that line of reasoning and you can figure out how to do maximum damage."

"Such as?" I ask.

"It works with anything. Let's say I wanted to do a simplified bioweapon attack. I'd start by getting the more dangerous strains of pathogens that are being worked on around the world," he explains.

"And release them in shopping malls and other public places?" I reply.

"No. Not at first. That would be too conventional. I'd release them at the doughnut shop across the street, infecting coffee cups. I'd put them in those misters they use in outdoor bars wherever you have soldiers. I'd be infecting everyone at the major disease-control centers. I'd infect the people who are supposed to protect us first. That's what Forrester was trying to do to our military forces."

"They said he never would have gotten that far," I reply.

"They desperately needed to convince themselves that's true," says Theo. "So many of their safeguards failed—why should we believe only the ones we didn't test would have held up?"

I don't know if this is Theo trying to make himself out to be some kind of great savior or if he's just stating simple truths. I'm leaning toward the latter, and it's frightening.

"And one more thing," Theo continues. "Depending upon what I could get from each lab, I'd release different variants and entirely different diseases around the world. That would cause chaos. We may be better prepared now for handling outbreaks, but this would overcome those preparations. While we're overwhelmed with one attack, we'd get hit by another. Then another."

"So you think it could be biological in nature?" I ask.

"It could be, but I'm a biologist. So I'm biased. Ask a computer scientist and they might point out that one of our biggest vulnerabilities is embedded systems. You know that already. Red Chain found a series of exploits in the power grid that they were able to use to cause blackouts."

And nearly tore countries apart through riots and misinformation. "They're supposed to be better now, and we have improved systems for controlling misinformation," I reply.

"Do we? Or did we centralize everything and make it even easier to spread fear? Now all it takes is one extra vote in a contested district for a VP of software at a tech company to have the authority to tell people what's true and not true. Is that a better system? Sometimes quick fixes are exactly what our enemy wants. Viruses learned to use our immune systems against us, and that's worked extremely well."

"We're still here," I reply.

"Cow pastures exist because we need meat, not because of any clever social thinking on the cow's behalf."

"Any other cheery thoughts?"

"No, just what I said. That if Heywood did want to use some kind of pathogen attack, then he'd do well to infect the people who are supposed to solve the problem. Taking them out of the equation like he tried with you and me."

I make some notes. "So, we should be monitoring infectious-disease researchers for disease?"

"It's probably worth the effort. Although I suspect that he'd use something rather mild in the beginning so as not to raise too many of their own alarm bells. He might even infect researchers with variants of their own research so they'd take longer to report symptoms."

"Because they'd assume it was self-contamination?"

"Yes. The only thing intelligent people hate almost as much as making mistakes is being wrong. When I was teaching, sometimes I'd deliberately mess up my students' experiments and see how many of them reported the errors in their results."

"And?"

"I'd call out the name of a student and read their lab report in class and eviscerate them for concealing the faulty results, giving the others a chance to make amends."

"That had to suck to be that student," I reply.

Theo shakes his head. "I made the name up. The other students were too focused on their own mistakes to realize that I was tearing into someone who didn't exist."

"Did you like to teach?" I ask.

"I miss it more than anything else," says Theo without hesitation. "I liked to teach and do original research. I didn't appreciate what I had back then, though. I didn't know what a gift it was to be around smart, young minds . . ." His voice trails off. "I should have paid more attention."

There's something profoundly sad about the way he just said that. I'd ask for more, but I might be probing too deep.

"You've circled the word *biological*," says Theo, pointing at my notepad.

"Well, you make a strong case. The thing is, we haven't had any reports of break-ins at labs . . ."

"First of all, you don't need to physically steal the specimen. You can get the genetic sequence from an online database. Then it's a matter of using a sequencer. If the strands are too short, you can use a growth medium like yeast to join them. After that, you take the DNA and convert it to RNA—if it's an RNA virus—and then infect a cell with it. Same with bacteria, although you can skip a step. For fun, you could mix and match genes to see what you get."

"It's that easy?" I ask.

"It's all relative. I've done it . . . unofficially. But some of my methods haven't been published because I'm afraid they make the process a little *too* simple. Any medium-size university or biotech company could pull it off. It just takes one or two steady hands and money. Do you think Heywood has access to those kinds of resources?"

"I wouldn't put anything past him. And I suspect he has access to a large source of funding, either his own or from a state sponsor. But I can't prove it."

Theo goes silent for a moment. "Hmm. I'll have to think about that."

"I hate to ask you this, but we need your help. Ongoing, I mean. This has already been helpful."

"Hmm," he says again. "Last I checked, the government was trying to put me into a cell."

"Some people still want to see that happen. And if you stay on board, it'll only create more suspicion for them about you."

"That's good. At least it shows they're learning. After the Forrester incident, I pointed out that because he'd been considered a leading authority on the kind of vaccine tampering they were trying to prevent, they never considered him a suspect. And yet he should have been the first one we looked at."

"So, you'll help us?"

"No, Jessica. I'll help *you*. The moment they take you off this or try to get me to talk to someone else, I'm done."

"That could mean sitting this out in some IDR secret detention center," I say.

"Then so be it." Theo shrugs. "Where do we start?"

CHAPTER TWENTY-ONE
THREADS

"I'd like to know more about the data centers," says Theo. "What was taken. That seems like our biggest clue yet. If we could get back in there, we might find something else."

"We can't. IDR has taken over that part of the investigation, along with the Koreans," I explain.

"Well, they seemed to be on the same track we were, so I guess it makes sense."

"Except they weren't. They got our position from Korean intelligence. They didn't show up at the data center to chase down a clue. They went because it's where *you* were."

"Ah. I see. And now they have access and get the credit, I assume?"

"Basically. The credit doesn't bother me. I'd just like to know what they know as soon as they find out. While I don't trust Kieren, the people working with her aren't stupid. They're bound to discover something, but I doubt they'll be sharing it with us," I say with a sigh.

"Why didn't the FBI put their foot down? You or Ambassador Ailes could have made a deal."

"We did. Sort of . . ."

Theo leans back and stares at me. "Oh. I see. *I* was that deal. I'm not in some IDR facility because you made a trade?"

"In a roundabout way," I say.

"Jessica, objectively speaking, was that wise? I think you and your colleagues might make faster work of whatever is in that data center than IDR can. This could be a setback."

I shake my head. "No. I'm making a bet, something my gut tells me."

"And that is?"

"That having you on the outside is better than whatever I can learn from the data heist. I bet on your freedom and your mind."

"Let me apologize in advance for disappointing you. I don't think there's anyone better at understanding Heywood than you. I'm afraid I'm not much more than deadweight."

"Let's hold off on that determination until later. Right now, we need another lead."

"What about the EMPs?"

"The FBI lab is looking for clues. All the materials except the carbon nanotubes are off-the-shelf. The suspects they've arrested have prior associations with anarchist groups. They claim they were recruited online and paid to carry out the New York attack."

"Paid how?"

"Bitcoin or some other digital currency. A hundred thousand each. Apparently, there were dry runs with small teams. Those might've been to see who could be trusted."

Theo nods. "They were run like terrorist cells. Nobody had enough information to compromise the others."

"Correct. And it seems they had no idea what the EMPs would do. They thought they were just bombs meant to disrupt traffic."

"Interesting. So that means that somewhere there's a bomb maker. Did we have any more sightings of demons or dementors anywhere else?" asks Theo.

"No. But I've asked if we could get hold of military radar recordings and satellite images. There might be something to be found there."

"It sounds like everything to do with the Void is being covered," says Theo. "I don't know what help I can really provide."

"Then let's look outside the Void. Let's look where nobody else is paying attention."

Theo considers this for a moment. "Patterns are hard because we can only know what we see. Great white sharks were a complete mystery to us because they'd show up in one region, then vanish for a year before returning. Where did they go? In retrospect it was obvious, but at the time it was a big nature mystery. The simple answer is that when an animal goes someplace else, it's either to eat, breed, or give birth.

"When they finally were able to tag great whites with satellite trackers, they found the places where the big sharks were doing all those things. The feeding grounds should have been obvious, because that pattern was enmeshed in another creature's pattern. In this case, great whites went to eat where seals went to give birth. A booming seal colony meant a great white buffet. When scientists found out where great whites gave birth, it turned out to be where they didn't have to worry about being fished or killed by orcas when they were at their most vulnerable.

"The lesson was: if you can't discern one species' pattern, look for the patterns of the other species it shares an ecosystem with."

"All right. How do we apply that here? Or do you just make up nature documentaries in your head as you go along?"

"Good question. I've been asked that before. As far as Heywood's pattern goes, he needs people. Maybe not informed people who know the whole picture, but people to do the physical work for the insanity he dreams up. Talking to some of the people he's recruited in the past would be helpful, but I suspect that he's smart enough to leave so many false trails that we'd be running in circles.

"If he's planning some bigger event, something to make the Void look like a warm-up, then there's got to be some other pattern we're not seeing. Maybe not one big one, but several interrelated patterns. Remember the collection of weird cases you showed me?"

"Yeah, but we're looking for a pattern. Those cases seemed pretty random."

"Yes, but you and your colleague selected them out of a huge number of weird cases. Why those particular ones? Were there some other criteria about them?"

I weigh how much to tell him. Do I really trust him? I believe so. Do I need answers?

Absolutely.

"I have a friend. Sometimes he sends me information that was obtained in ways that are . . ."

Theo holds up a hand. "I understand. What made these interesting?"

I've only told one other person this. If Robert Ailes found out, he'd kill me. It goes against so many bureau directives, not to mention violating the law, even if I'm not the one actually violating it.

To hell with it.

"My friend was worried about my safety and afraid that the FBI wasn't doing enough. So, he used a device to track cell phone numbers."

"Where?" asks Theo.

"Heywood's attorneys' offices. We suspected that while his own attorneys may have been acting within legal boundaries, a clerk or someone else there who had access to Heywood wasn't. So, we started tracking numbers and looking to see where they popped up."

"And anytime you saw a suspicious incident and a related number, or one associated to that, you put a pin in it?"

"Basically. I was looking for weird stuff. Test runs, whatever." I'm embarrassed to admit this. I may have broken not only the law, but my own ethical standards.

"Clever. You created contact tracing for weirdness in order to find the Warlock's hidden pattern," he replies.

"It was wrong." My cheeks burn at the mere thought of Ailes knowing what I did.

"Is it? I mean technically, yes. So is breaking a window. But if there's a child suffocating inside a hot car, breaking the window and committing a crime is the only moral thing to do. Sometimes we have to take extreme actions with the hope that we'll be judged for their impact and not the deeds. Or better yet, hope we never get judged."

I think about the allegation that Theo created an entire crime scene with body parts and wasted the FBI's and local authorities' time and resources. "Is this how you make decisions?"

"Yes. And I'm always weighing them, unsure if I made the right choice. I don't judge you for what you did. I'd do the same. In fact, I have, and more."

"So, do any of the cases stand out more than others?" I ask.

"The miracle cures intrigue me, but the one I fear the most is your missing chimpanzees."

"What would Heywood do with a bunch of chimpanzees?" I ask.

"Lots of things. Pound for pound, they're one of the most ferocious animals you could encounter," Theo replies.

"Wait . . . Do you think Heywood's trying to weaponize chimps?"

"I wasn't exactly going in that direction. But it is a horrifying thought. It could be another distraction, or it could be part of his bioweapon research. I don't know. But I'd love to understand how over two dozen chimpanzees went missing without a trace."

CHAPTER TWENTY-TWO
MONKEY VILLAGE

Theo is on his knees, face-to-face with a young orangutan that has ventured to the edge of her enclosure to study the curious man. His arms are outstretched in much the same way that apes balance themselves. His head is slightly tilted back, and he moves his face from his lips and upper cheeks, forming a kind of smile. Baba the orangutan is amused by Theo and reaches a hand out to touch the glass near his nose. She smiles, backs up, and tries it again, delighted by the show the man ape is putting on for her.

Theo sees me observing and says, "At this age, her brain and a human child's are far more alike than we care to acknowledge. It's not for another year that nature sets in and she becomes more orangutan and a human becomes more *Homo sapiens*. Same with chimps, bonobos, and gorillas. You could put all five of them together at the same age and they'd play, once they got over their shyness. The ironic part is the human kid would be the slowest one in the room, mentally." He blows Baba a kiss. She puts her hand to her mouth and almost mimics the gesture. I wonder if she'll master the action and if anybody will ever realize it was taught to her by one of the smartest people on the planet, who also apparently speaks orangutan.

"You must be Jessica," says a young man in a polo shirt and sunglasses, striding toward us.

"Jack?" I reply, assuming this is Jack Soonsiri, son of the Thai owners of the Monkey Village amusement park.

"Did they let you in without any problem?"

"There were tickets waiting for us. Thank you," I reply. "This is Dr. Cray."

"Nice to meet you. Sorry I couldn't be at the front gate. We have so many animals. Lots of hungry mouths. What do you think of our park?"

To be honest, it's nicer than I expected. I don't know how the captive animals feel, but I was afraid I'd find a lot of chains and exploitive demonstrations. "I think you've done a great job here."

"We love our animals," he says before kneeling down to look at Baba, who has retreated to the arms of her mother. "Hey, Baba! How are you today?"

Baba blows him a kiss. Jack looks at Theo and me with excitement. "Did you see that? I love you, too, Baba." He gets to his feet. "Her whole family was going to be sold for meat. They lost their home when her forest was destroyed to make a palm oil plantation."

"That's horrible." I can't imagine anyone wanting to eat something like an orangutan, but then I've never been starving and living in a world where people treated me as poorly as the animals around me.

"But you're not here about Baba. You're here to help us find our missing chimpanzees," says Jack. "Follow me."

Jack leads us down a tree-lined path with enclosures on either side. Part of what makes Monkey Village special is that most of the property is used for the animals, with the humans funneled through caged corridors. At the very least, it gives the illusion that the animals can roam freely.

We reach an open space surrounding a recess in the ground with a cage running around the top edge. It's probably a hundred meters across. Below is an island with a moat. Large boulders and trees landscape the area, along with a fake rock wall and cave.

Signs around the enclosure in Thai, Chinese, and English warn people not to throw things at the chimpanzees. Which would be helpful if there were any chimps here.

"This is it," says Jack. "This was their home, and then one day, no more chimpanzees. People thought it was a publicity stunt. I thought maybe Safari Kingdom stole them. But chimps are a lot of work. We had the largest population in Asia."

Theo goes up to the edge of the fence. First he scans the area, and then he does something I'd never have thought to do: he smells the air. "No idea?" he asks.

"None. Some people thought maybe the Chinese stole them to eat. I don't like that theory. Plus, people blame the Chinese for everything. Too much pollution? Blame the Chinese, even though it's our cars. Prices too high? Blame the Chinese. Without Chinese tourists, we'd be like the other zoos, making the orangutans kickbox and putting the chimps in bikinis. Imagine little Baba kickboxing? No. I want her to have a nice life. You want to take a closer look?"

I glance at Theo. "Your call."

"There hasn't been a chimp in here for a while. At least not living here."

"It's safe," says Jack. "No chimps. And ours are well trained, anyway. Nobody's lost any fingers yet."

"It's not losing my finger I'm worried about," says Theo.

Jack leads us around the fence to a gate that he unlocks. On the other side is a staircase that takes us down to the back side of the chimpanzee island. Behind the facade is a large enclosed cage with several smaller cages and sliding gates.

"During monsoon season we bring them in here. Otherwise they stay outside," explains Jack.

"Were they outside when they went missing?" asks Theo.

"Yes. We have watchmen who keep an eye on things."

"What about cameras?" I ask.

"Yes. But they don't work very well. We had one that shows the outside. We watched the footage to check if we could see any chimps escaping. There's another one." He points to the corner. "It was watching inside here."

"And the only way out would be to climb the fence or through here?" I ask.

Jack nods. "Which is why I get frustrated when people accuse us of doing this ourselves. Why would we leave the camera on in here? It'd be easier to believe someone just backed up a truck and stole them from back here."

"Can we look outside?" asks Theo.

"Sure. This way." Jack leads us through a side door that opens into a passage behind the fake rock cliff.

We follow Jack down the narrow corridor. I keep glancing around, worried some hidden chimp will come flying at my face with its teeth bared. Intellectually I know it's safe, but Theo's stories and my own online research have me on edge.

"Cages are confusing for animals," Theo muses aloud. "They don't understand the relationship between the cage and the person caging them. Also, from a psychological perspective, they don't fully understand captivity, but it affects them . . . They don't know where to direct their anger."

"I used to work with a tiger in my magic show," I reply. "She was an adolescent. Still dangerous, though. If I knew what I know now, I never would have done that."

"How did your parents think that was okay?" asks Theo.

"I had a weird childhood. My grandfather kept a pistol on him whenever the cat was around. So, there was that."

We reach the main area of the chimpanzee enclosure, the section where the chimps would hang out doing chimpanzee business among rocks and trees that look a lot less natural up close. Above us is the viewing area that wraps almost completely around. A family has stopped to look at us. A confused toddler in her father's arms points at us and asks something in Thai. He laughs.

"She wanted to know why the chimps are so white and wearing clothes," says Jack, translating.

Theo drops to all fours and scrambles on top of a rock and beats his chest like an ape. The little girl claps her hands, and the family laughs.

"I don't think your friend is all there," Jack whispers to me.

"Dr. Cray *is* unique."

I'm just glad he's regaining his health.

Theo stands up and surveys the enclosure, revealing the real reason he climbed on top of the rock. It's weird how his brain works. He's deadly serious one moment and then clowning the next, but then you realize that he decided to get from point A to point B by amusing a child.

He examines the walls and the fence, then turns to me. "That back door still looks like the best option."

"We have footage," says Jack.

"Footage can be faked," I reply. "Trust me. Besides, if not that way, then what? How do you steal thirty scared chimps that would just as easily maul you?"

Theo kneels on the boulder. "Maybe you don't steal them. Perhaps you just show them the door and they let themselves out? They're quite clever. Captive chimps observe people opening doors and unlocking gates."

That has me thinking. I start walking around the enclosure, looking at it from a chimp's point of view. I don't know that I'd want to escape, but then again, I might be curious to explore. But *all* of them?

I put that aside and think about it from a different perspective. Something Theo said. It's not like we're in the Louvre trying to figure out who stole the *Mona Lisa*. We're at Alcatraz, trying to understand how an entire prison block escaped.

My nose twitches, and I realize something. The curious part of my brain overtakes the rational, fearful part, and I act on a hunch.

Jack is the first to speak. "Where did she go?"

"Well, that's interesting," says Theo, trying to figure out how I vanished.

CHAPTER TWENTY-THREE
TRAPDOOR

Magicians have been using trapdoors to create illusions for centuries. What most people don't realize is that in a good magic show, if you think the magician is using a trapdoor, she probably isn't. When used poorly, trapdoors can make the performer look clumsy and undermine the effect. Used judiciously, they can add a dramatic touch to a trick.

When audiences came to understand that the stage could be riddled with secret entrances and exits, magicians had to think of new methods to rule out the possibility of a secret door in the stage.

I rarely had the luxury of performing in theaters with traps, so I had to use illusions that employed entirely different methods. For this reason, I rarely even consider trapdoors, thinking they would be too obvious, but my grandfather showed me that with the right misdirection, they could help you perform a miracle.

The chimpanzees vanishing was a miracle because people made either one assumption or another. The chimps escaped of their own accord yet somehow managed to go undetected in the larger world. Or they were stolen from the enclosure.

The truth, I now believe, is neither. Someone stole the chimpanzees by creating an opportunity for them to escape. That opportunity is the storm drain I'm now standing in.

Its entrance is a metal grate that had been covered with weeds and rocks. The reason Jack's handlers didn't consider this is because there was a large rock on top of it and a lock on the grate that I picked while pretending to tie my shoe after sliding the boulder to the side.

"Jessica?" Jack calls out above me. "Did your friend go back inside?" he asks Theo.

I can see a shadow walking past the crack in the grate. I can visualize Theo standing there. Is he using the same method I did? The method that he demonstrated when we arrived at the enclosure?

Smell.

That's what tipped me off. Even though the zoo staff must have washed the rocks off on a regular basis, plenty of chimpanzee poo and urine slid down here. It's why the smell is unbearable and I'm seriously questioning how far I'll go to prove a point.

The grate opens, and sunlight pours down. Theo is looking down at me. "Clever. Very clever."

Jack pokes his head over. "This isn't supposed to be here. They told me it had been filled in!"

"Somebody unfilled it," I reply, imagining chimps smuggling rocks out in their chimp pants.

"Or they made it look like it was sealed," says Theo. "Someone on the inside helped." He calls down to me. "Jessica, you want to come back up?"

I look down the dark tunnel at the bottom of the pit. "Yeah. We should get some flashlights. And nose plugs."

"And tranquilizer guns," adds Theo. "We need to make sure none of our little friends are still down there."

"Oh shit," says Jack.

"She's fine," Theo replies, probably more to calm me down than to state an objective truth.

I start climbing the rungs, slowly, then faster when images of chimpanzees pulling me into the darkness fill my mind.

I reach the top, and Theo helps me out, then shuts the grate, snapping closed the lock I picked. "That was . . ."

"Stupid?" I reply.

"That, too. But interesting. Jack, can you get a couple of your people here so we can see where this little tunnel goes?"

"I'll get right on it," Jack says, then pulls his phone out and starts speaking in Thai.

"Is there a back exit?" I ask.

"That way." Jack points to a line of trees that ends at a wooden fence.

Theo and I make our way out of the enclosure and toward the back exit. He already understands what I'm thinking. Instead of waiting for them to explore the tunnel and possibly meet certain death if there's a cult of chimpanzee doomsday preppers waiting to bite off any noses that come poking around, we can follow the general path of the tunnel and see where it surfaces—assuming that it follows a straight line and actually ends somewhere.

We reach another door, where I pick the lock instead of asking Jack to assist. Before I can push it open, Theo stops me.

"What?" I ask.

"Listen first," he says. "General precaution."

"Oh, good point." I put my ear to the metal door. A noisy truck passes. I'm pretty sure this is the street. When I push the door open, we're facing a street and a row of industrial buildings on the other side.

We run across the road, dodging small cars and motorcycles, and reach an alley on the other side, where we find a concrete manhole cover. I take out my phone and look at where we are in Google Maps.

"Does it line up?" asks Theo.

"Yep."

He kneels and inspects the cover. There are crowbar marks on either side that haven't been weathered or stained over yet.

"See those?" he asks.

"Yep. Looks like we have an exit point. But I have two big questions."

"Only two?"

"Well, for starters. Who builds a chimpanzee enclosure over a sewer tunnel? And how do you get a bunch of chimps to make the crawl all the way through here? These are chimps, not Mexican drug-tunnel workers."

"First, I don't think it was always a chimpanzee enclosure. That moat looks like it had more water at one point. It may have been a crocodile pen," he replies.

"Okay. Then who the hell puts a crocodile pen over a sewer? How does that make sense?"

"It's not like they pick locks . . ."

"I'm still putting that in the bad-idea file." I look around for video cameras on buildings but can't spot any.

"I'm putting chimps in cages in the bad-idea file," he replies. "As far as how you get them all in there? That's easy: food. Getting them out? I suspect you scare them out." Theo pauses, then stands up. He walks around the street, then kneels down by a concrete planter and sticks his hand in it.

"Careful, snakes," I warn.

"I've learned that one the hard way. If you ever get bit, just call me. My blood can be used as antivenom."

"Seriously?"

He nods. "Wait. What have we here?" Theo's hand emerges with a syringe-like object that has a fuzzy end.

"Tranquilizer dart?" I ask.

"It would appear so. They probably put some kind of cage over the top and took them one by one. Although I don't see how they'd coax the mothers with infants out of the tunnel."

"You might be able to do it with sound. And whoever the inside man was could have sealed the grate shut."

"We should ask Jack who he doesn't trust," says Theo.

"Or we could ask ourselves why we should trust the son of the owners of the zoo, who pretends to like apes but clearly doesn't."

"What are you saying?"

"Did you notice his shoes? Dolce & Gabbana. Thousand-dollar shoes don't seem like a good idea for walking around in monkey poo. Also, the sunglasses were kind of pricey and not the kind you'd want a spider monkey to grab and run off with. He was late meeting us because he wasn't even at the zoo. He wanted to intercept us first. Notice how he didn't have a walkie-talkie?"

"Not until now," admits Theo. "So, Jack helped arrange the theft right under his parents' noses? I still think he had one or two people inside helping him. We'll need to talk to staff and find out who Jack just sent home."

I see Jack running in our direction from across the street. I wave to him, pretending we don't suspect a thing.

"Hey, guys. What did you find?" Jack asks in his most helpful tone.

"This syringe. Theo pricked his finger, and I want to call a friend to make sure he doesn't need to go to the hospital. But I can't get a signal here," I lie.

"Oh, here, you can use my phone," says Jack, trying to be super-helpful while having an internal freak-out.

I take his phone and pretend to dial while I actually open the recent-call list. "Theo? What's your friend's number?"

He's already ahead of me and has his camera app open. Theo pretends to look up a number while he surreptitiously videos Jack's recently called contacts and numbers.

"Here you go," he replies and calls out a number.

I go through the motions of dialing the number Theo gave me.

A recorded message from a young-sounding woman answers: "This is Hailey. You better have a damn good reason to call my private number or I'll have you murdered."

Aware that Jack is probably listening, I continue the charade, "Uh, hey, um, I'm with Theo Cray, and he appears to have been pricked by a syringe that was used to inject a chimp with a tranquilizer. Uh-huh. Typical Theo. The syringe? Stainless steel. About three weeks old. Is he okay?" I glance at Theo for an answer, because god knows I have no clue.

Theo doesn't pick up on what I'm asking.

"Yeah, that's right, three weeks ago. Does Theo need to go to the hospital?" He still doesn't get it. How can a man this smart be this dumb? "What? You want to talk to him? Okay." I shove the phone into Theo's hands.

"Hello?" Theo looks confused for a second, then he gets it. "No. Not deep. Yeah. I shouldn't be worried? Uh-huh, I've had my tetanus shot. Okay. Thanks." He hands the phone back to me.

"Hey, thanks." I hand Jack his phone back. "Looks like we're okay."

Okay, except I need to give Theo some lessons on improvising with a partner. Well, that and we've got to get Jack to a police station or somewhere we can interrogate him before he takes off and we can't find out whom he sold the chimpanzees to.

CHAPTER TWENTY-FOUR
New Logistics

Jack refused to talk at first. The Thai police captain screamed and yelled in his face, and then his mother came into the interrogation room and started slapping her son. This startled him even more than the threats of the captain.

Even then, he held fast. That is until, at my suggestion, the police took the two zoo workers Jack had recently called from his phone and walked them past the open door to the interrogation room. Also at my suggestion? Neither was handcuffed.

This convinced Jack that they'd reached some kind of plea deal, and suddenly he was ready to try to bargain his way out of the situation. Which ultimately, depending upon his relationship with his parents and their willingness to bribe the whole affair away, could mean him walking.

But I don't want him thinking that now. I want him thinking he's going to be locked into his own cage with no hope of daylight.

While Jack was being yelled at, Theo and I read the police report, using Google Lens to translate it into English.

When the chimps first went missing, suspicion immediately fell upon park employees, specifically the two men that Jack used. Because

Jack was considered a victim and had an alibi for them, they were released and the case only lived on in the news.

"Who did you sell the chimpanzees to?" I ask when the Thai police let me take my turn asking questions.

Jack glares at me. "I thought we were friends."

"I thought you weren't a thief and a liar," I reply. "Who did you sell them to?"

"I'm not saying anything."

"Your chance of getting out of this will increase considerably if you can tell us. We're after the people that bought them, not you. I can make sure the cops go easier on you if you help us."

"Why should I believe you?"

"Let me put it this way: if those chimps are being used for what we think, you'd do well to cooperate now . . . or be charged with murder later."

"Murder?" he scoffs.

"You realize that if any one of those chimps harmed somebody, you'd be accountable. If one of those people is an American, we can have you extradited to the United States. You think you love animals—wait until we get you in front of a California jury."

"He said they were going to private zoos," Jack says defensively. "Good places. My parents put on a show, but the chimps were getting expensive. People only like them when they're babies. We have thirty. Who needs thirty chimps?"

"Who was this man?" I ask.

"Some American. I met him at a club. He asked me about the chimps. I complained about how expensive they were. We came to an arrangement."

"And he said they were going to America?"

"He didn't say that. He said private zoos. I was curious if he was double-crossing me or selling them to the Chinese for more money.

After they loaded the chimpanzees, I followed the trucks all the way to the port."

"So where do you think they were bound?"

"I don't know for sure, but I saw the name of the ship. The MV *Arcturus*. I wanted to make sure it didn't have a Chinese name. Then I'd know he was screwing me over."

Theo's typing the name of the ship into the burner phone I gave him. He shows me a web page with shipping tables. He taps the row showing the arrival of the *Arcturus* in Long Beach.

It already arrived.

I type a text message to Gerald, telling him they need to search the port, although I doubt the chimps are still there. Whoever shipped them probably arranged to have them smuggled out of customs as well.

Damn. If we'd come here a day sooner, maybe we could have intercepted the ship before they unloaded the chimps. There's still hope, but I'm not counting on it.

"What can you tell us about the man that bought them?" asks Theo.

"Thirties. Average-looking American. What can I say?"

"Do you have a photo of him?"

"What? No. All I knew was his name was Dave and he had a Hong Kong number I could reach him at. It's dead now."

"Could I have that number?" asks Theo.

Jack shrugs. "I know it by heart. He wouldn't let me put it in my phone." He recites the number for Theo.

Theo types something in his phone notes and shows it to me: Is this the number that flagged your friend's phone search for the Warlock?

I open a calculator app on my phone and enter a code that opens a secret file. When I search for the number, nothing comes up. I show Theo.

He nods, then accesses a website that looks like a private server. He types in what looks like some kind of programming language, and numbers scroll across the screen. He sets his phone down and looks up at Jack. "What about the men with David? Thai? American?"

"Filipino, I think. Maybe crew from the ship."

"Harder to trace," I note.

"Did they seem comfortable around the chimpanzees?" asks Theo.

I wish I'd thought of that question. Your average deckhand would be rightfully terrified of chimps.

"The Filipinos, yes, but two didn't: an older Chinese guy and his helper. They knew how to tranquilize the chimps and move them."

"You didn't mention the Chinese before," I point out.

"What? It doesn't mean they were Chinese *nationals*. I'm a quarter Chinese. Welcome to Thailand."

Theo picks up his phone and squints at something. He writes another note and shows it to me: Telephone calling card databases are very insecure, FYI. That Hong Kong number made three prepaid calls to another number, which called a public number belonging to this company: Pacific Data Storage Systems.

I look up at Theo. "Another server farm?" It occurs to me that we should check it against the numbers connected to Heywood's law firm.

"Yep." Theo pulls up a web page for the company. There's an image of row after row of servers, like in the Seoul data center. The address has it just outside Bangkok. "Want to get there before IDR finds out?"

"What's IDR?" asks Jack.

"None of your business," I reply. "If you think of anything else, let us know."

Theo and I get up and leave Jack to the Thai police. Having literally missed the boat on the chimps, we don't want to let the chance to catch a data heist slip through our grasp.

CHAPTER TWENTY-FIVE
SYSTEM MALFUNCTION

"For a high-tech facility, this sure is in the middle of nowhere," I say as I drive us down a desolate, jungle-lined road outside Bangkok.

"Data centers are often located where power is the cheapest. If you ever look on satellite images, you'll find them in some surprising locations. And some of them aren't exactly public. There are a number of companies that run shadow colocation facilities in case of disasters or attacks," says Encyclopedia Theotannica.

He's far from annoying. He's flat-out interesting.

There's the Theo who says whatever comes to mind, and then there's the Theo who tries to self-censor. The more obsessed he is by a problem, the less capable he is of keeping his mouth shut.

As we drive, his eyes wander to the flora and fauna around us. Asking him what he's thinking can lead to a graduate-level dissertation on how microbiomes can be more revealing about an ecosystem than the macro environment. One explanation typically leads to another—like how you can tell more about the level of industrialization by looking at the contents of our stomachs than satellite photos . . . or something to that effect.

A question leads you down a rabbit hole, and then suddenly you're discussing the rabbit hole itself.

And every answer, it seems, leads to two more questions.

Still, not once in our time together has he asked me a personal question. Nothing about boyfriends, relationships, kids, relatives, or anything else. I don't think it's indifference; I just think there's mind stuff and there's human stuff, and Theo prefers to live in the world of the mind.

I check the GPS on my phone. "We should have seen it by now. At least the road leading to it."

I'm not sure what he was expecting, but I was thinking we'd find a big sign or an industrial park. All we've seen so far has been the occasional farm and patches of jungle.

Theo takes out his phone and looks at a satellite map. "I think it's a kilometer back."

I turn the car around, careful not to land us in a ditch. I have no idea how reliable the Thai version of AAA is out here.

We continue back and pass a few small side roads, but nothing that says DATA CENTER THIS WAY, DUMMIES!

I bring up a thought I've been trying to avoid. "You don't think it's possible that the website is fake and the address isn't real?"

"It's occurred to me," replies Theo. "Still, let's look a little further."

"Anything on the map?" I ask.

"There're a lot of sections with construction. It could be one of those. Often these images are quite old."

We continue for another kilometer with no sign of the facility. "Now what?"

"Stop the car," says Theo.

"Okay. Need to take a leak?"

"A look."

Theo gets out and walks up to a concrete telephone pole and squints up at the wires and cables. He then gets back into the car. "That's a fiber-optic junction. Let's keep going."

We continue driving with Theo craning his neck to look at the cables. Occasionally the wiring will lead down another road, but he doesn't say anything until we're almost back where I first noticed that we hadn't noticed anything.

"Turn right," says Theo, pointing out an almost-invisible side road. I oblige.

"The fiber-optic goes this way. It's our best bet," he explains.

"At least we know we'll get good Wi-Fi."

A fraction of a second later, he smiles. God knows what kind of process my little joke went through in his brain. Did he consider telling me that fiber-optic internet doesn't necessarily equal a wireless internet connection? Or did he get it was a joke right away? Do words appear in his field of view like the Terminator? Has he been sent from the future to kill me?

The road is narrow but paved. Trees line either side, but they've been cut back to allow cars and trucks through. Occasionally I run over a branch, which tells me the road hasn't been maintained in the last few days.

We reach the end of the road and a large metal gate blocking the entrance to a dirt parking lot. At the far end stands a three-story, metal-sided building with no windows and only the numbers 88077 on the side.

"I think we found where they hide the aliens," I remark.

"Yeah," says Theo, studying the building. He gets out and walks up to the gate. There's a small guard shack to the side, but no guard inside. He looks back at me, shrugs, reaches into the shack, and presses the button that lifts the gate.

I drive in, and he hops into the passenger seat. We park next to an old Toyota and a pickup truck that are in front of the entrance, where a set of metal doors with a keypad and a camera face outward.

"Now what?" I ask.

"I guess we see if anyone's home."

We get out and approach the doors. Theo knocks, then presses the intercom button.

No response.

I pound louder. Still nothing.

Theo walks over to the keypad and stares at it for a moment, then picks up a handful of powdery soil and gently blows it at the buttons. He takes out his phone, aims the light at the pad, and then looks at it from a side angle.

Theo presses four of the buttons. Nothing.

He presses them in a different sequence. *Bzzzt.*

The door unlocks.

"Well done." I consider whether and how we should enter, but Theo already has the door open and is walking into the lobby.

I follow, trying to come up with an excuse for why we're trespassing.

Nobody is at the reception desk, which is literally a metal desk in a room with unfinished drywall and electrical cables hanging out of the ceiling.

Theo walks to the next set of doors. These have a traditional lock. He tries the knob, but they don't open.

He produces a strip of metal I never saw him acquire from his pockets and feeds it into the gap between the lock and the doorframe.

Click.

"Maybe they're throwing a birthday party in the back?" he whispers.

We're both dreading finding the bodies of the data-center technicians. I nod.

"But let me go first," I say, pulling my gun out and holding it to the side.

Theo doesn't stop me. That's when I notice he has a gun drawn, too. Where the hell did he get *that*?

No time now. I'll have to ask later.

We're in a long corridor with half the lights out. The nearest door to our right is another set of double doors.

Theo turns the knob and opens the one on the right. Inside is a large room. The only light comes from skylights high above. Underneath them stand row after row of server racks. Except these look only partially installed. Cabling still lies on the floor, and the cabinet doors are open, revealing empty racks.

"Are we too late or too soon?" I ask.

We walk along the wall, deeper into the huge room. I go down the center aisle, getting a closer look at the cabinets, trying to see if any of them are functional.

Something feels strange, but I can't put my finger on it. I stop walking and turn around to look at Theo.

He has a finger to his lips.

I nod. He points to the ground. At first, I don't understand.

Then I'm revolted.

Now I'm terrified.

It's a pile of crap.

Not just any crap.

Chimpanzee shit.

Theo is still staring at it.

That's when the real horror strikes me.

Embedded in the dung is a bone with a wedding ring on it.

PART FOUR

DARWINIST

CHAPTER TWENTY-SIX
Pan Troglodytes

The first chimpanzees brought to medieval Europe confused learned men and caused endless speculation as to whether this was another form of a human—a not altogether unreasonable position at the time, given that every group tends to see themselves not as equals but as pinnacles of the human species, with every other race falling further down the line.

Chimpanzees confused Europeans because the primates were a lot like them, but also so different. African tribes struggled with the chimpanzee-classification problem, too. While there were many stories of unpleasant interactions in which chimpanzees kidnapped and murdered children and (hopefully apocryphal) stories of chimps raping human women, chimps never made it deeply into African folklore. They were both too familiar and too weird.

And for every story of a tribe of chimpanzees killing a human, there were probably a thousand more of humans killing chimps. We may be cousins, but uneasy ones.

I've been up close with chimpanzees. I've helped sedate them. I've been there when their teeth have been cleaned. I've had young chimps cling to me and been hugged by a much older chimp who was as docile as a grandmother.

I'm still terrified of chimps.

I'm terrified of chimps in the same way that I'm terrified of a cornered man in an unfamiliar situation who is stronger than me, a more ferocious fighter than me, and programmed by evolution never to back down once a fight has started. You don't talk a chimp down from a rampage. You tranquilize them at best and shoot them at worst.

Right now, there could be as many as thirty chimpanzees closing in on us. Baring my teeth and showing dominance is more likely to get me torn to shreds than make the primates back down. These chimps were raised in a zoo, not a circus. They never got the beatdowns from an underpowered human with a weapon to force them into docility.

Zoo chimps, even the best-cared-for ones, can kill. Chimps at sanctuaries have cooperated to pull keepers into their enclosures to attack them. These chimpanzees, stuck in this unfamiliar environment, are capable of anything. And from the scat on the floor, it's clear what they've been feeding on.

Now fresh food has entered their territory, and they're trying to figure out how best to kill it. The alpha male and his lieutenants are probably closest right now. When they make visual contact, they'll look for a weakness and then attack. It'll feel coordinated, but in truth it'll be one chimp spotting an opening and the others jumping in a split second later.

Jessica and I both have guns, but the problem is that if the first shot doesn't scare them, the others won't make much of a difference. We have to use each bullet to kill. Even assuming perfect aim, one bullet per chimp may not be enough.

We're surrounded; we're outgunned.

I have to make a decision now, before the chimps do.

"I think I have a plan," I whisper to Jessica as quietly as I can and still hope she hears me. "We wound the most dominant one and make a run for it."

"That's a horrible plan," she whispers back. "Let's make it out of here alive with our fingers and faces intact."

I look down the dark corridor of empty server cabinets. In a moment we're going to be surrounded with chimps on either side and crawling over the top.

In a normal encounter, it might just be one or two aggressive males that do the attacking, but in this situation, as frightened and starving as they are, it could be a free-for-all of flying arms, hands, nails, and teeth.

Jessica's back is to mine. She's probably scanning the tops of the cabinets like I am, waiting for the attack to begin. I'm not sure she understands what we're up against. One adult male chimp could devastate the entire top tier of the UFC. It's not just their strength; their teeth are like bolt cutters.

Clank.

The echo of an object hitting the floor fills the air, followed by the buckling sound of something heavy climbing on metal.

"You mean hide? If we get inside a cabinet, they'll tear it apart. Chimps can rip off car doors if they're angry enough," I whisper.

"That's not my plan. This is a server facility, right?"

"Yes," I reply, watching a moving shadow in the distance.

"Where are all the cables supposed to go?" she asks.

"It's a floating floor . . ."

So, *underneath* us.

Server rooms are built several feet above the ground with a false floor where all the cables run. There's at least two or three feet of crawl space underneath our feet—enough room for cables and a human to connect them to all the junctions.

"I'm not sure it would be any better if we get trapped down there with them," I tell Jessica.

"Where do you think we stand a better chance? In a two-dimensional fight or a three-dimensional one?" she asks.

Okay, she knows my language. "Cover me while I lift a panel."

"Theo," she says under her breath.

I glance back in her direction and see a large male chimpanzee blocking that row. I look back to my end of the aisle and spot two more.

I kneel to inspect the floor, keeping my gun aimed in their direction. Chimps don't coordinate like we do, but they react and adapt so quickly, it's effectively the same.

The floor is perfectly smooth. I can spot the seams where the panels fit into their recesses but can't fit a fingernail in to pry one up, much less a finger.

Normally they use suction cups attached to handles to lift the tiles. I left mine at home. "They're moving closer. Should we try a warning shot?" asks Jessica.

"Um, yes. But let me do it."

I point my gun at the floor and aim it an angle. *Bang!*

My bullet tears into the flooring, leaving a thumb-size hole. When I glance up, the chimps are still advancing.

"That didn't work. I think they lost their fear of guns," says Jessica.

"It still may help us." I wave my gun at the chimps on the left side, then hear the scratching of nails on the cabinet to my right.

I'm about to tell Jessica my plan when her gun fires and makes a loud *clang* as the slug ricochets off the metal cabinet.

There's a loud thump as something jumps to the floor on the other side. I don't look back because my chimps are getting closer. If I had to guess, she just shot near the one trying to climb over the top. The vibration of the bullet hitting the metal was enough to scare it. But for how long?

They'll all go apeshit in a second.

I reach down, shove my thumb through the bullet hole I made in the tile, and lift it up.

"Jessica!"

I don't know how, but she manages to drop to her knees and slide under my legs and into the opening before I can get the last syllable of her name off my tongue.

"Theo!" she yells, pulling at my foot from the crawl space.

I slide my legs in, and she pulls me all the way under. I try to straighten the panel so the chimps won't have an easy time of getting it open, but with their strength, anything is possible.

"This way," she whispers, crawling in the direction of the entrance.

"Hold up." I crawl back and take a position with my gun aimed at the tiny spot of light streaming through my bullet hole.

"What?" she asks.

"I need to discourage them."

"With what? A backhanded Instagram compliment?"

An intelligent primate doesn't need to have watched a dozen prison-break movies to understand what just happened. Chimps hunt other chimpanzees and monkeys. They're accustomed to clever thinking and on-the-fly adaptation. They're extremely fast learners when it comes to matters of survival.

The light through the tiny hole suddenly vanishes, which means a chimpanzee is inspecting our means of escape.

Bang!

I fire through the hole just to the side of the creature, intending only to wound him. There's a loud scream, followed by angry thrashing as a chimpanzee starts flailing. Unfortunately, I don't know if I grazed or mortally wounded it.

Also, unfortunately, I just shot at a chimp. I didn't want that to happen. They're victims of circumstance like we are.

The light vanishes again. I fire a second time to the side.

There's a thud and the sound of feet running away. That should buy us a little time until the chimps realize they can just punch their way through the tiles.

When that happens, it's game over.

CHAPTER TWENTY-SEVEN
SURVIVAL

Jessica and I keep moving, or at least she gracefully moves through the crawl space while I drag myself through the tiny passage, feeling every pebble and loose drywall nail in my kneecaps. Our illumination is a small penlight she's using to guide the way.

We're about thirty yards from the server room entrance when she stops moving and rolls onto her back, angling her ear at the floor above us. I stop moving and do the same.

The footsteps are quiet and stealthy, but the chimps, or at least some of them, are directly above. They can hear us. How long before . . .

Scratch. Scratch.

Chimpanzee nails trying to fit between the gaps in the floor tiles.

Damn.

It's one thing if a chimp gets down here and we have a line of fire to shoot them. It's another if they figure out how to pull the tiles free and yank us out from our crawl space.

Scratch.

Scratch.

I'd fire again, but I'm afraid it will only create a new hole that they can use to lift up the tile.

"Keep going for the exit," I tell Jessica. "I think they're following my clumsy ass, not yours."

"What are you going to do?"

"Hope you figure something out? Maybe there's a fire-suppression system. You could try to reach that and turn it on."

"All right," she says reluctantly. "The Thai military is at least a half hour away."

"How do you know that?" I ask.

"I texted for help."

I have no idea when she did that, but I'm glad at least one of us was thinking a little more multidimensionally.

I weigh the option of sitting still and waiting for more men with guns to arrive. The problem is that if the chimps get smart and attack, it'll all go down in seconds. There will be no chance to buy more time.

I can see the outline of Jessica's body in the distance as she gets closer to the exit.

Hopefully she'll survive. She seems really good at that.

I've already decided that when I have one bullet left, that one's for me . . . if I can get the gun to my head. You don't survive a chimp attack like this without immediate help, and I don't want Jessica trying to save me.

Scratch.

Scratch.

Bam!

Dust falls into my eyes as a chimpanzee smashes at the tile. *Bam!* The whole floor rattles.

The chimp can feel it giving way. Now he knows he can smash his way through.

Bam! Bam! Bam!

A crack of light shines through the gap between the tile and the frame as the flooring bounces from the force being thrown at it.

Bam! Bam! Crack!

I'm bathed in light as the tile is thrown free. Three sets of chimpanzee eyes peer down at me. They stare at the metal object in my hand, trying to comprehend.

I fire a bullet an inch to the left of the one closest to me. He flees, and I fire another over the sloping forehead of his companion before the third moves out of the way.

I pull myself backward. *Bam!*

Another chimp strikes the floor directly over me.

BAM!

A chimpanzee fist punches through the tile over my stomach.

Just as quickly, it disappears.

I aim at the hole. Before I can fire, a fast-moving hand rips the tile free, exposing another section of the floor. I crab-slide backward, keeping my gun aimed at the openings.

A chimp drops into the gap and comes at me faster than I can imagine, a nightmare of fangs and fury.

I fire.

I fire again.

Another chimp drops into the crawl space. I fire near him.

Again. And . . . *click.*

I lost count of my bullets, and now I'm out. I didn't have a chance to steal a spare clip when we were in the police station. I curse myself for not being prepared.

I hear, but can't see, another chimp drop into the crawl space. His frightened brothers are waiting for the right moment to attack.

My hands scrape around, looking for a weapon. All I can feel is cable and electrical conduit.

The chimpanzee starts loping toward me.

All that talk about saving the last bullet for myself . . .

Well, the joke's on me, the computational biologist who couldn't count.

I grab for anything I can and feel the conduit rip free. There's a blue arc as it hits the metal of the struts supporting the floating floor.

Damn, this cable is live. Like twenty amps worth of live.

I feel something heavy land near my legs. Something snarling.

I make a tight fist, tucking in my thumb, and swing the electrical line in that direction. An impossibly strong hand grasps my wrist and starts to pull my fist into its mouth.

My wrist explodes in pain, but not nearly what the chimp must have experienced before the current made his heart skip a beat.

I can smell the scent of burning hair and flesh. I pull myself out from underneath the unconscious chimp and crawl in the direction of Jessica.

I hit a wall near the door. A tile is yanked free. I cower in fear, ready for death.

"Theo! Out now!" Jessica yells.

I pull myself through the gap and realize what she's done.

Jessica slid a large equipment cabinet in front of the door as a kind of barricade. She pushed it a meter forward so I could crawl out of the hole.

"Let's get out of here," she says, opening the metal door behind us.

The metal creak attracts the attention of a band of six other chimpanzees that had been watching the melee in the floor. They come running toward us on all fours and leap onto the cabinet.

Jessica pulls me through the gap in the door and slams it shut on the screaming chimpanzees.

We run through the next door and then the exit, making sure each is closed tightly behind us.

Finally, we reach her rental car and get inside, lock the doors, and catch our breath.

She starts to speak. "Holy . . ."

"Crap," I finish for her.

We're both pumped full of adrenaline, like some crazy drug rush. Neither of us is assuming it's completely over, but for a moment we don't have to worry about being attacked.

Jessica stares back at the facility. "What a damned waste. What a goddamn waste." She looks at me, eyes filled with pain.

I shake my head.

In this moment, I realize how much I respect this woman. She feels only sadness over having to hurt those poor animals. She understands compassion and accepts its burden.

"Now what?" she asks.

"We wait for the army to show up and find out what they were doing in the other half of that facility," I reply.

"Other half?" she replies.

"That was only half the interior. Someone bought it unfinished, maybe from a bankruptcy, and repurposed it for something else."

"Genetically modifying chimpanzees for aggression?" she asks.

"No. Those were normal chimps. Normal chimps stuck in a nightmare scenario. I want to know why."

"I want to know who," she adds.

CHAPTER TWENTY-EIGHT
WETWORK

Jessica and I kept a lookout on the building, guns drawn, in case any of the chimpanzees tried to make an escape. We debated whether it would be best to let them run and let Thai animal control deal with them, but we decided that an escaped chimp in an unfamiliar location is a dangerous chimpanzee. Never mind that we have no idea what's been done to the chimps and if they carry any infectious diseases.

When the Royal Thai Armed Forces arrived, Jessica explained the situation to General Phathanothai and his aide, who then directed his unit to surround the building and enter through the front.

Although they had tranquilizer guns from the Thai wildlife agency, Phathanothai wasn't taking any chances—his men were fully armed.

Jessica and I both stood outside at a safe distance waiting for gunfire. Other than a few warning shots, it never happened. They managed to tranquilize most of the chimps and get some of them into an armored truck. Afterward, General Phathanothai went in to inspect the facility before giving us the all clear to enter alongside the Royal Thai Police.

Captain Chuntakaro, a tall man who's worked in Thai anticorruption for years, escorts us into the facility. "We've found twenty chimpanzees," he explains to us in English with a slight Australian accent, revealing where he studied abroad.

We walk into the server room, where bodies of unconscious chimpanzees lie everywhere amid blood spatter across the floor. A few soldiers are holding the lifeless body of a chimp to take a photograph. Chuntakaro yells at them and they apologize, putting the chimp down and scurrying somewhere else.

"I apologize for their behavior," Chuntakaro says to me. He then addresses Jessica: "If this is too traumatizing for you, we can move on."

"Traumatizing for her?" I reply. "I'm the one who pissed myself. She took out the first chimp that attacked us."

"My apologies," says Chuntakaro.

Jessica gives him a polite smile, waving off the remark. How often does she have to deal with men assuming that because she's a woman, and not one who hides it, she can't roll with the best of them?

For a woman like Kieren, it's probably different. She broadcasts *military* from a hundred miles away. And Jillian, her soldiering days behind her, seems almost relieved to have men assume she wouldn't hurt a fly, let alone take down a crazed serial killer at point-blank range. Which she did, but I got the credit for it.

Jessica has to navigate a world of chauvinism and presumably chooses her battles carefully. Every subtle insult she protests, every condescending remark she calls out, would only get in the way of her trying to solve the problem at hand. It's a tremendous sacrifice of ego that I don't think I could ever manage.

Perhaps she realizes that she wins by catching her suspects and closing her cases.

Results speak.

"Twenty chimpanzees?" asks Jessica. She turns to me. "We're missing ten."

I kneel down to inspect the body of one of the chimps I wounded. There's a small metal band around his ankle. I put on my gloves and lift it for a closer look. I read a serial number and see a string of Chinese characters. Three other chimps have similar bands.

When I inspect the skin, I can see old scarring. They've had these bands for a long time.

Well before the chimps went missing from the zoo.

"What's up?" asks Jessica.

"You want the bad news or the bad news?" I reply.

"Oh jeez. You choose."

"Some of these chimps are from somewhere else. These aren't the Monkey Village ones. I think those over there are."

"Two groups of chimps?" she asks.

"At least. And, like you said, we're still missing more than ten chimpanzees."

Chuntakaro calls into his radio, ordering his men to spread out and look for escaped animals. I'm not sure if they're anywhere near here or not, but it's a smart precaution.

Jessica is taking photos with her camera to use for her report. She gets close-up shots of each chimp's face and extra images of the wounded ones. From what I can tell, she's treating them the same as she would victims in a human massacre.

Chuntakaro walks over to the section of the floor where I shot near the two chimps as they started to crawl inside. I can see the blood drops from where my bullet grazed one of them. Things got close.

"You were down there?" asks Chuntakaro.

I nod. "Did the army check underneath?" I ask, suddenly aware that since we don't have an accurate chimp head count, more could be hiding beneath us.

"The general crawled under himself," replies Chuntakaro.

Jessica finishes taking photos and walks back over to us. "So, what was going on here? I'm pretty sure these guys weren't doing tech support."

I point to the far wall. "We need to find a way through that. The interesting parts are probably hidden there."

"I know the way," says Chuntakaro. "Some of General Phathanothai's men found an entrance."

He walks us to the back of the room, where a large section of server cabinets has been slid aside, revealing an opening into another cavernous room. Only instead of being filled with row after row of cabinets for servers, this one is filled with large metal cages and operating tables. The back wall is lined with benches, refrigerators, and large medical equipment, like centrifuges. Broken vials and syringes litter the floor.

"What the hell happened here?" asks Jessica.

I kneel and pick up a tranquilizer dart. "It looks like they had a riot."

Chuntakaro points to a large enclosure. It's about ten feet tall, thirty feet long, and made from chain link. At the bottom of the far end, the fence has been ripped from the metal post with just enough space for an adult chimp to climb through.

"That is not very good construction," Chuntakaro remarks.

"No kidding. Something tells me this lab wasn't built to standard. Check out the benches. They look like they've been cleaned out."

"Before or after they started eating people?" asks Jessica.

"I'd say before. My guess is the people running the facility took off and left a skeleton crew behind that wasn't prepared for handling this many chimpanzees. They may have been in the process of euthanizing them when the chimps broke loose. You can't do that in front of them. They're not dumb. The chimps probably panicked, tore open the cage, and then . . . whatever came next."

At the back of the room is a large roll-up door. I walk over to the control panel. There's a lock on the button to raise the door. Jessica leans in to take a closer look.

There's blood on the lock.

"I'm guessing they didn't let the staff have the key to the only exit inside here," she replies. "Captain Chuntakaro, with your permission?" Jessica holds up a lockpick.

"Be my guest."

She has the lock open a second later and presses the button to open the door.

The metal groans and begins to retract upward. Too eager to wait to see what's underneath when it reaches eye level, Jessica and I both kneel to look. I was afraid there'd be another room of horrors, but instead, sunlight shines in from underneath, revealing a red clay loading area and an untilled field beyond.

Jessica and I step outside the building. There are large tire tracks on the ground, along with a pile of metal cabinets, buckets, and shovels.

Chuntakaro joins us. "Looks like they cleared out of here."

I step farther out into the loading area and look around. "Not quite."

"Are you thinking what I'm thinking?" asks Jessica.

"Probably," I reply as we start walking toward the overgrown field.

"What's out there?" asks Chuntakaro.

"I don't know. But where there's this many apes, there's got to be a lot of ape shit and whatever else you're trying to hide."

We climb to the top of a small berm and are greeted by a cloud of flies. To the left is a long pit filled with excrement. In front of us is another pit with a large pile of burned boxes and documents. To the right is a mound of fresh dirt at least a foot high and ten feet long.

"Our missing chimps?" asks Jessica.

"I'm afraid so," I reply.

"Why afraid?"

"If the chimps were part of a medical experiment, which ones are the control group, and which ones are the experimental ones?" I wonder aloud.

"What do you mean?"

"Are the chimps we encountered the lucky ones? Or are these?"

I step down from the berm and take a look at the burn pile. There are some file folders, IV bags, and lots of vials. I notice some unusual writing on one of them and reach down for a closer look.

"Step away from there!" shouts a man in accented English.

I turn and see a different general from Phathanothai standing on the berm with a row of armed men. That's the problem with the Thai military: they give out general stars like midtier colleges hand out honorary degrees.

Chuntakaro confers with the general, then steps down from the hill to explain the situation to Jessica and me.

"He's with a different division. You are being asked to leave. He says this is an internal matter."

"Great," sighs Jessica.

We back away and head to the front to wait for Chuntakaro to try to smooth things over.

Twenty minutes later, he comes walking around the building, shaking his head.

"They want you to leave here now," he says. "He yelled at me for letting you into the location. I'm sorry, there's nothing I can do."

"It's okay." I notice a fire truck parked at the outer edge of the parking lot. "Can I go talk to them about how to deal with the bodies in case they have to burn them here? I don't want anyone getting sick."

"I can give you my notes," Jessica says to Chuntakaro.

"That would be helpful," he replies.

Twenty minutes later, we're back in our car, and I have questions burning through my mind—plus one literally burning through my pocket that's too crazy to mention even to Jessica right now.

CHAPTER TWENTY-NINE
PARALLEL PROCESSING

I'm a difficult guy to like. I have very few friends. If people were pets, some would have to be dogs: everyone likes them. Others, like cats, are a bit of an acquired taste and come with the understanding that it's going to be a one-way relationship. I think I fall into tarantula territory—interesting to most people at first, but only worth the effort to a select few.

Hailey is one of my friends. She's put up with almost as much of my insanity as Jillian.

She even tracked me down when I went into my last downward spiral. I was too far gone to explain the method to my madness. Hell, I barely understood it.

She may have forgiven me, but she hasn't forgotten. I can tell by the way she's watching me from the other side of the coffee table in the Marriott hotel lobby.

Hailey is in her late twenties and runs one of the most successful mobile video game companies on the planet. I met her while trying to hunt down Forrester, and she's proved to be instrumental to my work on more than one occasion.

"So . . . I got an interesting voice message a couple of days ago," she says after we exchange hellos. "Care to elaborate?"

Jessica's in meetings at FBI headquarters, and I've been told to hang out here while I wait to be called in, arrested, or committed. I figured it would be smart to reach out to my one friend in Virginia in case I need help.

"Ah, that. I was in Thailand. We were looking for a group of missing chimpanzees. I needed to fake a phone call so I could copy a suspect's phone directory."

"Cool," she says in that way people younger than me say *cool* without it actually being cool. "No word from you for six months. Jillian worried that you were dying in some jungle, and this is *after* you had your psychotic break in Portland?"

"Was it a psychotic break?" I ask. "I mean, I did catch the most prolific serial killer in America."

"Alleged," says Hailey. "The trial hasn't finished yet."

"You taking demotivational lessons from Mylo? Speaking of which, where *is* your sidekick?"

Mylo is Hailey's best friend and probably the most sarcastic person I've ever met. Nothing I could say or do would impress her.

"We're running an online tournament right now. She's providing commentary."

"Does that include reminding your fans they're going to die virgins?" I joke.

Hailey shakes her head. "You of all people can't be the ultimate nerd hero and then point at other nerds and yell, 'Nerd!' It doesn't work that way."

"Fair point."

"So, the Void thing? Are you involved in that?" she asks.

"Kind of. Did it affect you?"

"Not too much. We run some servers from Manhattan, but everything was backed up. It was more of a problem for some friends there.

A lot of people had their entire businesses wiped. I'm hosting a used-laptop drive to help people get back on their feet," she explains.

"That's good of you."

"Good? If people don't have computers, they can't play my games," she jokes. "So, seriously, are there going to be more of those after Singapore and Seoul?"

"I don't know. Are you worried about your data?"

"Yeah. Like everyone else now. Companies are scrambling to add triple redundant backups. Some services are even offering servers in Faraday cages."

"Smart," I reply.

"Maybe. What can I do to help?"

"With what?"

"Your case, idiot. What can I do?"

"I don't have a case. They actually wanted to put me into some detention center in case I had some connection to what was going on. Some people were afraid that I was a secret criminal mastermind."

"Well . . . ," Hailey replies.

"Well, what?"

"You do have that 'decides who lives and who dies' vibe. Not gonna lie. I think it's kind of attractive, but I always rooted for Ming the Merciless and the Bond villains with the good plan."

"Maybe we should be looking into *you*."

She shakes her head, "Oh, Theo, you could never catch me if you tried. But seriously, if there's anything I can do to help, let me know."

"I will. Assuming they let me stay involved." I'm surprised to hear myself say that. A few days ago, all I wanted was to die or go home and sleep forever. What changed?

Idiot. You know what changed. You don't only need challenges, you need challenging people.

People like Hailey, who can run circles around you mentally; or Jillian, who can literally run circles around you hiking up a trail looking for a crime scene; or Johnny, who could grasp a concept so quickly you felt stupid for not seeing it his way; and of course Jessica, who underneath it all is as scarred as I am, but somehow manages to hold it all together.

"Earth to Theo." Hailey snaps her fingers. "You zone out on me again and I'll have you committed to a facility I control where Mylo can be your therapist."

"Sorry. I appreciate the offer of help. There might be a point where I need something in a hurry."

"Like what? A helicopter? Billie Eilish singing at your birthday party?"

"I don't know who he is," I reply. "Either way, I'll let you know."

My phone starts buzzing. I glance down and realize I've received five text messages from Jessica while talking to Hailey. Each one is marked Urgent.

"Whoops. Looks like I need to take this."

"I'm not surprised they need you," says Hailey. "But can they handle you?"

CHAPTER THIRTY
THE CLOCK

An FBI staffer greets me at the entrance to the J. Edgar Hoover building and escorts me all the way up to the sixth-floor meeting room where Jessica is seated at a conference table with five other people I'm given quick introductions to.

The only one I've heard of is Gerald Voigt, her acting supervisor for the Manhattan incident. He sports a boyish look but also has a certain gravitas that tells you he's intelligent and chooses his words carefully. The other obvious player in the room is an older man to his right, Assistant Director Thomas Pullman. While he shares Gerald's gravitas, he falls on the other end of the boyish spectrum. Pullman looks like a man who would rather be tying flies and planning his fishing trip to Montana than be here right now.

"Jessica, do you want to give Theo the update?" asks Gerald.

Other than a polite nod, we haven't interacted since I entered the room. We never agreed on an "official" version of the events, but we did dissect what happened enough to know we wouldn't contradict each other. The only tricky part is how I got the gun in Thailand. Since I still have a federal firearm permit from my work as a defense contractor, I'm not too worried about the legality of my having a gun, at least from the US perspective.

"Sure," says Jessica as she picks up a controller for the oversize video monitor at the end of the room. An image appears showing a countdown clock and the name MANHATTAN. She opens two more screens with SEOUL and SINGAPORE. "These website countdowns appeared five days before each city experienced its Void. The links to them were found in several Reddit forums from aliases that appear to be connected to Heywood." She clicks to another countdown timer that has four days left. "If this is to be believed, another city's going to be hit soon. We're obviously concerned about wherever gets hit, but we're especially concerned if it's in the United States."

"Agent Blackwood is convinced that Michael Heywood is either the originator or a conspirator in this attack," says Gerald. "What's your opinion?"

I'm not sure if this is a trick question. Are they asking me to contradict her? Do they want me to implicate myself?

"I would defer to her opinion on Heywood's involvement," I reply. "I'm not as familiar with his methodology or his motives as she is."

"Do you think it's possible?" asks Pullman.

Interesting. They don't know if they should believe her, or at least Pullman doesn't. Do they want an outside opinion? That seems odd. Do they want a scapegoat in case their judgment is questioned after the fact? That seems more likely.

"I'd say the chance is nonzero. And as to my understanding, we have no idea of his whereabouts after his custody was shifted to another agency. All of which is suspicious," I reply.

"That's not exactly a ringing endorsement of the theory," says Pullman.

Odd that he calls Heywood being behind this a theory, dismissively.

Wait a second. Why are they looking for every opportunity to look anywhere *except* at Heywood? Jessica suggested that Heywood had been feeding another agency false information and may be at the center of a spy ring embedded in the intel agencies. If that's the case, then they're afraid to find out if that's true. Heywood escaping, causing the Void, and also being involved in espionage and disinformation from within federal custody would be a huge blow to the government. It doesn't matter if it wasn't the FBI's fault. Everyone would look bad, and whoever would look the worst is probably trying hard to convince themselves and anyone who will listen that Heywood is a preposterous suspect.

They've done such a good job of it that the only reason Jessica was even brought into the case was because her former colleague realized she was essential.

Okay, I think I understand the game. This is a matter of risk management. So I need to try to point it out to them in emotional terms, not rational ones.

"If Heywood is involved in this and you don't follow Agent Blackwood's leads, I can't see how this would be anything other than a disaster for the FBI."

"I'm glad to see you have our best interests in mind," says Pullman sarcastically, possibly thinking of Butcher Creek and the other times I've frustrated federal investigators.

"I'm always for good law enforcement. Furthermore, what concerns me is that nobody seems terribly bothered by the fact that Heywood is still at large."

"We have a special unit dedicated to his capture," says Pullman.

"How's that working out?"

Pullman sighs. "We don't have nearly the resources you imagine."

I nod at Jessica. "And yet, the most valuable resource you have is kept at the academy teaching cadets card tricks."

She glares at me for a moment. I know she's not teaching them card tricks. At least I don't think so. What I do know is that if I'm going to be the most aggravating version of myself, I need to say things like that. At least that's the strategy I've decided to follow here.

Usually my "I'm the smartest guy in this room and if you don't do what I say, you're all going to look like idiots" approach has a fifty-fifty chance of working. Which is to say, shutting up might have the same outcome.

Pullman shakes his head. "I don't know how much of you is show versus real. I've got people at NSA and the CIA strongly hinting that I should take a closer look at you. They say you're far more dangerous than Heywood could ever be."

"And yet here I am, offering you my help. And he's on the run," I reply.

"But you have an angle. A book deal, a TV series, or a something."

I reach into my pocket and set my burner phone, hotel key, and twelve dollars on the table. "This is the entirety of my net worth. And both the phone and the money are borrowed. I transferred everything I own to my girlfriend over a year ago, with no obligation for her to give it back. I've been washing my underwear and socks in the sink every night because they're the only ones I own. I've never accepted a book deal because I find the idea of profiting off the horrific acts committed by the people I caught to be disturbing. I've never sold movie rights, tried to sell them, or had any wish to be a public person other than to what degree it helps me help other people. If you think I'm trying to profiteer from a situation, then I think I have a better understanding why you've failed to see the warning signs within your own agency of agents found guilty of corruption and espionage."

Pullman doesn't immediately respond. He sits back and sizes me up for a moment. "You're nuts. You're absolutely nuts. I just can't tell if you're the good kind or the bad kind."

"I can simplify that proposition for you. All you have to ask is if I'm the useful kind."

Pullman turns to Gerald. "Do you vouch for him?"

"That he's nuts? One hundred percent. That he's useful? Blackwood thinks so. And that's better than my own opinion."

"Fine. If Dr. Cray flips out and turns evil, I'm having you both put on trial as conspirators," says Pullman.

"If I went evil, there would be no one left on this planet to hold trials," I reply. Jessica groans audibly.

Too much?

"He doesn't know when to shut up, does he?" Pullman asks her.

"You get used to it," she sighs.

"No," Pullman replies. "*You* get used to it. Not me. Let's move on. Blackwood told us that you found evidence that Heywood or someone he's connected to is working on a biological weapon."

"We did not," I correct.

I can feel Jessica's stare burning into my face. "Pardon me?" says Pullman.

"We found a testing facility where they were using stolen chimpanzees and a mass grave where we believe more chimpanzees will be found. This could indicate a bioweapon. It could just be a clandestine pharmaceutical-testing facility doing under-the-table work for a major pharma company," I explain.

"Run that by me again?"

"Human trials are prohibitively expensive. Sometimes pharmaceutical companies will conduct secret trials using third parties to determine if it's worth the effort to spend billions of dollars taking a drug to the next stage of development."

"I'm not familiar with this."

"It's a kind of regulatory compromise. Either way, though, that facility *could* be a weapons-testing lab. It's illegal and probably has ties to the United States."

"So you want us to send you back to Thailand to investigate further?" asks Pullman.

"No. I want you to send Blackwood and me to Estonia."

Jessica's head snaps toward me. I didn't tell her this part because I knew she'd have to disclose everything to her superiors. Whereas I'm under no such obligation. I can also present only one set of facts to them while withholding other details.

"We've had one EMP attack in the United States, two in Asia. My guess is that if the target is data-storage facilities, then the next one will be in Europe. Estonia is a possible target. I'd like to start there."

"Estonia? What about the chimp research?" asks Pullman.

"We found that lab inside an abandoned data center. Estonia has quite a number of data centers. There might be a correlation." *But there's not . . .*

"Fine. Voigt, they're your problem. Got it?"

"They're definitely my problem," Gerald replies.

Pullman gets up and leaves the room, taking everyone else with him except Gerald and Jessica.

She makes a polite nod and waves as they depart, then turns to me. "What. The. Fuck. Was. That?"

"Yeah," Gerald chimes in. "What she said."

CHAPTER THIRTY-ONE
ZOMBIES

Jessica is looking at me like she's seriously considering turning me back over to Kieren and being done with me forever. Gerald seems ready to help her.

"Okay, let me explain things. Or not . . ." I think out loud. "Jessica, do you trust Gerald?"

"With my life," she replies flatly.

"Okay. Do you trust me?" I ask.

"Not at the moment. No."

"Okay, fair enough without context. On a meta level, do you trust that I have everyone's best interests in mind, not accounting for whatever brain damage you assume I may have?"

"Fine. Sure," she says impatiently.

"Okay, Gerald. May I call you that?"

"If it helps you get to your point faster, yes."

"You trust Pullman, right?"

"He's ethical. Yes," he replies.

"All right. But I can infer that somewhere between Pullman and the other agencies, there's someone we shouldn't trust."

Gerald glances at Jessica. She doesn't flinch. I'm assuming there's something deeper here.

"My name showed up on a list that it had no business being on. Someone's leaking misinformation. Which means somewhere in this huge circle of trust between the Justice Department and the intelligence community, there's someone being trusted who shouldn't be trusted. And if I were to have said certain things in this room that raised red flags, the party we do not trust could learn what was said . . . eventually." I turn to Jessica. "And that meant me withholding certain things from you until after your briefing so you wouldn't have to disclose them and have the enemy know what we know."

If they think I sound like a raving lunatic now, wait until I get to the good part.

"Go on," says Jessica.

"Well, first we have to solve the Gerald problem."

"And what problem is that?" he asks.

"If what I tell you is too sensational or whatever, you'll have to tell your superiors."

"As will Jessica."

"No. Not if you tell her to use her discretion," I reply.

"It doesn't work like that," she fires back.

"Of course it does. If I told you that I believe in aliens, does that have to go into a report? No. If I mentioned that one of the reasons I want to go to Estonia is to see if the mother ship is there, does that need to go in?"

"Aliens?" asks Gerald.

"Don't be ridiculous. I'm just making a point. I have a lead, and it would be better if only Jessica knew. You have the comfort of knowing that if she thinks I'm completely insane, she'll let you know."

Gerald shakes his head.

"See what I've been dealing with?" says Jessica.

"I'm shaking my head because I see his point," Gerald replies. He stands. "I'm out. Jessica, best of luck. Have fun ending the world in Estonia with Dr. Strangelove here."

"It may not be Estonia. That's the other thing," I reply.

"Don't care," he says as he exits, leaving Jessica and me in the conference room.

She rocks back in her chair and swivels in my direction, I assume assessing what just happened. She finally nods. "Clever, Theo. Very clever. I think I get you. You managed to clear the room yet still got us what we want. You've got the mad-scientist part down pat."

Er . . . do I tell her it wasn't an act?

"You have to use what tools you have," I reply.

"Okay, enough with the Estonia-and-aliens nonsense. What are you really up to?"

"Estonia was just a cover. And the aliens thing was just a joke."

"That's a relief," she replies.

"Yeah. We need to go to Chernobyl . . . to look for radioactive zombies."

Her hands go to her forehead, and she lets out an exasperated sigh. This may be the closest I've seen her to tears. "And why?" she asks in a strained voice.

I take the one item I didn't set on the table and place it in front of her. She picks up the burned piece of green plastic and examines it.

"Is that Cyrillic?" she asks, pointing at the Russian wording.

"Yes. I pulled it from the fire pit back in Thailand when you were distracting the general. It's a prepackaged syringe wrapper."

"Made in Russia?" she replies.

"Or Ukraine. Either way, they were trying to destroy this. Leaving behind the chimps didn't matter as much as this and whatever else was in that fire pit."

"Why is that?"

"Because there's a second facility. One that may still be active. But with human subjects."

"And why Chernobyl?" she asks, inspecting the paper more closely.

"Because that wrapper's radioactive."

Jessica drops it on the table and looks at her hands.

"Not *that* radioactive. But enough to measure. Remember when I talked to the Thai firefighters?"

"About disposing of the chimp bodies?"

I slap my forehead. "I forgot to tell them that part. Actually, I asked to use their Geiger counter. Fire departments carry them in case they have to go into hospitals or other facilities that have radioactive materials."

"And that made you think Chernobyl?"

"Indirectly. We know there are a number of research facilities in that part of Ukraine that are used for secret research because of its isolation yet relative proximity to major cities. Also, your Weird File," I add.

"Oh." Jessica thinks for a moment. "The zombie sightings outside Kiev?"

"Yes. Read one way, it sounds like science fiction, but in the context of a poorly run secret facility that may have had drugged-up, unwell people escaping, it kind of makes sense. And there's the fact that I was able to trace the number Jack gave us to another number in Kiev."

Jessica glances up at the ceiling and runs her fingers through her hair. It's quite nice hair, I realize for the first time. It reminds me of a raven's feathers.

"Theo. How does Jillian put up with you?" she asks.

"Well, I'm gone a lot. That helps. We do our best when I'm not around."

"Sorry," she replies. "I didn't mean that. Your thinking is of course sound. And I understand why you went about it in the way you did. I'd tell you not to do it again, but that would be pointless. So now what? Where are we headed, Kiev?"

"Yep," I reply. "We start with those zombie sightings."

CHAPTER THIRTY-TWO
THE PATIENT

Dr. Mayya Kosakivsky agreed to meet us at the Pesto Café in a small shopping plaza in Kiev. Her sixteen-year-old daughter, Olena, is sitting next to her, translating for her mother. Mayya watches the exchange and appears to understand our English but is too self-conscious to speak it herself. Fortunately, her daughter's English is excellent, and she even occasionally throws in an Americanism that I assume comes from television.

"She was the doctor on the afternoon shift at the clinic. It was just herself and two nurses when they brought the man in," Olena explains.

"Who brought him in?" asks Jessica.

We'd started off by asking Mayya about the news story involving a "zombielike" man found wandering outside the Chernobyl zone. He had no idea who he was and could barely answer questions. His dialect was unfamiliar to anyone who talked to him. Because of his hollow cheeks and the condition of his clothing, he was nicknamed the Kyyiv Zombi, which, phonetically, is almost the same as the Kiev Zombie.

The mystery deepened when, after the man's story hit social media that night and a ghoulish photo was posted to Facebook, a group of men identifying themselves as government health workers pulled up to the clinic and took him away.

The Ukrainian government denied any knowledge. When attention turned to the Russians, they insisted they had no knowledge of the man. Eventually it was dismissed as a hoax, but other regional news outlets ran stories about other *zombis* being spotted on roads or in forests.

We decided to talk to Mayya first, because her account was the most credible. She'd actually avoided talking to the news out of concern for patient privacy and seemed more worried about the man's well-being than the sensational aspects of the story.

"He was brought in by a policeman who patrols the roads," Olena translates for us. "He was a friend of a doctor there and brought the man into the clinic because it was closer than the hospital." Olena confers with her mother. "Dymytro is his name."

Jessica lays a map on the table. "Do you think he or your mother would know where the man was found?"

Without waiting for the translation, Mayya puts her finger on the map, then speaks to her daughter.

"Dymytro said the man was found wandering near the road close to the equipment cemetery," Olena explains.

"Equipment cemetery?" asks Jessica.

"It's where they buried all the trucks and machines used to handle the Chernobyl accident," I reply.

Mayya nods in agreement. Jessica puts an X where the doctor indicated the man was found and adds the time and date it happened.

"What was the health of the man?" I ask.

Olena relays her mother's comments. "She says he looked malnourished, but from some kind of digestive disorder." She points to her left arm. "There were needle marks there. The police thought they were heroin injections, but my mother said the needle was too big and looked like a . . . what's the word . . . intravenous drip."

Jessica nods, glancing at me for my reaction.

"My mother says he also had marks on his wrist," adds Olena.

"Like handcuff marks?" I ask.

Mayya nods again and seems agitated as she speaks rapidly.

"It looked like he'd been a prisoner somewhere. That's what she thought. Perhaps he escaped a prison infirmary. The problem is that Dymytro never would have brought him in if that was the case. He called the state police and the organization that would handle such a thing. They said check the mental hospitals."

"And they didn't know anything, either?" asks Jessica.

Mayya shakes her head, looks around the café, then whispers something in a low voice for her daughter to translate.

"She says that she spoke to a friend at another facility, and they had a similar patient two days before. But he'd only been there for an hour before the men in the trucks pulled up and took him away. Same condition. Same injuries."

"Where was that facility?" asks Jessica.

Mayya puts her finger on a spot twenty miles to the northwest of the other sighting.

"Do you know what time he was brought in?"

"A-bout ten o'clock," Mayya says in halting English. "Night."

"What do you think was medically wrong with these men?"

Mayya thinks it over, then speaks to her daughter for a full minute, pointing to her feet and her chest occasionally.

"She says it's quite odd. They had blisters on their feet and what looked like bedsores. These men appeared to be on the verge of death, but they were healthy enough to walk great distances. She didn't get to thoroughly examine the man, but she did see some surgical scars. There was another thing . . ." Olena asks her mother for clarification. "She says the man wasn't quite there. Not drugged. Not crazy, but not fully present. Like he had some kind of brain damage. Mother said when she was an intern, she met older patients that were similar. They'd been given . . . what's the word?"

Mayya points to her temple. "Lobotomy."

"That's curious," I reply.

"That's disturbing," says Jessica.

"There's also an odd connection here," I say. "António Moniz, the man who pioneered lobotomization, got the idea after watching a talk by a neurologist who severed the frontal lobes of a chimpanzee, making her docile and easy to work with."

"Too bad the people at the Thai research facility didn't do their homework," Jessica replies.

"Or maybe they did—the ones that abandoned it, at least. The Thai facility may have tried chlorpromazine on the chimpanzees to keep them calm, but I'm sure human-level dosages wouldn't nearly be enough."

"Lobotomies . . . patients escaping? What are they up to?" asks Jessica.

"I don't know, but if we can find the facility, that would be a start."

After thanking Mayya and her daughter for their help, Jessica and I plan our search. We don't have a lot to go on, other than two sightings twenty miles apart. The radiation from the syringe package was strong enough for me to draw a perimeter around where its origin point could have been, but that still leaves several hundred square miles.

Jessica is using her phone calculator to track on the map the range the men could have walked from. Both of their paths lead back into the Chernobyl protective zone, which is fenced off and patrolled—loosely. The security doesn't mean there aren't people coming and going from there on a regular basis. Within the zone there are a number of research facilities studying the effects of radiation on the wildlife around Chernobyl, as well as testing treatments and technologies for mitigating the threat of radiation.

Working within large parts of the zone doesn't pose much more of a radiological threat than being an airline flight attendant or working in a coal mine. That doesn't mean there's zero effect, but it's not enough to keep researchers away.

When I saw the syringe wrapper with Cyrillic, my instincts were to check for radiation, because the Chernobyl zone had been on my list of locations for possible clandestine operations. I didn't expect the Geiger counter to go off, but I wasn't terribly surprised when it did.

Having a facility in Ukraine would give the people behind the project access to highly skilled researchers in a depressed economy . . . scientists accustomed to keeping secrets. There's also the possibility that the project has, at least in part, some support of the Ukrainian government. I'm fairly certain they have no idea of the full scope of what is going on, though. This could be an offshoot of a research study where the researchers are doing something else entirely.

Jessica glances up at me from the map. "You ready for a road trip?"

"*Da,*" I reply.

CHAPTER THIRTY-THREE
WANDERERS

Mickey, the guide we hired to get us through the checkpoints, is an enthusiastic physics student we found through a contact of mine at the University of Kiev. Since Mickey works for one of the state-licensed tourist agencies that give tours of Chernobyl, Pripyat, and the other areas inside the radioactive zone, he has the right documents to get us through the checkpoints.

"What do you want to see first?" Mickey asks as we pass the first guard station. "The amusement park? The high schools?"

"I'd like to see what research facilities are still open," I reply.

"Okay. They're not as exciting, and they're a little farther out," he explains.

"It's fine," I tell him.

Jessica is sitting up front, making small talk, while I sit in the back of his old Mercedes with a laptop, scanning for Wi-Fi signals with a directional antenna that's letting me build a map of possible points of interest.

Some of them match up with buildings and institutions on the map. Other signals appear to be unlisted and, in a few cases, in locations that are supposed to be undeveloped.

After three hours of driving around, I have seven points of interest that could be where the wandering men came from. We need to narrow it down to one or two and convince Mickey to take us on an unscheduled side trip.

I figure it's up to me to choose the spot and Jessica to convince Mickey, which shouldn't be too hard, since the young man seems clearly smitten by her.

I stare at my map and think, *If I were a secret research lab that wanted to operate in a somewhat patrolled yet remote area, how would I go about it?*

I'm assuming the facility isn't any of the ones still listed as operational by the Ukrainian government. I'm also assuming that our suspects didn't build anything new. They took over an existing facility that was close enough to their needs.

For a small bribe and slightly larger payment to the state, a private individual could set up some kind of research project here, just as the tourism companies got permission to bring buses full of people through the zone.

"How are you doing, Theo?" asks Jessica.

"Great. Fine."

An internet search doesn't bring up anything that sounds remotely like what I'm looking for. While that doesn't surprise me, the facility would have to have some official reason for existing.

Or at least it did at *some* point . . .

If the Ukrainian databases don't have any listings, there might be another place I could look. If this facility had been on the radar under different management, then it is also possible that they applied for research grants, possibly in conjunction with a US institution.

I do a search of the National Science Foundation and Department of Energy databases for grants relating to Chernobyl research.

I get thousands of results back.

Okay, that's obvious. But what about facilities *in* the zone?

I refine the search using the postal codes for this region. The list gets considerably smaller. I write a script to list the names and addresses and put them on a map.

A moment later I have an overlay to accompany my map of Wi-Fi hot spots. One stands out from all the others: the Yaniv Workers Clinic.

I pull up everything I can on the institution. Apparently, it was a research project to study the impact on the cleanup workers of working in the zone. It operated for more than two decades, looking at the various impacts, and was shut down eight years ago.

Shut down . . . but it still has active Wi-Fi.

I look up the location. Interesting. Prior to being named the Yaniv Workers Clinic, it was the Yaniv Workers Spa, a retreat near the Red Forest for Communist Party members.

I think this might be the place.

"Mickey, could you take us to the Yaniv Workers Clinic?" I ask.

"The what?"

"The Yaniv Workers Clinic."

"I've never heard of it," he replies.

"It was the spa for the party members. It's near the Yaniv train station," I explain.

"There's nothing there. Unless you mean the train station. That we can see."

Well, that's at least a start. "That would be great."

It takes us forty minutes to get there. We park and get out of the car. As a precaution, Mickey uses a Geiger counter to check the background radiation.

While most areas outside the reactor are fairly safe, there are hot spots where the radiation levels can spike by a thousand percent. In some cases, rain or snow can bring about changes as soil shifts and hidden deposits of radioactive ash or irradiated soil become exposed.

I start walking to the west. Jessica follows. "What's up?" she asks.

"I think our facility might be a half mile that way. We need to figure out how to ditch our babysitter or bribe him to help us take a look," I explain.

"Let me try." She turns around and shouts, "Hey, Mickey, want to see what's this way?"

"Absolutely," he says before breaking into a jog to join us.

Here I was planning some kind of subterfuge to distract the poor kid, and all we had to do was ask. Or rather, have Jessica ask him.

We cross the tracks and follow a side road until it comes to another road that leads straight into the woods under a canopy of overgrown trees.

From the aerial image, I could see that there's another access road to the north of here, but it's in an inner zone and probably requires a level of access even Mickey can't provide.

The pavement is broken into uneven sections with tree roots occasionally rupturing the surface like mini mountain ranges. Weeds sprout from cracks everywhere, and insects crawl about their business.

What I'd give to be able to study these things more closely . . . As with other regions we've written off as uninhabitable, nature never got the eviction notice and has adapted in its own way here.

I'd be most interested in studying the microbial life near the main reactor. What survived? How did it adapt to the environment?

"Theo," says Jessica, pointing to something on the ground.

It's a dirty robe. I lean in to get a closer inspection, but Mickey puts his handheld Geiger counter between me and the robe.

It clicks with a not-insignificant number of rads, but nothing to worry about. Mickey still cautions me to step back. Not wanting to upset him, I leave it be.

We continue down the path and reach the start of a chain-link fence that's overrun with vines. Parts of it have been pulled open, and the barbed wire on top has been stripped away.

Jessica touches my arm to stop me. I glance over and see a figure kneeling on the other side of the road: a man, wearing only pajama bottoms. He's so skinny his vertebrae look like they're going to burst through his skin.

Mickey speaks first. "Hello?"

The man turns around; his eyes are sunken, and his lips are blistered and cracked against paper-white skin. His hands and fingernails are covered in grime from digging into the ground.

Startled, the man gets up and runs across the road, slides through a gap in the fence, and vanishes into the trees.

Shocked, Mickey lets out an expletive in Ukrainian and crosses himself.

I step over to look at where he was digging. It's just an empty hole in the ground. The man must have been out of his mind.

"This is messed up," says Jessica.

"Was that a . . ." Mickey starts to ask.

"A person with a mental disability? Yes," she says, trying to keep him from panicking. "Now what, Theo?"

"Let's find out where he went to."

I walk over to the fence and slide through the gap. Jessica follows. "Friends, I don't think we should be doing this," Mickey says.

"Wait here for twenty minutes, then call the police," Jessica tells him.

"I'm not sure if I'm comfortable waiting out here."

"It may not be better in there," I explain.

Torn, Mickey decides to follow us at a distance. We take a path through the trees in the direction the man ran and come to a clearing where the grass comes up to our knees. At the far end is a two-story building with barred windows. Behind the bars, a dozen pairs of eyes watch us from faces with sunken cheeks and listless expressions.

A door swings open, followed by a loud yell. Mickey starts running, but Jessica's hand goes to her gun.

CHAPTER THIRTY-FOUR
Skeleton Crew

I brace for anything to come running out of the doorway. So does Jessica; her hand stays on the butt of her gun inside her jacket. I trust her to decide when to draw it and when to wait.

A rotund woman with red hair and wearing dirty nurse's scrubs emerges from the door, shaking her fist in the air and letting loose a string of what I can only assume are Ukrainian curses directed at us.

A gaunt man appears in the doorway behind her. She spins around and shoves him back inside, then continues her tirade.

Despite the woman's intensity, Jessica lets go of her gun, and I breathe a small sigh of relief that we're not under immediate threat of being attacked by a zombie horde. Although anything is possible at this point.

Jessica holds up her hands. "Hold on. Speak slowly."

The woman stops cold at the sound of Jessica's voice. "Americans?" she asks.

"Yes," Jessica replies.

The woman stops her advance and crosses her arms. "You are not here to relieve me?"

"No."

"Then you are useless," the woman snarls before heading to the door.

"Wait!" Jessica runs after her. "We're here to help."

"Help me? Who is going to help them?" the woman replies. "For three weeks now, I try to take care of them. Just me since the others left!"

"What others?" asks Jessica.

The woman eyes her suspiciously. "I am not to talk to you."

"We're the only ones to talk to because you've been abandoned. Nobody's coming to relieve you."

The woman curses, not at us, but at the ground. "And what is to be done with them?" she asks, gesturing to the building behind her.

"Let's figure that out. That's Dr. Cray; my name is Jessica. What's yours?"

"I am Nurse Zlate," she replies.

"May we step inside?" I ask.

"Fine. But do not get too close," says Zlate, stepping aside to let Jessica and me enter the facility while Mickey waits behind.

The tiles are cracked, and the paint is peeling from the walls in the large open area. Two men sit on a couch, watching a television showing a cartoon. Another sits on a bed, playing with the drawstrings of his pajamas. Each looks listless and lost in their own world. Some of them watch us, but not with any great interest.

The conditions are horrific, but it's not dirty. Zlate, for her part, has tried to do her best.

At the far corner, there's a nurses' station in front of a small office. I can see the edge of a cot inside with a rumpled blanket.

"It's just been you here?" asks Jessica.

"Yes," says Zlate.

"And no help from the government?"

She shakes her head. "Help is coming, they told me. Don't worry, help is coming. But I do not believe them. Not since they sent the wrong medication."

"Wrong medication?" I ask.

"Yes. They gave me pills and told me to give them to each of the patients," she replies.

"What kind of pills?"

"Poison." Zlate walks back to her office and uses a key to open up a cabinet. She pulls a plastic pill bottle from inside and hands it to me.

The label says "Niacin," but when I open it up and take a whiff, I detect the distinctive scent of almonds. I show the bottle to Jessica. "Arsenic," I tell her.

Zlate nods. "'Did they eat the pills?' the man on the phone asks. I say no, they smell bad. 'No,' he tells me, 'the pills are fine.' But I don't believe. 'Then *you* eat the pills,' I tell them. And then they call no more."

"Who are these men?" asks Jessica.

"They said they were doctors, but I do not believe. One man is Russian; the other, Chinese? I took job from ad in paper. Nursing license not necessary."

"What did they do here?" I ask.

"Secret government research, they said. 'Where do these men come from?' I asked, but they say, 'Don't worry.' But I worry. Each man . . . his mind is gone, like scrambled. Here, let me show you."

Zlate motions us over to a man sitting on a bed, staring at the clock on the wall. "Medev, look this way," she tells the man.

He turns his face in our direction. Zlate points to a small scar at the side of his eye near the bridge of his nose. "When he arrived, he was still bleeding from here. Same as the others."

"A lobotomy?" asks Jessica.

"Yeah. Like the kind they did fifty years ago," I reply. "Apparently someone's kept the tradition going."

"I've heard rumors the Chinese still do it. Rumors, mind you, but it's easier than shooting patients up with Thorazine."

Medev turns his head back to the wall and goes back to whatever internal thoughts he was thinking. If it's anything like what I've experienced when I've had my brain tampered with against my will, it's not a lot of thoughts at all.

"Who are these men?" asks Jessica.

"I do not know. They do not say much. Their accents are from all over. Prisoners, perhaps? Patients of a mental hospital? I do not know."

Jessica takes out her phone and starts to walk around the room, taking photographs of each man. Most of them are barely aware that she's there. One reaches a hand toward her hair, and she gently pushes it away by grabbing at the wrist—a judo technique.

"I need to know exactly what happened here. What was the condition of these men when they arrived? Were they healthy? Were they sick?" I ask.

"Some were healthy. Some were not." She points to a stretcher. "Some arrived barely alive."

Interesting. Was this some kind of convalescence stop after treatment at another facility? Did the men who did this care what happened to the patients afterward?

"The sickest ones, the ones that arrived on stretchers, where are they now?" I ask.

Zlate points to Medev and five other men. "They are the ones that got better."

"What about the ones who didn't?"

She shakes her head. "They are buried outside with the rest."

"The rest?"

"Yes. The ones there was no hope for."

"How many was that?" asks Jessica.

"I lost count. Many."

Suddenly concerned, I tell Jessica to step back. "How exactly did they die?"

"They had the disease," replies Zlate.

"What disease?"

"*The* disease."

CHAPTER THIRTY-FIVE
ANATOMY

Jessica and I are sitting in an observation room, watching through a window as Dr. Leonid, Ukraine's top forensic specialist, performs an autopsy. Unfortunately, the chimpanzee mass grave wasn't the last hidden burial site that we encountered. There are four bodies in the room, filling up all the available tables, and another nineteen in freezers waiting to be examined.

Leonid is wearing hazmat gear from head to toe, not only to protect himself from the normal infectious agents you encounter when you pull a rotting corpse from the ground, but also because whatever killed these men may have been engineered.

Poor Zlate was arrested soon after we called the Ukrainian authorities. We've been given assurances that if she fully cooperates, they won't punish her.

Jessica and I explained as best as we could that only a saint would stay there trying to take care of those men by herself. It even turned out that she had tried calling Ukrainian authorities on multiple occasions and was either dismissed as crazy or handed off to someone else to deal with.

The surviving men were another mystery. Nobody knew where they came from until a sister of one the patients recognized her brother's photograph on the news. He'd been committed to a mental hospital in Belarus years ago and abandoned.

We expect that break in the case to lead to clues about the others. Jessica's suspicion is that they were acquired from various mental institutions throughout Ukraine, Belarus, and Russia. Many asylums are understaffed and might look the other way when offered the opportunity to make a difficult patient someone else's problem.

According to the sister of the one we identified, he'd been a problem teenager and prone to violent behavior. Regardless of his past, it's tragic that he ended up with his mind taken from him, the victim of some cruel experiment.

But what *is* that experiment? The other surviving men are now receiving medical care, but aside from malnourishment due to Zlate's dwindling supplies, they're otherwise healthy. Physically, at least. Mentally they're gone, but bodily, even the patients that Zlate said were incredibly ill when they arrived are doing fine. Just like with our chimpanzees, it's unclear which was the control group and which was the experimental group.

Dr. Leonid steps over to the microphone by the window, strips off his gloves, and speaks in English to us. "I can't find any sign of unusual infection. While antibody tests are difficult with this stage of necrosis, I was able to get some viable blood from deep in the tissue. But I don't see the symptoms of a respiratory infection. Their lungs and digestive tracts are also fine."

"Okay, then, what killed them?" I ask.

"This I don't know for certain. But if you were to ask me what killed this man"—he points to the nearest body—"his liver, spleen, and lymph nodes show all the signs of someone suffering from aggressive lymphoma. Cancer."

Cancer. When Zlate said they had *the disease*, that's what she was referring to.

"What does that mean?" asks Jessica.

I say the three hardest words for me to utter: "I don't know."

This wasn't what we were expecting. Our fear was that the experimenters had weaponized some infectious agent like a coronavirus into something even more deadly, but Leonid's autopsy looked for the symptoms of coronas, influenzas, even Ebola, plus a whole host of other infectious diseases. What he found was death by natural causes.

But was it?

"Theo?" asks Jessica.

"Some viruses can cause cancer. This is well known. And there are some forms of cancer that may be transmitted via a virus that we haven't identified yet. What if . . . ?" I think the question through, then shake my head. "I don't think that's it."

"That they've weaponized cancer?" she asks.

"You could, in theory. That is to say, you could take a very innocuous virus that we're already familiar with and maybe give it a payload that triggers a cancer response. It just seems like doing things the hard way."

"Maybe they want to do things the hard way. Maybe the point is to make us watch our loved ones linger."

The way she says this makes me suspect she has some personal experience with that, but I don't know if it's a good time to ask or get into the subject. I've never been good at understanding what lines we're not supposed to cross.

"I don't know. There's a pattern here, but we're just not picking it up. I don't think we understand the question well enough to know what's going on."

"We've got dead bodies, dead chimpanzees, and some kind of clandestine medical experiment . . . that's a lot going on," Jessica says. "God knows what other experiments are taking place we don't know about."

"Yes. But none of this ties back to Michael Heywood. At least not directly. It doesn't even directly connect to the Void. It's not impossible that we stumbled upon something completely separate."

"That seems highly improbable, to quote you," she replies. "I think it's time we push this to the next level. Gerald has kept our connection to this out of official channels, but I think we need more resources and more people on the case."

The news only mentioned that two tourists stumbled upon the facility. This was our attempt to make Heywood or whoever is behind this unaware that our investigation has reached this far. Now we're at the point where the cat is about to be let out of the bag. To bring in the kind of international cooperation we'll need to find out what's behind this means that the entire investigation and Jessica's and my role in it will all ultimately become a matter of public knowledge.

"I just wish we could use that to some advantage," she says aloud. "We know something that Heywood doesn't know we know yet. How can we exploit that?"

"Maybe to lure him out," I reply.

"Lure him out? What do you mean?"

"Why don't you see if the Warlock will talk to you?"

PART FIVE

ILLUSIONIST

CHAPTER THIRTY-SIX
JACKIE OSWALD COBS

I'm in my living room while Theo is sitting in a chair in my bedroom out of sight of my laptop webcam and the rest of the FBI is watching the interior of my apartment via their own hidden cameras and microphones. Twelve other agents live in this apartment complex, so it wasn't difficult to find a plausible excuse to have extra agents on hand in case something goes terribly wrong.

It's only supposed to be a video call, but with the Warlock, even the simplest things can go terribly wrong. Just ask the families of his many, many victims.

At first, I rejected Theo's suggestion to try communicating with Heywood. The Warlock loves to feed off my attention. I saw no reason to give it to him, let alone let him know that I'm personally involved in the case.

He's made attempts on my life in the past, and I saw no reason to encourage any more. Especially since news of his escape didn't seem to alarm people nearly as much as it should have. I got a welfare call from the FBI to let me know, but since my case with him happened almost a decade ago, nobody seemed to think he was much of a threat in light of the fact that the other attempts on my life could never be conclusively traced back to him.

We're a minute away from when he's supposed to call. Or at least the person who sent me an email after the FBI issued a cryptic tweet: Have a tip about the Void? Contact the FBI. To separate the thousands of pranksters and well-meaning overreactors, we included a screenshot of what looked like a standard stock image of a computer screen showing a bunch of random letters and symbols. It was actually a message meant for Heywood, using one of the encryption key pairs he's used. We sent the encrypted message to Heywood under the username Jackie Oswald Cobs: an anagram for Jessica Blackwood.

We assume that Heywood has been monitoring everything the FBI does, paying close attention to the people involved in the case. "Jackie Oswald Cobs" was meant to get him to respond. Which he did.

The Jackie Oswald Cobs account received a return email using his encryption key.

From: Michael (michael@eterniconhealth.com)
To: Jackie Oswald Cobs (jackie.oswald.cobs@fbi.gov)
Subject: Let's talk

Jessica,

I've been wanting to talk to you.

9 pm EST. Your computer, your place. Please at least go through the motions of pretending you're alone.

Michael

PS
I have something to show you that I think will be of
special interest to your new friend. Tell him there's
hope.

🦋

Theo said he had no idea what Heywood was talking about. I put it down to another one of the Warlock's typical mindfucks, which is why my pulse is racing.

I have no idea what to expect from a video call with the man who was using deepfake technology before there was even a word for it to lure his victims to their deaths. The only thing that derailed him from his ambitions was his obsession with me. Heywood's cordiality is a lie. He never hid his hatred for me. We were never polite adversaries.

I know that engaging with him like this is only going to reignite whatever fixation he has on me. I can only hope that Theo's idea to contact him pays off in some way.

The clock hits 9:00 p.m. I stare at the screen. Will he call? Although it's counter to what we're trying here, part of me—most of me—hopes he won't.

9:01. Still no call.

Maybe it's not going to happen. At 9:05, I'm still staring at the screen. I start to relax.

The ringing tone from my computer jars my nerves, and I almost jump out of my seat.

I have an incoming call from michael@eterniconhealth.com . . . a URL that has a masked owner and an IP address that employs untraceable proxies.

I have to answer.

I touch my trackpad and reluctantly accept the call. "This is Agent Blackwood," I say into my microphone.

"No video?" says a familiar voice. "That's okay. I understand."

The screen blinks, and I'm looking at the face of Michael Heywood. His camera is tilted up, and I can see ceiling lights and a bookshelf in the background. He appears to be in an office.

His face is exactly as I remember: slightly older now, a little grayer, but the same midwestern, not unattractive but not overly handsome face that could belong to your insurance salesman, your child's school principal, your doctor. Heywood doesn't have the piercing stare of Ted Bundy or the murderous facial expressions you see in serial killer mug shots. He looks normal. In a courtroom, he could be the prosecutor, the judge, the bailiff, or maybe a witness, but "suspect" isn't something you'd ever think.

Heywood has never admitted guilt. He's protested his innocence to me whenever confronted in person. We arrested the wrong man, he has insisted, while subtly hinting that we are playing a more complicated game.

"May I call you Jessica?" asks Heywood.

The FBI shrinks told me to build a bond with him. They want me to foster trust so that he sees us as strange allies in all this. They told me to be informal.

They can go screw themselves. "Call me Agent Blackwood," I reply.

He nods. "Fair enough. I see that you're taking your own advice. I respect that about you."

"What's your game, Heywood? What's this all about?"

"I'm not sure if we're on the same page about what 'this' is, but I can tell you that I'm working on something important. Soon everyone will know." He says this casually, like he's talking about an ad campaign for a breakfast cereal and not some potential biological weapon that could kill millions.

"Why don't you turn yourself in and explain it to us?"

"If only it were that easy. The reason I'm not in custody right now is that I found prison wasn't conducive to my life's work."

"Yeah, that's the thing about prison. It tends to put a crimp in your style."

"I've missed you," says Heywood, like we're old colleagues.

"The feeling is not mutual."

"I know. I know. The only reason we're even speaking is because you're desperate to make sense of recent events. You're hoping I slip up and reveal some kind of clue. Which would be unfortunate for everyone if I did."

For a moment I wonder if I'm even talking to the right man. I'm getting none of the bravado I'm used to from him. In fact, this new version of the Warlock is downright congenial.

"So why are you talking to me?"

"Don't you have a list of questions your superiors want you to ask me first?"

He knows how this game is played. The list is next to my computer. I didn't even plan to bother with them, because he's too smart.

"Will you answer them?" I ask.

"Let's hear them." He tilts his head like I'm interviewing him on a podcast.

"Fine. What do you want?"

"That's easy. More time to finish what I've started," he replies.

"Not a million dollars and a pardon?"

"The first would be immaterial to me. The second won't happen in my lifetime."

"What would it take to get you to surrender?"

"In time, I'll let the world judge me for my actions," he replies.

That bit of grandstanding sounds more like the Warlock I know. "What can you tell us about the events known as Voids?"

"I'm not the one responsible for those."

"Do you have any involvement in them? Did you design them? Did you plan them?"

He holds up his hands. "I can't answer any of that right now. Not in a way that would be convincing."

Is he on Xanax? He's being evasive but in the most nonchalant way. Should I provoke him? I was warned not to, but I want to see what lies under that facade.

"How do you live with yourself, knowing the pain you've caused?" I ask.

He hesitates. His eyes look down for a moment. "Not easily, Agent Blackwood. Not easily. I haven't done nearly what people think I have, but the things I *have* done, I'm embarrassed for. I think people will understand, once they've had a chance to see everything for themselves, but still, this is something I live with." His eyes rise to meet the camera. "And to you, Agent Blackwood, I'm very, very sorry for the harm I've caused."

What the hell?

"What about the harm you're continuing to cause? What about the people in the graves in the clinic at Chernobyl?"

Something changes. His face freezes for a moment. Not an emotional freeze, but a video frame freeze. Did he hang up?

His face starts moving again. "I wish I had answers for everything. But I don't. Some of the things I've done will have to be seen in the light of the greater good I'm trying to bring about for humanity."

Theo's standing in the doorway, holding up a pad of paper that reads, ASK HIM WHAT IT WOULD TAKE TO GET HIM TO SURRENDER.

I already asked that question. I point to my list. He nods and points again to his notepad emphatically.

"Jessica, are you there?" asks Heywood. "Are you conferring with your friends? I won't hang up if you are."

"Yes," I reply honestly.

"I appreciate your candor." He gives me a small smile.

"Next question . . . What would it take to get you to surrender?"

"In time, I'll let the world judge me for my actions."

What? That's the same response he gave when I last asked the question.

Theo is writing something on his notepad again: **WHAT CAN YOU TELL US ABOUT THE VOID?**

I ask Heywood the question.

"I'm not responsible for that," he replies.

He's got the patience of someone overdosing on Prozac. From the apology to the mindless way he repeats himself, he sounds like he's going through some kind of twelve-step program.

"You said you had something for my friend? What is that?"

"I emailed it to you. But answer me this: Has he figured the other thing out?" *The other thing?*

Theo nods.

He writes something else on the pad and turns it around to show me. *Jesus. Christ.*

I've been played again.

It's three letters that explain everything.

CHAPTER THIRTY-SEVEN
Avatar

I stare at the pad in disbelief. Not because I don't believe it's happening, but because I can't believe I let myself fall for it.

Theo simply wrote **Bot**.

As in, a virtual chat bot. Meaning, I haven't been talking to Michael Heywood. I've been talking to some sophisticated AI he created to answer for him.

"Jessica, are you there? Are you talking to your friends? I won't hang up if you are," Heywood's avatar says, repeating itself again.

"Are you a bot?" I ask.

"Yes. But I speak for the man you call Michael Heywood."

"Isn't that his real name?"

"I don't believe it is, but you'd have to ask him," the avatar replies. I press the mute button. "Is this even possible?"

Theo leans over to make sure we're muted. "Yes. It's an advanced text transformer trained on the things he wants to talk about. Spooky, but not self-aware. He'll tell you he is, but he won't remember what you asked him an hour ago. Maybe."

"So now what?"

"The real Warlock is probably listening. He wants to see how you'll react."

"I'm sure he's getting his jollies."

"Agent Blackwood, are you still on the line?" asks the avatar.

I unmute myself. "Yes. I'm just trying to figure out the point of talking to a homicidal Alexa."

Frustrated at myself for getting fooled, I hang up.

"I'm not sure that was wise," says Theo.

"What? And keep looking like an idiot?"

Ring.

I look at the screen. He's calling again. "Now what?" I ask Theo.

"Answer."

I click "Accept." "What?"

"It looks like we got disconnected. I'm not sure if that was on my end or yours. Would you like to continue talking?"

"Not really. I've had enough of this game."

"I assure you, I'm more than a game," the bot replies. "Feel free to call me back anytime you like. I'll be here."

I disconnect the call and slam my laptop shut. Theo has a smirk on his face. He sits down in the chair opposite mine. The one with the hole in the fabric on the side. I suddenly become conscious of the fact that I haven't updated my furniture since I moved in. "That was useless," I say, fuming.

"I think otherwise. He revealed quite a lot. I'm just not sure what it means."

"Well, that makes two of us." Gerald will be calling any minute for an update. I'm already dreading that conversation.

"For one, we learned much more than he realizes. Or at the very least, we learned a lot more than he assumes we already know," Theo replies.

"Explain," I say a little too quickly.

"What he just did, that chat bot, it's incredibly sophisticated. Using the AI to respond to you and drive a video image of himself? That took considerable resources. It wasn't cheap. More importantly, for a man who has supposedly spent the last several years behind bars and with only limited communication with the outside world, he's remarkably up to date on the latest artificial intelligence research."

"They couldn't stop him from reading. Only accessing computers and choosing who he communicated with," I reply.

"I understand that. But this is more than reading some research papers. This implies experimental knowledge, or at least contact with someone with that background. Also, the sophistication of what he did in the past, well before the deepfake algorithms were published, suggests he was in some kind of position where he had access to government research. Moreover, he had access to government-scale resources."

"Are you saying that he had help from the government?" I ask.

"Not necessarily. Access doesn't mean cooperation. Look at it another way: I can point to a building from your balcony that's actually a top secret NSA facility. It's got an innocuous name out front, but three floors underground there's a server farm five times the size of the one we saw in Seoul and an entirely separate floor with a quantum computer system. Do you know who operates it? I don't. I can tell you the agency, but the contractor is a complete mystery. They're some shadow company formed to build the system and keep it running. Who owns the company? Some other company. I ran a company like that, and I can't even tell you where our funding was coming from."

This helps confirm a suspicion of mine and reinforces Gerald's mole fear. "Heywood was a spook."

"At some point I think the man called the Warlock was deeply involved in the intelligence community, building computer systems for them. The problem, or at least what I've seen in my experience, is that the people writing your checks have no clue how much power they've handed you."

That would explain one of the other mysteries about the Warlock. He has no past. A man who helped install systems for intelligence agencies could also have erased his own history.

"How does this happen?" I ask.

"He could have been a brilliant college kid with a clever paper that the intelligence community saw potential in. They recruited him in some company they contract with. In time, he creates his own company and sells them on some application they're willing to throw money at."

"That's also a chance for fraud," I reply.

"Maybe. But not in the way you probably think. Those agencies are used to throwing dump trucks full of money at projects, but they like to see receipts. At least for what you spend your money on. With one exception."

"And that is?"

"The power bill. If you're running some supercomputer cluster that's trying to intercept North Korean radio transmissions and build an org chart based on each official's digitized speech patterns, then the CIA isn't going to care if you spent thirty thousand or four hundred and fifty thousand dollars on your monthly electric bill. They assume it's the price of running that kind of complex computer system."

"How do you defraud the government that way?" I ask. "Besides stealing computer time?"

"Lots of ways. It's a commodity in and of itself. I don't know what he might have done. Run his own research, for sure. See, you have to look at computation as a valuable commodity. Amazon is one of the largest companies in the world, not because they deliver your flat-screen television the next day, but because of their computer-services division, which runs the computer systems for half the internet. That's what makes them powerful. Heywood likely had access to that kind of power."

"And used it to make chat bots?"

"I don't know what he was doing, and that's what scares me. And here's another thing: I suspect that the heists he pulled off in those data centers may have been to steal his own data."

"What do you mean?"

"I'm just guessing, but let's say he managed to get a government computer cluster or somebody else's supercomputer to run a huge computational problem. Maybe running in the background or masking itself as a background process. Getting it to run is one thing, but if the result is terabytes in size, or if they've locked down the system, then the only way to get it out might be to physically steal it."

"But why, Theo? What is he doing?"

He shakes his head. "I don't know. I just can't think that way. Not yet, at least."

"Well, we need to think of something." I gesture to my laptop. "I think he wants us to keep playing twenty questions with his virtual self. You can have at it if you want, but I want to take a more physical approach."

"What do you mean?" asks Theo.

"If Heywood was up to all this while he was supposed to be in custody, that means he had somebody looking the other way pretty hard. Until they decided to 'move' him to another facility, that is . . . at which point he escaped."

"Have you considered that he was moved to a different facility because someone in the intelligence community finally realized who he was?"

"Or maybe someone knew all along. Yeah, I've been thinking along those lines. That's why I think I might need to go through channels that aren't official," I reply.

"What do you mean?"

"If Heywood was able to reach out from a detention facility that he was specifically put in because he wasn't supposed to be communicating, then that means somebody was doing their job pretty badly. I say we go talk to them."

CHAPTER THIRTY-EIGHT
ACCESS

Theo and I pull up to a Tudor house in an affluent Virginia neighborhood where I'm fairly certain nobody has so much as touched the mowers that keep their Wimbledon-short lawns so well trimmed. Two trash cans sit out front—one for garbage and one marked for recycling, which will end up in the same place as the garbage.

It's ten past seven in the morning, and at any moment we expect Nick Weir to leave his house and get into his car to go to work as general manager for Mesa Detention Facility.

Before Heywood escaped custody during the ill-fated transfer, he was an inmate at Mesa Detention Facility outside Richmond, Virginia. What makes MDF unusual is that it's a small private prison that houses federal prisoners who are considered intelligence risks. The owners of MDF are part of a conglomerate that provides services to military installations and is allegedly the operator of numerous black sites overseas where suspected terrorists have been held and interrogated.

Heywood's transfer caught even the FBI off guard, and—in retrospect—it had all the earmarks of something plotted by the intelligence community. Such exploits are not unheard-of. Sometimes a suspect in federal custody turns out to have information relating to the war on terror, like a drug-cartel accountant who has knowledge of illicit arms sales to the Middle East.

If the intelligence community's powers that be decided Heywood was useful to them, there's little they couldn't do to make him available at their discretion. And, much as he probably gained privileges while assisting an intelligence agency in jail, he must have also been assisted by somebody high up inside the prison. Private facilities are scrutinized to make sure this doesn't happen, but it happens. All the time.

In the case of Heywood, it's not only that he could have been given access to a computer or even a phone that he could use to carry out his plans remotely, it's also that the people who should have been monitoring his jail time closely didn't do so.

Someone was looking the other way . . . a lot.

Theo made the case that all Heywood would have needed was an iPhone or an Android device with internet access. Therefore, any corrupt guard would have sufficed.

While Theo's technically correct, I know Heywood better than that. He needs to control everything and everyone around him. He wouldn't want to wait until late at night to use the phone when nobody is watching. Nor would he risk having a random search of his cell turn up the device. No, he'd want to do whatever the hell he wanted, when he wanted. And to achieve that, he'd need to corrupt the man in charge of the whole facility. But to corrupt an official who's already well paid and works under the scrutiny of government officials, Heywood would have needed to come up with something incredibly persuasive.

"Here he comes," says Theo, indicating the middle-aged man with a military haircut emerging from his house.

Nick Weir immediately notices us.

Prior to working for the company that operates MDF, he served as the commanding officer for several military prisons. From the look of the man, it's easy to see why he'd be a good candidate to run a facility for federal inmates.

I climb out of the driver's-side door. "Excuse me, Mr. Weir? I'm Jessica Blackwood with the FBI. I spoke to your office yesterday."

I meet him at the bottom step. Theo hangs back in the car, texting on his phone, or at least making it look like he is.

"Yes, Agent Blackwood, I thought our appointment was supposed to be at 2:00 p.m. at the facility?"

He's looking a little frustrated. That was the point of intercepting him here. I wanted to catch him off guard and see how he'd react. Right now, not so well. He keeps glancing over at Theo.

"That's Dr. Theo Cray. He's advising the FBI," I explain.

"Advising them on . . . ?"

"The Void events. That's why I wanted to speak to you."

Weir was led to believe that I had some background questions on Heywood, which should have him alarmed but not panicked. If he has something to hide, he'll want to be helpful . . . to a point. As a contractor running a federal facility, he can only be so defensive before it starts to look suspicious. Weir's a smart man who will try to play it as safely as he can. It'll be interesting to see at what point he tries to shut me down.

"Can this wait until later?" he asks.

"Unfortunately, no. We got an update and are under extra pressure. This will only take a few minutes of your time."

"Okay," he says, crossing his arms. "What can I help you with?"

"Do you know how frequently Michael Heywood had visitors at Mesa?"

"I sent your office the logs. All that's in there. You know that, Agent Blackwood."

He's being condescending. That's a tell. I need to play with his expectations a little and see how he answers.

"Yes. But I've been told that meetings with national security officials wouldn't be logged. Is that correct?"

This is a safe question for him. He knows I already have the answer to it, and it gives him an opportunity to deny any lapses in procedure.

"In some situations, with approval of the court, inmates can receive visitors that are not officially logged." He says it like it's a prepared response.

Theo gets out of the car and Weir glances in his direction, but Theo just stands at the front bumper, drinking his coffee and texting on his phone.

"In instances where Heywood might have had off-the-record visitors, would the rules of his confinement not be applied?" I ask.

"I'm not sure what you mean."

"Yes, you are. If Heywood met with someone from the CIA, would that interaction be monitored?"

"Not necessarily. If a prisoner is a low risk or the agency that wishes to speak with him takes responsibility for their own safety, the visit would not be monitored by us . . . *if* the agency so requested," he hedges.

"Were they allowed to bring in computers or other items that Heywood was forbidden from using?"

Now he sees where I'm going. This actually comforts him, because he's not obligated to lie for the CIA or whoever was "consulting" with Heywood.

"It's outside our jurisdiction. In instances like that, a prisoner's custody enforcement is the responsibility of the agency that requested the interaction," he answers dryly.

"So Heywood could have had access to computers while he was meeting with them?"

"I wouldn't know what he or anyone else would have access to in that situation."

"Not even if you see them enter with a computer and they ask you for an extension cord?"

"Agent Blackwood, you understand that legally I can't give you any details about that hypothetical situation. These are questions you should be taking up with whoever you think was accessing Heywood."

He's trying to draw the conversation to a close, comfortable that he's not the real target. I'm planning to lure him in a little bit more before switching up on him, when a new question suddenly comes to me. "Did any agency ever take Heywood out of Mesa for any period of time?"

Weir hesitates, making me think I'm onto something I hadn't expected.

"I would not be able to disclose that."

I'll take that as a yes. More importantly, I think I have a better understanding of how Heywood was able to escape. It happened when the CIA or another agency was bringing him to a different location, possibly Langley or an off-site office where they could interact with him outside prison. Maybe they only sent an SUV and one or two armed escorts.

For someone like Heywood, this would be an easy extraction to pull off. He could do it with a handful of armed men and a bluff—like having a "police car" pull over their vehicle.

Something like this would be so profoundly embarrassing for the agency responsible, it would explain why we only learned that he escaped during a "transfer" and not how it happened.

Weir still believes my suspicions are about an intelligence agency giving Heywood computer access. What he doesn't realize is that I'm fairly positive that Heywood would have been extremely closely monitored while he was cooperating with the intelligence agency. While their physical security may have sucked, they're no dummies when it comes to computer security around suspect hackers.

The suspicious stuff that Heywood was doing probably didn't happen when he was drinking lattes and typing away on one of their laptops in a conference room.

"Outside of access to computers or the internet that he may have had via a government agency, was Heywood ever allowed unsupervised use of computers while he was your responsibility?" I ask.

Weir doesn't answer right away, because this is the question he didn't want me to ask him. "I'm running late and need to continue this conversation later." He glances over as Theo lifts the lid to his garbage can and tosses his coffee cup away, then looks down the street at the approaching garbage truck before returning his attention to me. "Look, Agent Blackwood, I'm just as frustrated as you are about Heywood's escape. Unfortunately, my hands are tied about what I can speak to you about. But it seems like you have a pretty good idea who you should talk to."

That was a smooth way of saying he's stopping the conversation because he doesn't want to be found guilty of lying to a federal agent. *Go talk to the CIA, it's their fault . . .* It's a credible gambit.

Weir nods at me and heads back into his house. "I have to go take a conference call I was supposed to have at the office," he says over his shoulder. "If you have follow-up questions, please email them to me."

"Thank you, Mr. Weir."

I get back into the car, where Theo is sitting in the passenger seat examining his nails. "How did it go?"

"About as well as I predicted."

"He's still watching us," Theo says.

"I'm not surprised." I spot the garbage truck in the rearview mirror heading our way, so I start the car and drive up the street and out of view of Weir.

"When you called yesterday and asked to meet at the detention center to talk, do you think it spooked him?" asks Theo.

"Definitely."

"Did you notice how nervous he was when I went near his garbage can?"

"A little. Why? Oh shit." I glance back in the direction of his house. If Weir had incriminating information like bank slips or anything else connecting him to Heywood, he might have tried to dispose of it after I called him.

The garbage can's still there, two houses away from being picked up. Do I go back and grab his garbage? Legally, I *think* I can do that. Although I wouldn't be surprised if Weir put up a legal fight.

One house away . . .

I take the car out of neutral, then hesitate. If I run out and grab the garbage with Weir watching, he's liable to lawyer up and prepare for whatever else we may try next, including destroying other evidence.

"Considering the legal options?" asks Theo.

"Should I?" I ask, deflecting the question to a civilian with a reckless relationship with the law.

"No," says Theo.

Behind us, the garbage haulers are dumping both types of receptacles into the same truck. The recycling illusion apparently ends at the curb.

"Did you manage to see anything when you opened the can?" I ask Theo.

"Not exactly," he replies.

"What does that mean?"

"We should probably follow the garbage truck."

"And stop them?" I ask.

"No. Just wait for them to dump the garbage. Weir might be paranoid enough to contact the sanitation company if anybody stops their truck."

"Okay. But you understand that by the time the truck is full, there could be several tons of garbage bags mixed in there?"

"Yes. But only one has my cell phone."

CHAPTER THIRTY-NINE
TREASURE HUNT

Theo and I are watching the garbage truck that picked up Weir's trash back up to a small ridge and prepare to dump out its contents. A bulldozer sits idle nearby. Once the day's garbage is emptied into the landfill, the bulldozer will flatten it out and lay down a covering of dirt and clay to create a barrier below the next layer of refuse. We need to get to Weir's trash and Theo's phone before that happens.

I used my badge to get us through the gate. The guard had no questions for us. I'm not sure if that was indifference or if they're used to law enforcement making frequent visits to landfills.

I know that in some missing-persons cases they send cadaver-sniffing dogs to landfills as a first step. Often, the first place people choose to dump bodies—especially those of small children, sadly—is in the garbage.

The truck releases its haul, spilling its contents onto the piles of garbage below. We wait for it to drive away, then exit our car.

I open my trunk and take out gloves, a pair of sneakers, and the orange vests we use when we work near traffic. "Put this on," I tell Theo, handing him a vest.

"Ah, a disguise," he says, sliding it on.

He's not wrong. If you don't have a badge, an orange vest can be very useful for getting into places that would otherwise be hard to sneak into. You become almost invisible. When I was a teenager and working on my grandfather's magic show, I found I could go into the audience and not be recognized if I wore glasses and had on a lanyard and a walkie-talkie—even when I'd been onstage minutes prior.

"First time I wore a vest like this was when I was fifteen," says Theo.

"What for?"

"Picking up roadkill," he replies as we walk toward the ridge where the garbage was dumped.

"Community service?" I ask.

"Not directly. I was collecting dead animals out of personal curiosity," Theo says over his shoulder.

"Uh . . . didn't Jeffrey Dahmer do that, too?"

Theo stops and turns around. "I really should provide more context for these things. Some of the pets in my neighborhood had been acting erratic and run away. I was curious if it was rabies. So I started inspecting roadkill."

The landfill foreperson is walking toward us. I need to explain what we're doing, but I really need to hear the rest of Theo's story.

"What happened?"

"It was rabies. I contacted animal control and the public health agencies. They put out a warning and told my mother I needed counseling."

"How did she handle that?"

"She'd already given up hope. My stepdad, on the other hand, was okay with it. He'd grown up in the woods and skinned animals as a kid. He understood."

"Can I help you?" asks the foreperson, a stocky man with a neck tattoo of a dragon visible above his blue jumpsuit.

I show him my badge. "We need to do a little searching, if it's not an inconvenience."

He shouts over to the man by the bulldozer. "Hey, Sergio! Do you have anything to hide? No dead hookers, right?"

"Not this week," Sergio replies.

"Have at it," says the foreperson. He glances down at my shoes. "Looks like you came prepared. You're doing this at your own risk, yada yada yada, and so forth. Now if you'll excuse me, Sergio and I are going to go take a smoke break so we don't have to testify in case you find something." With that, he leaves Theo and me alone with the garbage.

Theo starts down the small cliff first, walking sideways until he reaches the first bags of trash. He looks up at me. "You don't have to come down here."

"Legally speaking, you shouldn't be down there at all." I make the hike to the bottom of the ridge and pull out my phone with the app we're using to track his phone. "This way," I say, indicating a pile about ten feet from us.

Theo steps over the garbage bags and makes his way to the spot. What looks like the shadow of a cloud passes over him, but when I look up I see a flock of gulls circling overhead, waiting to swoop down and get at the contents of the dump. He glances at the sky, then starts sorting through trash.

"If I were a biologist looking for new antibiotics," he says as he paws through the trash, "I'd be checking the stomachs of those birds and all the rats around us. They've spent so much time eating our infected garbage, you'd have to imagine they have evolved some new coping mechanisms."

"I know you miss teaching," I say. "Do you miss doing research as well?"

"In a way, yes. But in another way, no. The problem with pure research is that you make a discovery, if you're lucky, and then move on to something else. The real work is figuring out how to apply that knowledge and make it useful. I think I'm more useful now. At least I hope so." Theo pulls aside a mound of fresh trash and stares at a large green lawn bag. "You look familiar."

"Weir's?" I ask.

Theo points to a tear in the side of the bag. "This would appear to be where I shoved my phone." He pulls the bag out of the pile and hands it to me. "Ah, we found your friend." He lifts another bag of the same color.

"Is that it?" I ask.

"I only saw that one in the can. But I think it's safe to assume the other is from the second can."

"Okay. Let's bring them back up to the car and have a look."

We haul the bags to the car trunk to have a look inside. First, I open the one Theo ripped and extract the coffee cup with his phone inside. "I guess that answers that question. This is definitely Weir's trash."

I take two unused garbage bags from the trunk and slide Weir's trash bags inside them so nothing falls out as I dig through.

I reach in, start sorting through the trash, and feel a smaller bag inside.

Theo can read the expression on my face. "What's the matter?"

"It's a good news/bad news situation. The good news is I think I found what Weir was hiding. The bad news is it took a trip through a paper shredder."

"Strips or confetti?" asks Theo.

"Strips, from what it feels like. Thin ones."

"Then it's all good news," he replies.

"Okay . . . explain."

"First, we need to take these someplace safe to examine them."

Obviously we can't take them back to FBI headquarters or Quantico, because there are too many eyes there. Even Gerald was paranoid. "Will a hotel room work?"

"Yes. Ideally one with a walk-in shower," says Theo.

"You don't smell that bad."

"What? No. I'm going to show you how to make a dinosaur," he says with a straight face.

CHAPTER FORTY
THEOSAURUS REX

Weir's shredded documents are sitting on the hotel room table like a pile of twisted paper ribbons. An airplane flies overhead, rattling the windows as it comes in for a landing at the nearby Richmond airport. Theo is seated, looking at a single shred from the pile.

"If that's your plan, I'm going to get another room and take a thirty-day nap," I tell him from my position sitting on the bed.

"What? Oh no. Just checking them and doing some math," he replies.

"Okay. But you promised me a dinosaur," I remind him.

"I promised to tell you how to build a dinosaur. There's a difference. So, there's the relevant part to what we're doing and the irrelevant part. I'll just give you the thumbnail version of that. DNA degrades over time. There's a kind of half-life we use to determine how long a strand of DNA will last before it loses fifty percent of its information from the molecular bonds breaking down. But unlike the half-life of a radioactive element, this isn't a law of physics. DNA's half-life has more to do with the environment DNA is preserved in and how it deteriorates over time.

"I can put uranium in a freezer and come back in a thousand years and it will have lost just as much radioactivity as if it had sat on a counter, more or less. That DNA in that same freezer—okay, maybe not the same freezer next to the radioactive uranium—won't have degraded at all if kept in the right solution and temperature. The problem is, with nature, you never get those kinds of ideal conditions, except when an animal gets frozen after getting stuck in the mud or a snowdrift. Even then, its own body chemistry can break down and cause the DNA to deteriorate. That's why we don't have museum refrigerators filled with dinosaur DNA. And if a mosquito trapped in amber *were* to have a stomach full of dinosaur DNA, the stomach acids and breakdown of the insect's body would lead to the DNA deteriorating."

"So *Jurassic Park* is a lie. Got it."

"Actually, not quite. When I was a kid reading that book, it got me to thinking about how you could restore dinosaur DNA from small fragments without having to insert segments from other animals. Also, about how you could know what was dino DNA and what wasn't.

"The hard part is to find that DNA, because it's not meant as a long-term storage solution. Well, technically it is, in that DNA replicates and carries genes through time. Some for over a billion years, so it's actually highly efficient for small bits of information. Not so much for whole animals. But that's another discussion."

"Oh, this is a discussion? I thought it was a TED talk," I reply.

"Sorry. I guess I'm way off on a tangent here." Theo picks up a handful of shredded paper. "Let me go work on this."

"Finish your point about dinosaurs. You can't leave a girl who dreamed about having a pet velociraptor in suspense."

"Velociraptors? Even the small ones were terrifying. Why would you ever have wanted one of those?"

"Revenge."

"Ah. Good point. So, anyway, the idea of getting dinosaur DNA, let alone resurrecting one, was considered a lost cause. And probably still is for right now, but not from an informational point of view. A velociraptor's whole genome might be more useful than a living velociraptor."

"You clearly never had your heart broken in the eighth grade," I reply.

"Tenth-grade science camp, actually," says Theo.

"What happened?"

"She fell for another kid in my cabin who was into physics. That's what motivated me to learn computer science as well as biology. I was tired of those hard-science guys getting all the girls."

"Every time," I reply, shaking my head. "So, dinosaur DNA . . ."

"Biologists, like other scientists, tend to like hard rules. We want to know exactly the parameters to work within, because otherwise it can drive you crazy. This kind of thinking was why you'd hear the term *junk DNA* when we encountered a sequence we didn't think was a gene. Or that DNA is the only way information is inherited. We now know things are much more complicated. Proteins on the surface of DNA contain information. Your mother's body can activate certain genes while you're in the womb. Even the bacteria in our stomach helps determine how our genes express themselves."

Theo picks up a handful of paper shreds, walks into the bathroom, and wets them briefly in the sink. I follow him to the doorway to watch.

"Anyway, we had some pretty specific ideas about how DNA degrades and just accepted the idea of a DNA half-life, which dictated that we'd never recover any DNA that was more than a few hundred thousand years old. That was until scientists started discovering that DNA might leave fossils, too. When scientists started cracking open the bones of sixty-five-million-year-old dinosaurs—something that had been ingrained in them *not* to do—they started to make interesting discoveries: fossilized cells, collagen, and in some cases, tiny balls of iron that appeared to be bound to a molecule . . . DNA. Not long strands. Only tiny pieces. By themselves, not very useful." Theo holds up a wet strip of paper and shows me the print. "But you can make out certain parts, like letters and parts of words." He places the strand on the glass of the shower door, where it sticks, then places another next to it. "These two sequences aren't immediately related to each other, but they might be from the same document. Or they might deal with the same topic."

He starts putting more strands on the shower glass, some upside down. He doesn't examine them individually, he simply flattens them on the glass like linguine noodles.

"All the information is here, but it's scrambled. With the dinosaur DNA, the problem is that little ball of DNA probably only has a fraction of the whole genome. Unlike our shredded documents, which we can assume contain everything. However, unlike our pile of shredded documents, inside the dinosaur bone that we grind down to look for balls of DNA, there could be millions and millions of copies, each one broken at a different place. It'd be like a thousand boxes of the same jigsaw puzzle, each one randomly missing different pieces. Mathematically, I can tell you how many boxes we need before we can fill in the rest. It would be a lot. Nobody has figured out how to extract enough remnant DNA. It might be there aren't enough bones on the planet to make that happen. But I don't think that's the case. Too many people were saying none of it could be done while others slowly chipped away at the problem.

"Here it's a different problem. We don't have two different strands with the same sentence split in different places telling us how to overlap them. We only have one copy, but presumably the whole copy."

Theo has covered the upper half of the shower door with strands. I can't see any rhyme or reason to them. It just looks like he pasted a bunch of shredded paper to the glass.

"We could try to match each piece to another. That's what the Iranian government did with all the shredded documents from the US embassy when it fell. But that took thousands of people working nonstop forever."

"We don't have that much time."

"Correct." Theo takes out his phone. "What we do have is computers and the same AI tools I've been playing around with for the dinosaur problem."

"Wait? You were trying to build a dinosaur?"

"Not quite. I was trying to tackle the problem to see what solutions I could come up with. I play with the problem every now and then to develop better tools. When I started, nobody knew you could find bits of DNA in tiny balls inside of fossils. And admittedly, there's some question that that's really what it is. But from a mental-exercise point of view, imagining that one impossible idea is no longer impossible can help you imagine several other things that are possible."

Theo takes a photo with his phone and uploads it via his browser. A moment later, he shows me the screen. There's an image of several of the strands from the glass window now next to each other, forming words. It's at best ten percent of one document. But that's one hundred percent more than we had before.

Theo points to the shreds of paper in the sink. "It's all there. We just have to take photos and let the computer do the rest, matching sections to each other."

"And the velociraptor you promised me?"

"Let's find out what Weir wanted to hide. Then you can help me break into a few museums to steal bones and we might just get somewhere."

Nothing about his body language or tone of voice indicates that he's lying or joking. Either he's not as crazy as I think, or it's contagious.

CHAPTER FORTY-ONE
PAPER TRAIL

While Theo pasted the shredded documents to the shower and started assembling them back together using whatever black-magic computer program he has hidden away in the cloud, I went to the office supply store across the street and got a printer and a ream of paper so we could print out all the documents Weir thought had been destroyed.

I only have a handful of them so far, and no smoking gun, but a curious picture is beginning to emerge. Most of the documents he destroyed are financial statements relating to stock holdings in about six different companies.

When I looked them up, having never heard of any of them, I learned that they were either technology or biotech companies. The total value of the stocks is approximately six million dollars. It's not a small sum, but what's interesting is that most of the companies are penny stocks with wildly fluctuating values.

Theo walks into the room and grabs another pizza crust from the box lying open on the bed next to me and my spread of papers. He sits on the opposite bed. "What have you got so far?" he asks, reaching for my leftover crust on the plate by the nightstand.

I glance at the half pizza still sitting in the box. "Don't you like pizza?"

"I love it," he replies between bites of the crust.

"Then why don't you try eating some?"

Theo glances down at the two crusts in his hands. "Oh. I didn't realize . . . When I was after N2—Angelica Covel, the serial killer nurse—I spent some time on the streets." He looks at me for a moment, perhaps realizing that I don't know most of that story. "Living on the streets, I kind of adapted."

I put a slice on a napkin and hand it to him. "It sounded like you went a little crazy."

"After a fashion. What I was trying to do was to find her pattern. Sometimes I can tell how to find a serial killer by looking at their history of crimes and finding tells. With Joe Vik it was how he buried them. This allowed me to go back to his earliest murders, when he wasn't as careful. With Covel, for decades she was so good at covering her tracks, I couldn't trace her back to when she made mistakes. She also knew all the weaknesses in hospital systems and nurses' lifestyles. She could assume identities and keep moving, burying her past. Although I didn't quite understand it at the time, I had to catch her by becoming a victim. I had to fall into the same kind of situation that her next mark would. In this case, she was murdering homeless people in a city she hadn't been to before." Theo takes a small bite of the pepperoni pizza. "I forgot how much flavor there is."

"So, there was a method to your madness," I reply.

"Yes. The method *was* madness. Coming out of it was hard. I lost a dear friend who'd been my mentor while I was away. I also made some bad choices, hurting people around me," he says somberly. "I don't know how you manage it."

"Does it look like I'm managing things?" I ask.

"I don't think you were living off scraps in trash cans."

"No. But I still feel alone. I'm closer to my family than before and . . . other people. But the circumstances have changed. I keep moving forward because I don't know how to stop. If I look like I'm holding it together, it's because I've been faking it for so long, I don't know how to not pretend. Speaking of faking it . . ." I hold up the printout nearest me. "Weir is up to something. But I don't get it. I found a name associated with all the investment portfolio statements. It's Joshua Scanlon. Scanlon is his wife's maiden name."

"Interesting," says Theo. "That's not a very good alias."

I finish doing the internet search I'd started. "Oh. This is interesting. Joshua Scanlon is her brother."

"So Weir is helping him manage his investment portfolio?" asks Theo.

"It would appear so, but according to this, Joshua died eight years ago in a motorcycle accident when he was twenty-two. Three years before Weir married his wife," I reply.

"Clever way to hide his assets," says Theo. "Do you think his wife knows?"

"I was tempted to call her until I saw this." I hand Theo the printout of the envelope he resurrected.

"This is addressed to Scanlon, but at a PO box," Theo replies.

"Yep. A box that's on the route between his house and the detention center. The odd part is that Weir's portfolio seems pretty unbalanced." I hand Theo a printout with the stock holdings.

"Interesting. I've never heard of any of them. It looks like they're pretty volatile, too," he replies.

"You think that Heywood might have told him to buy those stocks because he was going to try to influence the market?"

"You know Heywood better than I do. That seems almost beneath his skills. If a company like one of these has a suspicious increase or decrease in value and the SEC is curious, they start looking at who holds large stakes. That would lead to a dead man and more questions. You have anyone you trust at the FBI who knows more about this?"

"Hmm. Maybe Mandy Umbra. I worked with her years ago when I was chasing crooks through bookkeeping. I think I trust her. Also, I want to tread carefully, given Weir's wife's condition."

"Condition?" asks Theo.

I hand him the printouts that show the pharmacy receipts for her medication. "Cytarabine and dexamethasone. Leukemia?" asks Theo.

I nod. I didn't have to look them up to know what they were used to treat. "From the dosage, it looks like she's on the recovering side. If I'm reading that right."

"I don't know enough to know," Theo says in one of his rare admission-of-ignorance moments.

At least he has them.

"Let me make a couple calls and see if Umbra can meet with us so we can make more sense out of this before telling Gerald what we've been up to."

CHAPTER FORTY-TWO
Diversification

Mandy Umbra is already waiting for us at a diner that's a thirty-minute drive from FBI headquarters, where she works. She gets out of the booth and wraps her arms around me. I don't know if this is the Peruvian or the Italian side of her, but whenever we meet outside the office, she treats me like a long-lost sister—emphasis on the *lost* part.

She looks Theo up and down. "Wow. It's really him. I don't know if I should congratulate him or have him arrested."

"I'd prefer the former," says Theo. "But even then, I don't do well with praise."

"Well, it's nice to meet you," she says politely. "Have a seat. I can show you what I found."

Theo and I take the side of the booth opposite her, Theo on the inside and me on the outside. Mandy glances at us, then smirks. "I see you two have been working together closely."

"Come again?" I say, a little surprised. I look to my right and realize that Theo and I are sitting almost hip to hip in the large booth. "We've been through a bit together."

"I'll say," she replies.

"Killer chimps," says Theo, not helping and only sounding crazy.

"No worries. Not judging. We know Jessica's type. And normal isn't it," Mandy says as she makes an exaggerated eye roll.

"Pardon Mandy's judgy-bitch routine," I say to Theo. "She doesn't get to do that in the office."

"You can't do a lot of things in the office," she replies. "Apparently the field is where the real fun is, hanging out with brooding bad-boy scientists and their killer chimps."

"Wait? I'm brooding?" asks Theo.

"A little," I reply.

"Huh."

"You're thinner than the guy that played you in the TV movie," says Mandy.

"I didn't see it," says Theo.

"He was better-looking, too."

"I'm sure that actor didn't spend the last five months in a Southeast Asian jungle, fighting off death squads while trying to prevent genocide," I shoot back a little too sharply.

Mandy gives me an all-knowing smirk. I want to slap it off her face. I glance over at Theo, but he's staring at the saltshaker, probably counting the grains—accurately. Then I realize it's not that he was suddenly distracted; it's that when he feels uncomfortable, he uses things like that to distract himself.

Did this happen when his father died? Was that when he decided to retreat? It would explain why he can be extremely social one moment, downright funny even, but on another planet a moment later. I wouldn't put him down as someone on the spectrum, because I think for him it's a clear choice. It's not so much a retreat as a force field he chooses to raise.

I realize that my hand is on his knee, reassuring him. I feel his rough palm cover the top of mine and give me a gentle squeeze. His hand is warm and completely engulfs my own.

"Let's talk about what you found," Theo says to Mandy, putting his hands on the table after letting go of mine.

I realize that in that little moment it was me who needed the reassurance. Theo provided it, then found a way to redirect the conversation without being awkward.

"Those companies are interesting," says Mandy. "I only had time to dig into two of them heavily. The first is Autopharmix. It's a company that makes software for pharmaceutical robots that manufacture customized medication. They got bought for a sizable amount by a Chinese conglomerate. The other is Z-Prime Biotech. They are a large holding company that acquired a number of medical patents and then bought a smaller company, which they tried to bring a product to market with. It failed FDA trials, but Z-Prime was able to raise some more capital and keep researching. You might be able to make better sense of what they were doing." Mandy passes Theo some documents.

He scans them for a moment. "Artificial intelligence for drug discovery. It's kind of a big area right now. It has promise, but it's still early. Hmm, this is interesting. Their primary area of research was using modified viruses to insert DNA into cells. They were doing a whole-genome approach. Basically, the virus was the cure."

"Or was it?" I ask. "Didn't you say you could use viruses to deliver a bioweapon?"

"It's plausible," says Theo.

"Well, *somebody* thought they could do something and invested four hundred million dollars in the company back in September 2018," says Mandy. "That's when it gets—"

Theo cuts her off. "September 2018?"

"Yes. Why?"

"Nothing. Sorry. I didn't mean to interrupt you."

"Anyway, the mystery deepens, because the investor was an overseas investment fund that nobody knows who was putting money into. The suspicion was that it was a sovereign wealth fund of the Saudis or possibly a Russian oligarch."

I start a timeline on the back of my place mat, putting down when this happened along with Heywood's incarceration history. "Do you think Heywood was like a Jeffrey Epstein character? Posing as a financial adviser? Maybe he convinced the Saudis or Russians to put money into the company as a kind of pump and dump?"

Theo is typing away on his phone and using the calculator app. "Maybe. What else, Agent Umbra?"

"Well, for one, that company acquired a few small labs around the world. It's odd . . . the acquisitions didn't make financial sense until I realized what they were really buying was labs that had approval from their respective countries to do advanced trials—and, in two cases, work with infectious diseases."

I feel my stomach churn. "Heywood talked someone into buying him an illicit bioweapons program? Who'd be that stupid or evil?"

"He probably lied," says Mandy. "He may have told them they were working on one thing while doing something else."

"I don't think Heywood had to talk anyone into anything," says Theo.

"What do you mean?" I ask.

"In August 2018, Mount Gimli, a Bitcoin exchange, lost eight hundred thousand coins to a hack. The total value was almost half a billion dollars. What was odd was that when it happened, the coins were liquidated very quickly and none of the other exchanges showed an increase. Usually you can see stolen coins move from one market to another in the form of valuation."

"What are you saying, that Heywood stole it?" I ask.

"I've looked at his timeline." Theo gestures at the paper in front of me. "All his major acquisitions are preceded by a theft in the Bitcoin market. In some cases, they're big ones. In other situations, it's something like a bad wallet app that Android users installed that took twenty percent of their money."

Something that should have been painfully obvious to me comes into focus. "Heywood's a legendary hacker, so I guess it makes sense he'd go after Bitcoin exchanges and wallets."

"It gets better or worse, depending on how objectively you look at it," says Theo. "There have been rumors that some of the initial coins mined were actually done on government computer systems, either with the knowledge of the agencies or behind their backs by people who had access to the systems. Some even suspect that Bitcoin could have been a CIA or NSA invention. I don't know if I buy that, but it wouldn't surprise me if people who worked for either agency had been involved. In any event, Heywood may have seen an opportunity. It would also explain the resources he's been marshaling for his attacks."

"Heywood is a Bitcoin millionaire?" I say out loud, trying to wrap my head around the concept.

"No," Theo interjects. "If this theory is true, Michael Heywood is a Bitcoin *billionaire*."

CHAPTER FORTY-THREE
ICO

In a secure conference room inside FBI headquarters, Gerald stares at his laptop screen, tabbing through the different parts of the spreadsheet we prepared and shaking his head. He looks up from his computer and across the table at Theo and me. "Is this legit?"

"It's credible," I reply.

"A good portion of the wealth he amassed happened while he was in federal custody," says Gerald.

"And increased when we think he had especially lax oversight. Also, another thing. We wondered how he was able to retain such a high-priced law firm—Keller and Olson? They have a subsidiary that does cryptocurrency investing. Heywood's made them very rich," I say.

"That would explain an odd request we had a while ago," says Gerald. "Nauru, a tiny island country near Australia with huge corruption issues, wanted to have Heywood extradited there to go on trial, prior to completing his sentencing here. Now it makes sense. Heywood probably tried to bribe them so they could bring him under their jurisdiction and give him a new identity."

"It gets worse," says Theo.

"How worse?" asks Gerald.

"Heywood may have been behind a number of other cryptocurrencies. We might have no real idea of his true net worth."

This makes Gerald more agitated than I've seen him in a long time. "We've sent more than a few billionaires to prison. Almost none of them stayed billionaires. I can't think of a single one that got richer while he was in custody."

"We need to figure out a way to go after him," I say. "He has to be at the center of the Void. He's got the money and the opportunity to pull it off. I think it's clear that when he wasn't leading the CIA around by the collar, Weir was granting him complete, unmonitored internet access."

"But why?" asks Gerald.

"Why? Because he paid Weir off."

"Yes, but what did Weir think Heywood was up to? Why was he okay with letting a suspected serial killer and convicted hacker have access to a computer? Weir may be compromised, but he's not stupid or evil. And that brings us back to the Void. If that's Heywood's doing, what's the point of it?"

"If it's not data theft? Chaos? Fear? Death? We have all three. Plus, it's a distraction for whatever he's been cooking up in those secret labs," I reply.

"And what do you think he's doing?"

"A new plague? Perhaps those health companies Weir was investing in were going to be the first ones with a cure? Heywood would stand to get even richer."

"Heywood doesn't need that to get rich," says Theo. "Using them in some kind of stock scheme doesn't make sense to me. However, I do think he used them for their labs."

"We need to put together a team and go take those labs down right now," I tell Gerald. "Before word makes it back to Heywood through the grapevine."

"That's on the table," says Gerald.

"I hope so . . . Wait, what? Since when did you know about those labs?"

"We've been looking at a lot of facilities since you and Dr. Cray found the chimpanzee research lab. The ones you mentioned were among the list of suspect labs."

"Who is 'we'?" I ask.

Gerald lets out a sigh. "I was going to tell you. There's another team out there looking into the Warlock. It's an interagency task force."

"Sounds like a leaky ship," I say, frustrated at being outside the loop.

"These are good people. All information is contained within the group. We've had to compartmentalize because of the leaks."

"Why wasn't I part of this? It would have helped when I was dealing with IDR."

"IDR has members on the task force. And your job was him," Gerald says, pointing to Theo.

"Well, I found him. Why wasn't I put on this team?" The thought of being left out is making me angrier by the moment.

"To be honest, Jessica? Not everyone trusts you. Some worry that your connection to Heywood makes you irrational."

I'm about to show him how irrational I can be when I feel Theo's hand on my arm. He's more present than I realized and possibly as agitated as I feel. I take a breath to calm myself.

"What has this task force determined?" I ask as neutrally as possible.

"Nothing yet. But the best guess is Heywood is after something atypical," says Gerald.

"Like what? Disneyland shut down for his own amusement? A trip to the space station?"

"Some think he may be trying to build a bioweapon and ransom it back to the United States," says Gerald.

"Excuse me? How exactly does that work? Since when does the United States pay off bad guys not to do bad stuff?" I ask.

"I'd say the billions of dollars we've sent to the Middle East with no accounting says otherwise," replies Gerald.

"But you're talking about sovereign states. Countries and regimes. Not a person," I protest.

"It all comes down to power. A bioweapon that can kill more people than a nuclear bomb is a lot of power."

"This is madness! The government can't be thinking about taking an offer like that seriously?"

"It hasn't reached that level yet. And as far as it being an offer, we think if and when Heywood approaches us, it won't appear to be extortion. He'll probably present this as part of the intelligence that he stole from Chinese and Russian bioweapons research. He won't say, 'Give me what I want or I release this death virus.' He'll be offering to become a government informant."

"Wasn't he doing that already?"

"Probably. But even the CIA didn't have the power to free him."

"No. But they had the stupidity to make it easy for him to escape," I reply.

"That's being looked into as well. And I'll tell you one more thing." Gerald glances at Theo. "This doesn't leave here. Understand? We may have an informant who knows more about what Heywood is up to. We're going to find out what that is."

I make a loud sigh. "Right. Like that doesn't smell of a Heywood setup."

"Perhaps. But what you don't know is that informant tipped us off to five shipping containers in Chicago that had enough chemical EMPs to take out the city. There was a countdown timer that stopped shortly after we found them. We think we preempted an attack."

"Or Heywood set us up to think so," I suggest.

"Possibly. But why?" asks Gerald.

"So you'll buy whatever bullshit this informant feeds you. Come on, you have to see that."

"We have to explore all leads, whether or not my gut tells me otherwise," says Gerald.

"And does your gut tell you that this may all be a waste of time so Heywood can distract you?"

"It does. But the question you and I haven't answered is, to distract us from what? Heywood likes creating chaos, but his goals have never been apocalyptic."

"People change," I reply. "Besides, what better way to reset the social order than with a minor apocalypse?"

"Dr. Cray? What do you think Heywood's up to?" Gerald turns the floor over to Theo.

He thinks it over. "I told Agent Blackwood earlier that I don't have enough information to discern his pattern. The problem is like when we try to imagine what aliens or a superintelligent artificial intelligence would do in a given situation. You can't emulate a mind you don't understand. What we end up doing is either projecting our own ideas or playing a naive game of opposites, where we try to determine what's evil by our understanding of what's good. Some of the worst people I've gone after thought they were doing good, albeit in horrific ways. For example, if you were the conjoined twin a surgeon had to kill to save the other, you'd think he's evil. In the case of Heywood, my question is for Jessica: Does he see himself as a force for good or a force for evil?"

"Red Chain thought they were doing good by attempting to kill off half the planet. Does it matter?" I ask.

"Very much so. A man who sees himself as good and has multiple options will likely try the ones that cause least harm first. Michael Heywood has an incredible pool of resources. If he sees himself as good, then I can't comprehend what he'll attempt."

"He wants people to see him as a god," I reply. "Good gods, bad gods—they all have one thing in common: they define themselves by their ability to kill."

"And create life," adds Theo.

"So what does that mean? He's going to have a kid?" I ask, frustrated by Theo's semantics.

"No. Perhaps not. But he does like to create. The Void, as destructive as it is, is a sight unto itself. His little AI trick with that video call was another act of creation. He could have done something destructive."

"Like murdering a young girl so he can use her corpse in a macabre display in a cemetery, making it appear she crawled out of her own grave? By luring another girl hundreds of miles across the country to then throw her out of an airplane so he could pick up the broken pieces?" My hand goes to my side. "Is my scar an act of creation? Were the bodies I found hanging in the vault an act of artistic expression?"

"That's not what I mean," Theo says.

"He's evil. Evil does as evil is. Can't you see it?"

"Yes," says Theo. "Yet even Satan, a fallen angel, saw himself trying to restore the world to a more perfect order before man came along. From your account, Heywood doesn't derive any kind of sexual pleasure from what he does. He sees himself as a surgeon. Sometimes temperamental and vindictive, but his larger purpose is one I can't fathom. And it would be best if we stopped him before he accomplishes whatever it is."

I take a long breath and let my blood cool. Everything Theo said was maddeningly correct. But it was also cold and logical. Michael Heywood wounded me on a number of levels. The faces of his victims will never leave my mind. It's hard to see him as anything other than the embodiment of evil.

"Okay," I say. "What should we do?"

"Find him," says Gerald. "If you two can't, I don't know who can."

"Find him? Just like that? The man escaped federal custody and outsmarted the CIA and apparently your task force. So we just find him?"

"Start with his pattern," says Theo. "There's a flaw in his thinking. What is it? We know he took risks trying to kill you. So that tells us he's vindictive and probably feels threatened by you. He even built an AI to act as a go-between because you intimidate him. What else?"

"He's arrogant."

"Okay. I know from personal experience that can be a fatal flaw. In what way is he arrogant?" asks Theo.

"He likes to show you how close you came before he outsmarts you. We know he watched several of the crimes he committed in the past from up close. That's why I had our agents record video of all the onlookers at the Manhattan Void. But we got nothing."

"Yet you think he was there?" asks Theo.

"A hundred percent," I say without hesitation. "The question is, where?" Then it hits me like a ton of bricks. "Oh shit."

"What?" asks Gerald.

"I'm so, so stupid. He was right there. *So* close. And I think I know exactly where."

CHAPTER FORTY-FOUR
Operations

The Department of Homeland Security's temporary operations center in Manhattan is located in the Ritz-Carlton ballroom. Here, hundreds of federal agents, NYPD officers, and other law enforcement personnel are scattered around tables, going over computer screens and documents as they try to identify the perpetrators of the Manhattan Void.

Rachel Penn, the FBI liaison for the operation, greets Theo and me at the check-in station by the entrance. She's a tall woman dressed in a blazer and slacks, like me, though her clothes are newer and more stylish than the utilitarian wardrobe I've sported lately.

"Agent Blackwood," she says, offering her hand. She gives Theo a more circumspect nod. "Dr. Cray. My station is this way."

She leads us to a table in the corner of the room where her laptop rests next to stacks of folders and rolled-up posters. Gerald said that Penn was the one to ask about details of the investigation and that she could provide me with whatever we needed. From her response to Theo, I'm beginning to suspect that offer might be conditional.

Both Mandy and Gerald have made it clear, albeit indirectly, that there's a faction within the FBI that's no fan of Theo Cray. I'm not too surprised. There's a faction that isn't fond of me, either.

Not all of it is unearned, I have to admit. Besides my proclivity for chaos, I had a relationship with a man who is a person of interest to the FBI and a suspect in several cases. While I know Damian has broken more than a few laws, as far as I know he always acted in the interest of protecting me . . . perhaps too zealously.

I suspect that working with Theo is only making me more of a suspicious character to people who already had their doubts. There's not much I can do about that. In desperate times we have to look at alternate ways of getting things done.

"How is the investigation going?" I ask.

Penn glances at Theo, then back to me. "We've made some arrests. We're pushing for more information."

Okay. So that's how it's gonna be. She just gave me the verbatim response they've been feeding to the press. Penn considers me untrustworthy, at least with Theo around. I decide to keep this short and to the point.

"I need the thermal-imaging maps from the night of the Void."

"Do you have authorization?" she replies.

"Check your email from Gerald Voigt again if you have doubt," I say flatly.

"Fine." She picks up a rolled-up poster from the table and hands it to me. "Here."

She expects me to thank her and walk away, but I want to make sure this is what we came for. I take the rubber band off and spread the poster out on the table.

It shows an overhead thermal image of Manhattan taken by a satellite one hour into the event. There are half a dozen bright splotches on the grid, showing locations where power was still running. Some of them are the size of a block and contain dozens of buildings. Searching them all could take months.

I look across the table and notice three more poster tubes by her computer. "May I see those?"

"Fine." She hands me the other posters.

I unroll them all and lay them on the table. They also show thermal images of the city but with different bright spots. "Why the difference?" I ask, pretending Penn hadn't been hostile.

"Some of them had backup generators that came online, only to be taken out by EMPs or overloads," she replies.

"Is there any reason you didn't want to show me these?" I ask bluntly.

"You didn't ask for all the thermal images. I wasn't clear on what you were looking for." She checks her watch. "I have a meeting I have to go to. I need the other images."

"Hold on," says Theo. "May I?"

I step back. Theo takes the images and stacks them on top of each other, lining up the outline of Manhattan. He then flips through the posters, letting them flutter like a children's flip-book.

"There," he says, putting his finger on one tiny bright spot that never lost power throughout the event.

"What's that?" I ask Penn.

"The Acropolis Building. They had a generator and battery backup in the sub-basement."

"Who was in there when the event happened?"

"Only its residents. There's no public access," she replies.

"What about the residents?" I ask.

"What about them?"

"Have they been interviewed?"

"Yes. Anything else?"

"Could I see the interviews?"

"I'll look into it. You have to understand that the Acropolis is one of the most expensive pieces of real estate in the city. It's not as easy as going door to door. I have to go now. Please call the switchboard here if you need anything else." She shuts her laptop, gathers her posters, and leaves.

The fact that she didn't offer her cell number, which I already have from an email, was her polite way of telling me to go to hell.

"She seemed nice," Theo replies.

"I'm not used to having bureau people be so hostile."

"You know it's because of me, right?"

"Not all of it. I've stepped on a few toes."

"Perhaps. I didn't want to say anything before, but I have reason to suspect that once this is all over, you're going to be put into an uncomfortable position," he says.

"What do you mean?"

"Because of me. See, even if we catch Heywood, we have to remember that he wants me stopped. And others have been eager to help him. I know it from Myanmar. The bill's coming due," he explains.

"Don't be so dramatic."

Theo leans on the table and lowers his voice. "I'm not. You'll see. But I want a promise from you when they come and ask about me."

"What's that?" I ask, worried where this will go.

"I want you to tell the truth," says Theo. "Every correct action. Every questionable one. Just be honest."

"Okay . . ."

"Because they're going to get me, one way or another. We can't let them get you, too."

"Whatever," I reply. "But it's not going down like that. You've already done so much." I point to the hot spot on the map. "Now, let's go find out if Heywood slipped up."

CHAPTER FORTY-FIVE
FRONT ROW

The Acropolis Building, on the south end of Central Park, is one of the newer, ridiculously tall and thin skyscrapers that's started to appear along the Manhattan skyline. I don't know if they're a sign of skyrocketing property prices or some new construction techniques, but as I stand on the sidewalk, craning my neck to look at the top of the building, it looks like an impossible object—something that should not exist.

Theo gets out of our FBI SUV and momentarily glances up. "It's tall," he says before heading to the front of the building.

It's tall. For Theo, everything is a one or zero. But I'm certain if he saw an ant walking the wrong way on the sidewalk in front of the building, he'd stare at it for half an hour, asking how it's possible.

I join him in front of the entrance. He's looking at an app on his phone and making an odd face, which is Theo's tell for something's suspicious.

"What's up?" I ask.

Theo glances over his shoulder and speaks in a lowered voice. "It's a kind of contact-tracing app I made. I installed it when we were back in DC."

"What does it track?"

"MAC and Bluetooth addresses we've been in contact with. I think we might have someone following us," he replies.

"Who?" I ask without turning around.

"I don't know. It just keeps track of phone IDs, not the people attached to them. But I think these are government phones."

Would Gerald have put a tail on me? I trust him . . . but does he trust me? *Are* we being followed by our own people?

Whatever. It's out of my control. I need to focus on why we're here. I turn my attention back to the building.

"The Acropolis has a good view of the city from the top floors. When I was on that helicopter, I saw a lot of people at their windows and some on the roof. This building has a sky penthouse that's owned by a real estate investment firm," I tell him.

"And you think that's where Heywood wanted to watch the Void from?" asks Theo.

"Given that it had power and seems to have one of the best views in the city, yeah. Hopefully there's security camera footage, although I doubt it, or someone remembers seeing him. If it were me, I'd have disguised myself as maintenance or security. I don't think the security inside the building would stop him."

"You're stalling," says Theo. "You don't want to go inside."

Busted. "We've come this far, and I'd hate to fall for one of his pranks . . . or worse."

"You're worried that it might be a trap?" asks Theo.

"I'm afraid the moment I touch that door, the whole building is going to collapse on me." I can feel the shortness of my breath and my knees going soft.

"That's not going to happen. Come on. Let's see if he slipped up." Theo reaches down and grabs my sweaty palm and holds open the door to the lobby with his other hand.

I step inside and take a breath of the air-conditioned air. The concierge, a twenty-something woman with the looks of a fashion model, stands at a counter to the right.

"Welcome to the Acropolis. Are you here to visit someone?" she asks.

I let go of Theo's hand and take out my badge. "My name is Agent Blackwood. I want to see about access to the penthouse."

"May I take a look at that?"

I hold the badge so she can see that it's authentic. She types something into a computer. "No problem." She reaches down and pulls out a small plastic card. "Just use this to access the elevator."

This was easier than I thought. "Is it currently unoccupied?"

"I don't know. But Mr. Heywood left specific instructions that you were to be given full access when you arrived."

My heart stops. The last time I stepped into one of Heywood's secret lairs was the first time he tried to kill me.

Theo's hand wraps around mine again. It's the only thing stopping me from hyperventilating.

We walk to the elevator lobby, and I turn to Theo. He can read the question in my eyes before I even say it.

"Should we go up?"

"That's up to you," he replies.

"You're not helping. Should I call the bomb squad? Bring in reinforcements?"

"It's your call. I'm with you either way."

"Even if we're stepping into a trap with five tons of C-4 ready to kill us?"

"Yes."

The way he says it without hesitation soothes me a little. For the first time, I realize that it's not dying that scares me; it's the thought of dying alone.

I touch the plastic card to the elevator sensor, and the door opens. Theo steps inside first. I panic for a moment at the thought of the doors slamming shut and taking him away from me.

But they stay open.

I step inside and stand next to him.

The doors close, and we feel the sudden acceleration upward as the elevator takes us to the eighty-fifth floor. Theo gives my hand a squeeze, letting me know he's present.

I reach my other hand up and touch it to his stubbled chin and turn his mouth toward my own. I pull him in, and his lips make contact with mine. My tongue probes his mouth for the briefest of moments, and I feel every blood vessel in my body open wide. I want to pull him closer, but instead I let him go.

I pull back and release his hand. "I'm sorry."

"It's okay," he says.

"I know you just . . ."

"I think she'll understand," he replies.

"I don't think you understand women."

PART SIX
THEORETICIAN

CHAPTER FORTY-SIX
ASCENSION

Our kiss may have killed us.

Jessica is calm, collected, and outwardly fine, but from the perspiration on her hand and the pulse I sense with my fingertips, she's experiencing what feels like a minor panic attack. All my enemies are dead, in jail, or ten thousand miles away in another country, dreading the day they encounter me again. Jessica's enemy has been watching her the entire time.

While chasing Heywood, she found herself in the exact spot he wanted her to be in—or at least he made it appear that way. He may be in love with her, but he doesn't love her. The distinction is the difference between wanting a thing and wanting what is best for it.

I can convince myself that the kiss was just a platonic reassurance to a friend in a terrifying situation, but I know there's a deeper truth. The moment I gave Jillian the papers to the bakery, the house, and everything else, she treated it like a divorce. A polite one, but a separation.

I felt so horrible for everything I'd put her through I wanted to make sure that if I didn't return from Myanmar, she'd be able to make a clean break of it. The reality was that I didn't expect to return.

I went there to die.

I'd become a dangerous thing. A creature willing to crawl through the gutter to strike at my enemies while casting off my few friends and the people that loved me. I was more reptile than man.

At first, I blamed it on the Hyde virus, a pathogen that I may have come in contact with while hunting Forrester, the biomedical researcher who wanted to infect the US's armed forces, but I slowly came to realize my behavior was my own choice.

Having been the victim of a cruel and indifferent universe that stole away my father, I wanted that power for myself.

When they came for us in the jungle, I got to be who I truly wanted to be. I didn't hold back like I did with Forrester or Angelica Covel. I didn't hesitate like I did with Oyo. I didn't even wait to be physically threatened.

When Johnny ran, he wasn't running from them. They were all dead. He ran from me, terrified by what I had become.

Jillian never saw it. She didn't know the man she slept with each night when we were together was thinking up a thousand ways to kill all the evil in the world. She saw my light and my shadow but didn't realize that the real me was the shadow.

When I was in that cell, expecting to die, I hid away knife blades and picked the locks at night to see if I could do it . . . but I didn't want to leave. I was too tired.

And then light walked in. A light with a long shadow, but a light nonetheless.

I've watched Jessica as she faces each difficult decision. She's learned that sometimes the right thing isn't written down anywhere. Sometimes it's the opposite of what we've been told.

I didn't know if Heywood, this man who calls himself the Warlock, really wasn't going to kill her when we set foot in the elevator. What I did know—and I at least suspect Jessica realized on some level—was that Heywood was watching us.

For my part, I accepted her kiss in an act of defiance. I wanted him to see that I have the thing that he desires. I wanted him to see that instead of being pushed off the chessboard, I got the queen.

And if in some petulant act, Heywood pulled a trigger from wherever he's hiding, he'd do it knowing that he'd permanently lost the one thing he could never have.

A tone chimes in the quiet elevator car as we reach the top floor. Jessica is standing perfectly straight, and her eyes are facing forward as she waits for the doors to open. Her hands are at her sides, not ready to pull the gun from her waist like when we first met.

Like me, she must assume that whatever situation we're about to set foot in, a sidearm won't decide the outcome. Heywood is playing a game I can't fathom and one that I don't think Jessica understands, either. We're simply incapable of understanding him.

The elevator opens to a foyer. The large double doors to the only apartment on this floor stand before us, ten feet tall and presumably leading to a penthouse with a high ceiling and expansive view of the city. And quite possibly a trap set specifically for us.

Every rational part of me says we should leave. A voice in the back of my mind whispers that whatever's on the other side of those doors will change us. More specifically, it's been designed to change Jessica.

I grasp her elbow. "He wants you to step through those doors."

"I know," she replies. "I know." Her beautiful green eyes search the wall around the doors and land on a small section near the ceiling where a camera is visible, mounted on the trim. "He's been watching."

She uses the word *been*, letting me know that she understands the potential consequences of the kiss. Perhaps intentionally letting me off the hook for the guilt I feel.

A small smile forms at the corner of her mouth. "We could just flip a coin. Heads we enter. Tails we don't." She shrugs. "We'll have to find out sometime."

She unlocks the doors with the key card, and her hand reaches for the knob. She twists it and opens the door. A twenty-foot floor-to-ceiling window stands at the far end of the room. Three white couches sit in the middle, and a stainless steel telescope is aimed out at the city.

Jessica turns to me and rolls her eyes. "Of course. It's one big scavenger hunt."

She strides across the room and leans over the telescope to look through the eyepiece. I consider stopping her in case it's a trap, but it's too late.

Instead, I join her and watch as she adjusts the focus on the scope. Her free hand tucks a loose strand of her hair behind her ear as she squints.

"The first time he saw me was in Fort Lauderdale, when the FBI brought me onto the case. He watched me from a telescope."

A familiar voice speaks from within the room. "No, Jessica. The first time I saw you was long before that . . ."

CHAPTER FORTY-SEVEN
BACKPROPAGATION

Jessica's eyes go wide, and there's a flash of motion as she pulls her gun from her waist too fast for me to see her arm move. The barrel of the pistol is already pointed at the far end of the room by the time I realize what she's done.

"FBI! Hands behind your head. On the floor! Now!" she shouts as she advances toward him.

He raises his hands and drops to his knees on the tile floor.

He's an ordinary-looking man. He could play a dad in a car commercial. Midforties. Slight but athletic build. Graying hair at the temples. But there's something about the way his eyes watch her and me. They dart back and forth like he's looking for something between us.

Jessica puts the barrel of her gun at his temple and pushes him flat.

Heywood complies and allows himself to be cuffed with his wrists behind him.

Jessica pushes him down and tosses a set of keys and a phone to the side. "Theo, call the dispatcher. Tell them we need a team here now."

I pull my phone from my pocket and look at the screen. There's no signal. "I don't have reception."

Jessica pulls her phone from her pocket with her free hand and slides it across the floor to me. "Use mine."

"Yours won't work, either," says Heywood. "This apartment's a kind of Faraday cage."

"Unbelievable. Fine. Get to your feet. We'll go to the lobby. Theo, get the door."

I reach for the door handle, but it won't move. "I believe he has us locked in," I tell her.

"Actually, it's me who's locked in," says Heywood. "There are cameras controlled by a computer designed to keep me from leaving but not you. If Jessica releases me, you'll find that the door will open. If you try to prop it open, the elevator won't operate."

"Why?" asks Jessica, holstering her gun.

"I wanted you to hear me out. Both of you."

"Tell DHS," says Jessica. "We're done playing games."

"This isn't a game. This is a promise. Just let me say what I have to say and I'll deactivate the system and surrender," Heywood tells her.

"Theo, take a look around. If you see anything that looks like a computer, hack it or break it."

I start to search the room before moving to the rest of the apartment. The decor is sparse and modern without a lot of ornamentation. I knock on the walls, looking for hidden panels.

"The controls are inside a walk-in safe in the bedroom closet. It would take some time to get to them. Considerably more than it would take to hear me out," says Heywood.

Jessica glances in my direction. She really doesn't want to give Heywood his chance to monologue for us. I understand, but I don't think it's going to change the outcome one way or another.

"Give him ten minutes," I reply. "Then leave the room and I'll beat the access code out of him."

"Dr. Cray, your capacity for violence amazes me," says Heywood.

"It'll more than amaze you when you discover my capacity for throwing you out an eighty-fifth-story window."

"Do you know what the amazing part is, Jessica? Dr. Cray thinks he's bluffing, but he's actually secretly afraid that he's capable of doing it," says Heywood.

"It's no secret."

Heywood is still lying facedown. "May we move ourselves to the couch? I have something to show you. No tricks. I promise."

Jessica grabs the chain between the handcuffs to control him. "Get up. Move the wrong way and I shoot you."

She walks him over to the couch and pushes him into a seated position, then sits opposite him. I slide a chair between him and the door and take a seat, concerned that a trapdoor or spikes will be sprung at any moment.

"This is better," says Heywood. "I'd prefer it if my hands were in front of me. But I understand. Fortunately, I anticipated this and acquired exceptionally well-padded furniture."

"Nine minutes," says Jessica.

Actually, he has eight minutes left, but I don't correct her.

"Fine. First, I don't expect you to believe anything I have to say. In time you'll find that it's true. Right now, I just want you to hear it in my own words. My virtual avatar didn't come off as sincere as I would have liked, and I'll be honest, I was stalling for time."

His voice and body language seem sincere. But so do those of a sociopath. Jessica is watching him carefully, not reacting. She's waiting for the trick. I have the sneaking suspicion that this *is* the trick—some kind of mind game.

"I am very sorry for everything I've done. To you and to all . . . my victims. I can't even describe what I feel. But if you think that I have no remorse, please know that that's *all* I feel."

"Right. Is that it? Can we go now?" asks Jessica.

"There's so much more." He glances in my direction. "We could talk about the unusual nature of my ventromedial area, couldn't we?"

"What's he talking about?" Jessica asks me.

"It's the part of the brain that controls moral judgment," Heywood answers for me. "It's what Dr. Cray was afraid was deteriorating in his own brain after he was exposed to the Hyde virus."

Jessica scoffs. "Okay. A brain injury made you do bad things. Got it. Did it prevent you from seeking help, too?"

Heywood nods. "I understand. I don't expect you to believe me. But I have a question: Do you think a perfectly functioning brain would do the horrible things I did?"

"Maybe not the brain, but the mind. This is tedious. You're not going to spin me some bullshit story where you had a tumor or an accident that made you do the horrible things you did. And if this is the dramatic revelation you wanted to share, it was a waste. You failed."

"Everyone in this room is a killer, Jessica. All of us believe it was for the greater good," replies Heywood.

"This conversation is done. Open your doors before I shoot them open."

"They're bulletproof. But the good news is that they will automatically open ten minutes from now. We can use this time for me to answer any question you want. I'll either tell you the complete truth or pass. I promise I won't lie to you."

"Fine. Did you cause the Void?" she asks.

"Yes," he replies without hesitation.

This takes her aback for a moment. "Why?"

"It was a condition forced upon me by an anarchist collective when I sought their cooperation. I didn't have an alternative," he replies.

"All right. What was your purpose?" she asks.

"I needed to steal something."

"What?"

"Data," he answers.

"What kind of data?"

"Pass."

"This is pointless," she says. "Whose data?"

"Mine," Heywood replies.

"Was it Bitcoin or some kind of cryptocurrency?"

Heywood laughs and shakes his head. "Nothing so . . . trivial."

"Is it a neural network model?" I ask.

Heywood nods. "Very good, Dr. Cray. You are correct."

"What's he talking about?" Jessica asks me.

"A neural network is a program that emulates the neurons in the brain. It's how your phone recognizes your face or his little avatar demo carries on a conversation. He probably created it by stealing time on computers around the world and inputting billions of parameters."

"Trillions," says Heywood. "I used a scalable cloud cluster bigger than anyone could ever imagine." He smiles. "I had NSA computers working alongside Chinese People's Liberation Army clusters. It was massive."

"To create what?" I ask, trying to hide my curiosity.

"The most sophisticated neural network ever made."

"To do what?"

"Jessica gets to ask the questions," says Heywood.

"To do what?" she asks with a sigh.

"Pass."

"Well, that was completely useless," says Jessica. "So you made a nerd thing. Yay for you. I'm sure all the other nerds in nerd prison will be proud. Oh, wait. When we extradite you to South Korea, they'll probably give you the death penalty. Too bad. Or maybe Thailand."

Heywood shakes his head. "Nobody will be extraditing me. And if I go to those countries, it'll be because they'll be hailing me as a hero."

Jessica stands. "All right. Let's go. This is just sad now."

"Not yet," says Heywood. "We have to wait for your friends to arrive."

"My friends?"

"Yes. I'm not surrendering to you—no offense. I had something more strategic in mind. You'll understand." He looks to me. "And Dr. Cray, this will be the part where you kick yourself and wonder why you didn't think of what I did. You certainly have the capability."

"What the hell is he talking about?" asks Jessica.

The computer clusters. The secret labs. Heywood's grand proclamations. I finally see it now. The picture is coming into focus.

I was too close before, but now I see the entirety of what he's done.

"Oh my god," I say out loud.

"What?" asks Jessica. "What is it, Theo?"

"Holy shit."

Heywood is grinning from ear to ear. "You see it now."

"Theo . . ." Jessica's scared.

"He . . . he . . ." Words fail me. I've wasted my damn life.

If he's done what I think he's done, then I should be the one taking the dive out the window.

"Theo!" Jessica says sharply.

Heywood's practically bouncing up and down on the couch, waiting for me to say the words.

"Heywood won."

CHAPTER FORTY-EIGHT
PAPERCLIP

Jessica is staring at me furiously as I try to find the words while Heywood savors every nanosecond. This is the moment he wanted. Not what comes later. Not the accolades. Not the praise. Not whatever reward he may receive. This is the moment when someone else finally realizes why Heywood's name will become immortal.

"How many?" I ask.

"Hundreds right now. Thousands with more data. All of them, eventually," says Heywood.

"What. Did. He. Do?" asks Jessica.

"Heywood built the largest neural network ever," I reply.

"We know this," says Jessica.

"A neural network solves problems. Heywood built one to solve a very specific problem."

"What problem?"

"Death," I reply. "He built a neural network to develop cures for disease."

"Bullshit," she says.

"The angels, Jessica. Those miracle cures around the world? You heard of those?" asks Heywood.

Jessica turns away from me and toward Heywood. "What are you talking about?"

"I cured them. My model found treatments that had never been tried before. It looked at the human genome and the millions of medical records and research articles I trained it on, and it learned how to cure diseases. It saw patterns medical science never considered. It noticed why certain drug types would only work on certain genes. It figured out how to boost a treatment with a slightly above average success rate to near one hundred percent." Heywood is beaming.

"This is bullshit, right?" Jessica asks me. "Somebody would have thought of it."

"Lots of people thought of it," I tell her. "The problem was two-fold: one, you'd need more medical records than anyone legally has access to; two, you'd need more computational power than anyone has ever had access to. Not to mention an intelligent-enough algorithm to begin with. Basically, you'd have to be willing to invade the privacy of hundreds of millions of people and then steal billions of dollars' worth of computer processing without anyone noticing."

"You're mostly right," Heywood chimes in. "Although I did pay for a considerable amount of that computation myself. But essentially correct."

Jessica searches my face, trying to make sense of this. "Is he saying he cured cancer?"

"Some forms," Heywood answers for me. "The model is still learning. But yes, eventually all disease will be cured in time. Immortality is within our grasp."

Heywood's eyes dart to the left for a moment, like he's listening to something. "It appears the other guests have arrived, and they've sent a tactical team up the elevator first. Dr. Cray, you might want to go ahead and open the door so they don't knock it down. I would myself, but I'm afraid Jessica might accidentally shoot me."

"It wouldn't be an accident," Jessica replies.

I open the door at the same time an FBI SWAT team bursts through. My hands are on my head and I'm on my knees before they even have to yell at me.

An agent fastens a zip tie around my wrists and pushes me to the floor without too much force.

I turn my head to see that Jessica has her badge out. The SWAT team fans out and searches the rest of the penthouse while the commander speaks to Jessica.

"Are you okay?" the commander asks her from under his mask.

"Fine. Can Dr. Cray get off the floor?"

"We have orders to hold him for now."

"Whose orders?" she demands.

"The director's orders."

"I want to speak to him."

"You can once we clear the premises." The commander walks over to the window to confer with another agent.

"Theo, I'm sorry," says Jessica.

"This is the politest arrest I've had in a while," I tell her.

To be honest, my mind is still racing with what Heywood says he accomplished. Intellectually I can grasp what he did, even the finer details, but the scope of it is beyond comprehension. I've done some illegal and shady things in the name of helping people, but hacking the largest medical databases in the world, intruding upon that many computing clusters? It's a work of evil genius. But *is* it evil?

If he's telling the truth about the so-called miraculous recoveries and he can prove that his system cured them, the millions of lives he'll save will outweigh the many he's taken. Some might even forgive him. A generation from now, many will think of him as a mad-scientist hero. If his neural network continues to evolve, he could go down in history like Pasteur, Darwin, or Newton.

If his goal was to be thought of as a kind of living god, he may have accomplished that.

As hard as it is for Jessica to see it, we live in a world where leaders of nations can send missiles into other countries to clumsily murder enemies, kill innocents with drones, and still be given the Nobel Peace Prize. How would humanity look at the man who cured cancer—and had a viable explanation for his reckless behavior? Would people even remember him for the evil things he's done? Would they care?

Jessica walks over to me and kneels as two FBI agents frisk Heywood on the ground. The Warlock's looking in my direction and grinning.

"What's going on, Theo?" whispers Jessica.

"I think he won."

"He won? That's all you have to say? What exactly did he win? He killed some people and used a computer to say he cured some other people. We don't know if any of that is true."

"You're right. But we'll find out pretty quickly. And in theory, it makes sense."

"Does it?" she asks.

"In theory. Up to now, nobody's ever been able to put this kind of effort into solving disease."

"Why not? If it was so easy?"

"It wasn't easy. And the answer is more complicated, but even when we were trying to decode the human genome, the National Institutes of Health vetoed using supercomputers to decode it faster. They only relented when a start-up company was about to beat them and showed that their methods were hopelessly antiquated. Medicine is conservative. Sometimes for the right reasons. Sometimes for the wrong reasons. We'll let people die from a pandemic because we don't want to give them a cure that might also kill them. It's easier to deal with the repercussions of a death by natural causes than a death from an experimental procedure. We worry about fallout more than data. That's why it takes a sociopath to do what Heywood has done."

"They're not going to give him what he wants," says Jessica. "They can't."

"Sure they can. The entire US space program was led by a former Nazi officer who ran a slave camp. When we landed on the moon, he became an American hero. Did we make the wrong decision? I don't know that we did. If they want what Heywood's offering enough, then anything is possible."

"I'm going to be sick," says Jessica.

CHAPTER FORTY-NINE
The Gift

"Please have a seat," the unfamiliar Department of Justice attorney tells me, directing me to a chair opposite him and a dozen other people. Gerald and Jessica are already sitting to my right. They've been speaking to the committee today and for half of yesterday. As I sit, I scan the names and badges. There are scientists from the National Institutes of Health and the FDA, some advisers from different universities, and some Senate staffers. A few others don't have name tags and could be people from the CIA, NSA, or some obscure computational agency dedicated to artificial-intelligence security that's rumored to exist. IDR director Vivian Kieren is here as well.

"Dr. Cray, thank you for joining us," says the justice official who greeted me, Benjamin Elliott. "You had a chance to hear Mr. Heywood's claims. What do you make of them?"

"I think the phrase is, 'Big, if true,'" I reply.

"Could you be more specific?"

"Everything he said made sense, in its own right. If you had access to that amount of processing power, and if you had the right data, you could make some interesting discoveries. The key is putting them to the test. Knowing which ones worked."

"And do you think they worked?"

"I'm not a medical doctor. I haven't examined anyone he claimed was cured."

"You saw the patients in Chernobyl," says Elliott. "Heywood says that he'd asked an outside organization for independent verification. He claims that those patients were cured."

Interesting. So Heywood's claiming that he asked some folks to check his numbers and *they're* the ones accountable for the horrific treatment those men suffered?

"I saw malnourished people who were the victims of cruel experiments," I explain.

"But ambulatory and showing no signs of the diseases they had been suffering from," says a woman named Dr. Wheeler.

"I have no idea what they were suffering from," I answer.

"What about the chimpanzee facility? What was the condition of the animals?" Wheeler asks.

"They, too, were in a malnourished state."

"Were they ill?"

"Again, not my area," I reply. "I know the ones buried out back were pretty ill. And I suspect the Chernobyl facility has more skeletons. But I don't think you brought me here to get my opinion on those horror shows. You have experts on the ground."

"We wanted your assessment, Dr. Cray. We have some very challenging decisions. We've looked at eighty of Heywood's so-called miracle cures and found what appear to be eighty spontaneous remissions. When we ran the pharmaceutical combination that Jessica suggested in our own computer model, we came up with a pattern match."

"I'm sorry. *Jessica* suggested . . . ?" I look to Jessica.

"Not me." She shakes her head. "That's what Heywood named his computer model."

"Jessica in Aramaic means 'to see,'" says Wheeler. "He claims he chose the name before he knew Agent Blackwood."

"We're aware of Mr. Heywood's criminal activities," says Benjamin Elliott, taking the floor again. "We're not here to discuss them. We're trying to determine the viability of the computer model."

"Then take a look at it," I tell him. "Have it make some predictions. Test them on mice."

"Before we can do that, we need to come to an arrangement with Heywood," says Wheeler.

"Oh. He's extorting you. I got it."

Wheeler's not having any of that. "Actually, Dr. Cray, he's been very forthcoming with the data from his neural network model. In order to implement the full model, we'd need considerable help to get it running."

"You seem persuaded," I remark.

"I'd say that he has provided us with an overwhelming amount of supportive evidence. And I've examined the 'angel' cases myself. I believe he's made a breakthrough. My question is, do you, Dr. Cray?"

"Like I said, it's within the realm of possibility. His approach is sound, albeit illegal and unethical, but it doesn't contradict anything I know."

Prior to the meeting, I'd been given a two-page document outlining how Heywood built and trained his network. It was a good thumbnail sketch, but it didn't get into specifics. I sent a copy to Hailey for her take, since she's more knowledgeable about this than I am. Her response was, "Yes, in theory. But too vague. This looks like bullshit meant to fool investors. This is how Theranos happened," referencing the crooked health start-up that promised to detect hundreds of diseases from one drop of blood.

"And what is your opinion of the research summary?" asks Elliott.

"If he actually used the resources he said he did, then it's possible," I suggest.

A man in the corner with a thin crew cut and five-o'clock shadow speaks up in a British accent. "We've managed to verify that part of it."

"Using NSA and CIA computers? How did he pull that off without inside access?" I ask.

"We're not here to get into specifics of legality," says Elliott.

I can see that Jessica is fuming at them. I decide to say what she can't. "It sounds to me like you're ready to give him a free pass on being a mass murderer for this."

"Mr. Heywood may have had a condition that impaired his judgment," says Wheeler.

"Was it contagious?" I ask.

"Can we get back to the discussion at hand?" asks Elliott. "I'll be forthcoming. Mr. Heywood has offered convincing proof that his system has discovered effective treatments for Kaposi's sarcoma and myxofibrosarcoma, using off-label medications. He's also shown that the model has the ability to create entirely new classes of pharmaceuticals with tremendous impact. Pursuing this will take a considerable effort and his cooperation."

"His cooperation . . . ," I echo. "Let me guess. A pardon?"

"The specifics aren't your concern, with the exception of one matter. But first, a philosophical question: If what he says is true, what is the value of his system?"

"Something that could save millions of lives a year," adds Wheeler.

"What sacrifice wouldn't be justifiable?" Elliott chimes back in.

"I guess you have to ask whoever is making that sacrifice," I explain.

"We are, Dr. Cray," says Elliott. "Mr. Heywood's terms are for the most part understandable. But he appears to have a grievance with you."

"Who doesn't?"

"Heywood claims to have evidence that you've done unlawful network intrusions into government computers. His condition is that you be convicted for this."

I can't keep the smirk off my face. "The guy who was using NSA computers for his science fair project is calling *me* a hacker? That's just incredible."

"Did you show Agent Blackwood an application that tracked the device IDs of cellular phones belonging to federal agents?" asks Elliott.

"I think that's a question for a lawyer. But would said app work in exactly the same manner as a contact-tracing app and within the same legal boundaries?" I ask.

"That would be a question for a courtroom. Let me put it this way: right now, the only thing standing between us and Heywood granting us access to his system is you. He wants a conviction. Obviously, we can't promise him an outcome," says Elliott.

I know where this is going. "But you can ask me for a confession, a guilty plea, and a waiver of my right to a trial."

"This is bullshit," says Jessica.

"Agent Blackwood, you were allowed to sit in on this on the condition that you remain quiet," snaps Elliott.

She stands and points at Elliott. "Go fuck yourself."

"Blackwood!" shouts Gerald, jumping to his feet. "Out of the room, now!" He ushers her to the door.

"Don't do it, Theo. There's another way. There has to be," she says before the door shuts.

"As you know, Dr. Cray, there is another way. That way is called time," says Wheeler. "Unfortunately, as we wait for alternatives, people die. What Heywood has presented us could accelerate research by decades. If we can prove the model works, we can get funding to build quantum clusters and systems much more powerful than what he could cobble together."

"We'd ask for the federal minimum," says Elliott, returning to the issue at hand. "We can expedite you to a minimum-security prison."

"We can give you access to research," says Wheeler.

"All I have to do is take one for the team?" I ask.

"There's another matter," adds Elliott. "When Agent Blackwood retrieved you from Myanmar, she forged several government documents to get you out of the country."

I look over to Gerald. His expression is stone-cold. Did he know about this? Jessica may have intercepted a request, but I'm not aware of any forgery she committed. She's too smart for that.

I notice that Gerald has underlined something on his notepad and is tapping his pen lightly on it for me to see.

THEY ONLY WANT YOU.

I understand. If I don't make the choice they want, they'll come down hard on Jessica and force me.

Fine.

I was ready to die in prison before she found me. I'm ready to die in prison for her now.

"Whatever you want," I tell them. I feel like adding in that if Heywood's system doesn't work out the way they plan, then maybe they should spring me sooner than later. But that's not the way it works. Worst case, he'll show only modest improvements to the tech and they'll keep hoping for a miracle. Best case, his system delivers. Either way, these folks will forget about their promises to me.

"Director Kieren, tell your agents that the IDR can take Dr. Cray into custody," says Elliott, already breaking one promise.

CHAPTER FIFTY
COLD STORAGE

Lagrange comes to move me. That's not his name. None of the guards in the Death Star have names, at least not ones they tell us. And by *us*, I mean the other inmates I assume are in this black-walled detention center. I've only passed by the others in the halls. Or at least I assume I have. When they move you from one room to another, they put a hood over your head.

Shortly after Kieren had me escorted out of the conference room, I was hooded, placed on an airplane for three hours, and brought to this facility. A government lawyer explained from the video screen behind the thick sheet of glass in my cell that I would be held indefinitely as a security risk because I had access to state secrets.

Apparently, you can have your citizenship taken from you when the right judge signs a certain document. I'm sure it was a well-intentioned rule to help fight a war on terror through a legal system not meant to fight wars, but like any power, it has the potential for abuse, and whoever holds that power will avoid relinquishing it at any cost.

Lagrange shoves me against a wall. "Stay here."

His footsteps fade on the concrete floor, and a door closes. My hands are still bound and the hood is still secure around my head.

The Death Star is an interesting place. It's incredibly efficient, cruel in certain ways, but not in others. I've never been brutalized by a guard. The meals are adequate, and my health is checked weekly by a physician. I get the feeling that this is the product of the government learning from other black sites and detention centers.

Somewhere in this facility, I'm convinced there's an office where they have Christmas parties and plan baby showers. The inmates are numbers on a board and somebody types up a weekly report, then checks Facebook.

It feels like a prison built by a machine. There're no shower sexual assaults or illicit drugs that I'm aware of, but there's also no library, classes, or church services. I have a cell with a toilet and a shower. At the end of my bed is a television that I can only control with my voice.

With a little human interaction, it could be a model for prisons everywhere, except for one detail—it has to cost a ridiculous amount of money to keep me here. This is a place reserved for a certain kind of criminal, though I haven't a clue what that kind of criminal is supposed to be.

Maybe like me? I don't know.

There are footsteps that sound like heels. I can smell a whiff of perfume. This would be Dr. Diane. She's one of the psychologists who interview me twice a week. She's never been formally introduced as a psychologist, and I'm sure Diane is merely the name she shrinks under. I can tell from her questions that she is highly educated but horrible at statistics and has only a weak understanding of world events.

She asks me questions, usually through the television, about my well-being, then random ones about potential network vulnerabilities or whether I've communicated with certain hacking groups.

I imagine that somewhere at the other end of those questions is an intelligence analyst typing into a web form like they're ordering Korean food.

"Dr. Cray, you have a visitor," says Dr. Diane. "I'm here to remind you that we've made you aware that the procedures and practices in this facility are national secrets. You may talk about your well-being, shows you've watched, and books you've read. But you may not discuss our conversations or any other aspects of our facility. May I get a verbal yes from you before you're allowed to see your visitor?"

"Yes, Dr. Diane," I reply.

Diane's footsteps retreat, and I hear the heavy plodding of Lagrange as he enters the room.

He tightens the hood on my head, puts a hand on my back, and walks me to another room.

"Sit down," says Lagrange, using a powerful hand on my shoulder to remind me which way is down.

"Face forward."

I look straight ahead as the hood is pulled away. When my eyes adjust, I see my reflection in a pane of glass. The room around me is white, like the interior of an Apple store.

A light flickers to life on the other side of the glass, and I see a mirror version of the room I'm in. A door slides open, and I see the face that I've been thinking about constantly—and feeling guilty about it.

"Theo," says Jessica as she steps forward and sits opposite from me across the glass.

"Hey, Jessica," I reply, giving her a smile to let her know I'm perfectly fine.

"I am so, so sorry," she says. I can tell from the puffiness around her eyes and the dark circles she's tried to cover with concealer that these last three weeks have been worse on her than on me.

"It's not so bad. Last time I was in a jail, I was pretty sure I was about to be killed or one of the guards was going to try to make it all the way to third base with me. Possibly in that order."

She shakes her head. "Theo, Theo. I've been trying to get you out of here and to the minimum-security prison. I've also reached out to Heywood . . . ," she adds hesitantly.

"What?"

"I want to talk him out of this."

"No! That's what he wants. You can't put him in a position of power. He's a cruel man. He'll just use that to torment you."

"Knowing you're in here is tormenting me. It's not right." Tears start to well up in her eyes.

"Hey, it was only a matter of time. I deserve worse than this. I'm okay. More importantly, how's your father?"

"My father? What do you know about my father?" she asks.

"You had very specific knowledge of Weir's wife's cancer medications, and I've seen you receive texts on multiple occasions from someone named Dad on your phone," I reply.

"I didn't know you knew."

"I didn't think you were ready to tell me. It's a heavy burden to put on someone," I say. "And I suspected you didn't want me to revisit what happened to my dad."

"He's doing okay. We think he has a good chance of remission. That could give him several years." Jessica pounds her fist on the counter. "That asshole."

"Your dad?"

"No. Heywood. He made sure I saw the list of diseases they wanted to test for once the system was up and running. He wanted me to know my father's form of cancer was one of them."

"I only see that as a good thing. Assuming it works."

"Assuming it works," she repeats. "I've been looking into the miracle-cure cases. There are a hundred and twenty of them now. Something's still bothering me about them."

I raise my eyebrows and wait for her to tell me.

"I was thinking that maybe he looked for spontaneous remissions and then tried to take credit for them, but that's not the case, as far as I can tell."

"How exactly did he administer his treatments?" I ask.

"Well, that's one more reason that it's frustrating that you're in here instead of him. He hacked the medical diagnostic software hospitals were using and added in the recommendations for off-label treatments. A number of doctors just blindly followed what the software told them. Most of the senior oncologists didn't, but the younger ones were willing to try it in dire situations."

"And it worked? Have you looked to see if there were cases where it didn't?"

"Some people didn't react as strongly, but that's the extent of it. We've been calling around to hospitals trying to find out if any doctors tried recommendations that didn't work out. So far none."

"You wanted to see if he was randomly trying different treatments."

"Not randomly, but off-label therapies the FDA hasn't approved," she replies. "The scary part is how many people are okay with this. Heywood broke just about every ethical and legal law you can imagine, yet people in all these agencies are rushing to evaluate the results. I don't understand."

"Well," I say, "you have to accept the idea that this could be real. Bad people sometimes do brilliant things. The Soviets starved millions of people but put a man in space. Columbus discovered a new world at the expense of the people who already lived there. This could be the real thing. I hope it's real."

"Yeah, I understand. I just have trouble separating my feelings. I want him to be wrong because he's so vile. But I understand that also means that millions of people would die."

I point to the ceiling, reminding her that we're being listened to. "I understand the philosophical quandary."

"The part that really gets to me is his obsession with you," she replies. "You threaten him. I'm not sure why. He already got what he wanted. We didn't stop him."

"Some people are vindictive." *And strangely obsessed with me.*

"I guess so. I'm embarrassed they went along with this. I had to pull every string I could to come see you. Have you been able to talk to anyone else?"

"They let me send basically a form letter to Jillian."

"I talked to her. I explained the situation as well as I could. She already knew about Heywood. That's another thing. The asshole hired some elite publicity firm to promote him and his cure system. It's insane. Thankfully some people are calling it bullshit. But a lot aren't. Anyway, she sends her love."

Of course she does. But I know it's a different kind of love now. When Jillian responded to my letter, she said that there would always be a room for me when I get back.

She used to tell me her bed would always be waiting. Offering me a room is her way of telling me that she'll be there for me as a friend, but not as a lover. In a way, it's the most loving thing she could say. She's releasing me from the guilt of holding her back emotionally. Jillian deserved so much better than me. They all did.

"You okay, Theo?"

"I'm fine. Everything is fine. I should go now."

"Go? Where? Oh crap, Theo, are you okay?"

I wish the hood were back on so she couldn't see me like this. "Everything is fine," I say again, trying to convince myself.

CHAPTER FIFTY-ONE
Palace

Sometimes I lie in bed at night and try to see the entire world. Instead of creating a memory palace, in which I could store and organize memories and experiences, I try to remember the world in its entirety, every place I've visited, every person I've ever known.

I visit my mother and stepfather, who are so used to my infrequent visits that often our only communication is a Christmas card listing the places we've been.

I watch Jillian in her bakery as kids in dusty baseball uniforms crowd the glass cabinets, pointing at cupcakes.

I imagine Hailey at her company, eating lunch and tossing insults back and forth with Mylo.

I travel back in time and sit in Amanda Paulson's living room and watch a slideshow of some subterranean ecosystem that my mentor explored.

I follow Johnny as he rides his grandmother's bicycle, making deliveries.

I follow Jessica on her run around the lake near her apartment complex.

Then I imagine him. Heywood. The Warlock. My enemy.

He's sitting behind some computer at a secure facility, typing away, knowing he's being watched but also knowing they're too afraid to do anything to stop him if he veers off course.

I see that blank face and try to peer inside that brain, which is impossible . . . but I still try to understand him by attempting to make sense of the things he's done.

I have no trouble accepting the idea that some kind of trauma or brain defect impaired his ability to feel compassion. It's the only way I can conceive of a mind doing the evil things that he's done.

We're both men driven by curiosity, but mine has limits. I'll kill to protect the innocent.

But I won't kill the innocent to protect myself, except for in the most ridiculous hypothetical cause-and-effect scenarios.

If I found out that right now Jillian was in the arms of another man, I'd only want to know that he treated her well. In fact, the idea that someone else was looking after her would relieve me beyond words.

All this is why I can't understand why Heywood fears me. If his neural network is bogus, artificial-intelligence researchers will figure that out. If his cures are snake oil, the doctors testing them will cry foul.

Moreover, if it's a sham, why turn himself in? It doesn't make any sense. The only conclusion I can come to is that it's only part sham and Heywood is trying to buy time because he thinks he can make it work.

But that still doesn't explain his hatred of me. Jealousy's part of it, perhaps, but long before Jessica and I had our embrace in the elevator, Heywood still wanted me eliminated.

Why?

What does Heywood see in me that I don't?

I ask that question over and over and can't find a single answer. Maybe I'm asking it the wrong way . . .

I slip back into my mental model of the world and start watching someone I've never watched before.

Myself.

What do I see?

A man sitting in a prison cell that he accepted as his home because he thought he was doing the morally correct thing.

A man who breaks laws and lives by his own moral code.

An intelligent man who sometimes lets his arrogance lead him into trouble.

Perhaps the better question is, what do other people see?

To some I'm brilliant.

To others I'm dangerous.

This is how people see the Warlock as well. From a certain perspective, we have a lot in common.

If you were one of the child-torturing soldiers I killed back in Myanmar, you wouldn't feel much different about me when I slit your throat in the latrine than Heywood's victims felt about him when he killed them for his stunts.

Heywood is afraid of me because he fears I think like he does . . . that I *understand* him. He doesn't realize that I can't possibly fathom his twisted mind.

The difference between us is easy for me to see. Jessica sees it. Jillian saw it.

I can't think like Heywood because, no matter how dark I get, how much wrath I feel, I never see the innocent as pawns. Every life is precious. I only kill to protect life, and even then with conditions.

That's the line he doesn't understand.

Or does he?

What if what he's really afraid of is me learning to cross that line?

Let's imagine the world again. This time we're picturing a man named Theo Cray who sees people not as lives to protect, but as objects whose innocence has no meaning or value.

What would the world be like for that Theo? What dark things would he do? What *great* things could he do?

What holds *me* back that doesn't hold back Dark Theo?

If I wanted people's awe and respect, I wouldn't need to steal super-computer time and build a massive neural network to cure disease.

I'd do it myself.

I'd make the world my laboratory. I wouldn't waste my time tweaking the parameters of a neural network and laboring to find precise data to fine-tune its training. I'd take the most promising ideas in research journals and go straight to human trials. Many would die. Many would also live. I could advance medicine by decades.

All I'd have to do is . . .

I bolt upright out of bed.

That goddamn monster . . .

I pound my fists on the door to my cell and scream, "I have to talk to someone!"

The guards probably think I'm going mad. They don't realize that this is the clearest my mind has ever been.

CHAPTER FIFTY-TWO
MEMETICS

My desperate attempt to find someone to listen to me didn't fall on deaf ears. Unfortunately, it fell on the wrong ears. After pounding on my cell door, demanding to talk to someone, I saw Dr. Diane's face appear on my video screen.

"What's the emergency?" she asked.

"I need to speak to Agent Blackwood."

"We can provide you a form to relay a message."

"No. It has to be now. It's about Heywood and what he's been up to," I added hastily.

"I'll see if there's someone who can assist with that."

Eight hours later, Lagrange and another guard were at my door with the hood. This time I wasn't taken to another room. I was led down a corridor and into a garage and placed into a van and driven for two hours.

The hood was removed when we neared the processing center for the Stone Creek ADX, a supermax federal prison in Pennsylvania. I breathed a sigh of relief, glad that I'd finally been transferred to a public facility and out of the black-box detention center.

Here I'd have the right to counsel and to send messages. I'd be able to tell Jessica what I realized and what we needed to do to stop Heywood. For the first time, I saw the light at the end of the tunnel.

That light went dark the moment I was handed over to the Stone Creek correctional officers. I was told to lie facedown in the back of the van—I assumed to change my restraints. A moment later, I felt a sharp stab in my neck as a hypodermic needle found a vein.

The man's face is blurry. He's sitting on the fixed stool by the metal desk. He has a clipboard in his hands. He's been talking to me, and I've been nodding.

". . . any violation will result in you losing privileges. Any attempt to communicate with other inmates will also result in punishment. No outside communication without prior approval," his voice drones.

Drool is sliding out of my mouth. I'm upright and have some control, but I can't seem to make sentences more complex than yes or no. I'm on a psychoactive I'm unfamiliar with, no doubt courtesy of the same minds that thought up the Death Star.

I make out the other words the man is saying and slowly grasp what he's telling me. I'm in the secure wing of this ADX. No visitors. No communications. I won't be able to talk to anyone.

"With good behavior we'll allow you limited access to the other facilities. Do you understand, Mr. Cray?"

I try to form words. I want to tell him what's really going on. I want him to understand why they drugged me. All I can do is nod.

"I'll take that as an affirmative," he says.

The blurry man leaves and the cell door is shut, making an echo that reverberates around the tiny room. The reality of what is happening to me is starting to come into focus.

I wasn't transferred from the Death Star for my benefit. I was transferred so that whoever's strings Heywood is pulling could have me killed.

They couldn't do it at the Death Star because it would have raised too many questions. If I died there, Jessica would no longer have any reason to keep her mouth shut, and others at the FBI would begin to wonder what kind of deal the Department of Justice made. Someone would talk.

The longer I'm still alive here, however, the greater the risk for Heywood that I'll get to talk to somebody from some other agency, even if it's to interrogate me. Which means that someone will be coming for me soon. Possibly as soon as this drug wears off and breaks down in my system so it won't be detected in an autopsy.

I have two options. One is a set of small cylinders that I inserted into the inside of my right forearm several years ago. I consider those my nuclear option.

The other is an implant in my left arm the size of a quarter and twice as thick. Wrapped in layers of silicone to prevent it from creating an odd indentation on my skin, it's close enough to my elbow that when it occasionally sets off metal detectors at close range, the assumption is that I have a metal pin in my joint.

I'd considered less invasive measures, but I knew that if I found myself in a worst-case scenario, I'd be subjected to a thorough exam that would reveal anything I'd swallowed or tried to retain rectally.

Hence, my under-the-skin solution.

Fortunately, in this age of body modification and biohacking, others did the pioneering work for me. The challenge was deciding what to implant myself with.

I decided on a tiny microcomputer that would find any open Wi-Fi network and send out a blast message to a list of people, giving them my location. I put Jessica at the top of the list.

It was a clever idea.

I can tell from the bandage on my arm that they removed my little device before I left the Death Star.

Now I think I have a better idea who that facility was meant for. It wasn't hackers, terrorists, or drug lords. It was built for spies.

The cylinders still remain in my other arm. They're plastic and would only show up on a close X-ray. I'm tempted to cut them out and mix the contents. But we're not there yet.

I have one other trick left for getting a message out of here. It involves my fingernail and the skin of my left forearm.

I bite away the tip of the fingernail of my right pinkie, giving it a jagged edge, then stick it into my flesh. The first line is just a red mark. I have to scratch it repeatedly until it bleeds. Then I move on to the next mark.

If I had time to secure a needle or, even better, a prison tattoo gun, I could do a better job of this. But I don't know how much longer I have. I need to get the message out while I'm still alive.

As I carve the last letter into my arm, drops of blood begin to drip down onto the floor and form a tiny puddle. My skin is on fire; I need to wash it to prevent an infection.

But first I have to get the message on my arm outside the walls of this prison. I need someone to see it other than me. Hopefully at that point it will become a kind of mind virus that will force the powers that be to do something. The message is my version of the Cordyceps fungus, which turns ants into zombies to spread its spores. My message will work the same way to a lesser degree, but it should still serve my purpose . . . assuming anyone sees it.

There are footsteps in the corridor and the jangling of keys. The slot slides open, and a guard yells at me to stand in the circle by the far wall with my hands interlocked behind my head.

I comply. Blood drips down onto my shoulder. Plastic cuffs are fastened around my wrists, and I'm placed onto a gurney, cuffed to its rail, and rushed out of the cell.

"Why wasn't this asshole on suicide watch?" one of the guards asks another.

"Special case," replies the one pulling the gurney forward.

I'm moved to a clinic at the end of the block and placed in a room where a male nurse who apparently bodybuilds is waiting.

"He's a no-contact," says a guard.

"I understand the protocol," the nurse replies.

"Prisoner, will you cooperate? Answer only in the affirmative," says the guard, shining a light in my eye.

"Yes."

"I just want to take a look at that arm. Can you uncuff him?"

One guard releases my bloody arm while another watches a few inches from my head, ready to take me down with a stun gun. All their procedures are airtight—developed over decades of containing the most dangerous elements of society.

The nurse, his face obscured by a mask, pours water over my arm, cleaning away the blood. "What is this?" he asks.

The cold metal tips of the stun gun are shoved into my neck—a warning that if I speak, I'll experience an incredible amount of disabling pain.

Whoever planned my detention here wanted to take absolutely no chances that I would speak to anyone. Which only reinforces my certainty that I now know what has Heywood scared shitless.

Why didn't he kill me in the penthouse? I can only guess that it would have jeopardized his attempt to come to an agreement with the government and, worse, set Jessica against him even more than she already was.

The nurse dabs my arm with gauze, wiping away the blood. The writing is clearer now and the incisions mostly clotted.

He walks over to a cabinet and takes out a camera. "Hold your arm out."

"That's not permitted," says a guard.

"Actually, I have to photograph every wound," says the nurse.

"He's a no-contact prisoner," the guard fires back.

"Fine. Then you take care of him." He sits on a stool in the corner of the office. "He's all yours."

"All right," says the guard. "But the photo goes to the warden only, and he can decide if it stays in the record."

The nurse stretches out my arm and takes several snapshots of the wound with his digital camera. He then sprays my arm with disinfectant and wraps it in a bandage.

"He's yours now. Take him to iso."

They wheel me out of the room and down another corridor. Instead of returning me to my room, they place me in a much smaller one with my arms and legs strapped to the rails of the bed. "Twenty-four hours of isolation for self-harm," says a guard. "Try it again and it's seventy-two." He shuts the metal door, and the lights go out.

This is how they treat me for going crazy . . . by driving me even more insane.

CHAPTER FIFTY-THREE
Iso

As I lie in the dark, trying not to let the itching and the smell of my own urine get to me too much, I realize that the self-harm incident may have bought me more time. If someone wants to kill me, they will need to put me in a position where another inmate can commit the act.

The majority of correctional officers in charge of me do not want me to die under their supervision. A prisoner death leads to questions and paperwork. If one of them is found to have been culpable, then they'd face an even more serious investigation and possibly charges.

As vulnerable as I am right now, I don't think my concern is some guard slipping in here with a pillow and suffocating me. An autopsy would reveal quite a lot and would almost certainly be performed in such an instance.

An injection of some drug that could stop my heart is another possibility. But that has its risks, too. A guard has to come here and administer it, in full view of security cameras, including the one that's watching me right now.

The way to kill me is to make a simple mistake, like with Heywood's prison transfer. One administrator somewhere in the prison system has to put in an order that I'm to be transferred to the general population. From there, snuffing me is merely a matter of economics.

One study found that the average price paid for a professional hit was approximately fifteen thousand dollars—which coincidentally is the average amount of money a person can withdraw on their credit card.

I don't know what the average price is in a prison. If it's not less, it can't be too much more. While killing someone inside a prison increases the chances of the killer being caught—and therefore, rationally, should command a higher fee—prisons aren't full of rational people.

Given Heywood's resources, I suspect that more than one inmate may be prepared to kill me as soon as I'm free from isolation. Once they escort me out of here, I have to be ready for anything.

My best chance of survival is to defend myself long enough that I can get near a guard who'll have to intervene in some way, with all the cameras watching. If they're too slow to react, then suspicion will fall on them. That doesn't mean that they're required to perform a heroic intervention on my behalf, but they at least have to go through the motions of pretending to stop the assassination attempt.

After what I guess is ten hours of my isolation, the light comes on, and two guards enter the room. One of them inspects my bandages and unlocks me from the gurney.

"Prisoner will stand up," says the other guard. I comply.

"Prisoner will face the wall."

I face the wall and let them put the restraint belt around my waist and hands and the bindings around my ankles, making me incredibly vulnerable.

"Prisoner will exit the cell and stay on the yellow line," says the guard with his hand around my left arm.

I'm moved out of the cell and down the corridor. When we pass the infirmary and the wing where my cell is located, a knot forms in my stomach. Somebody isn't wasting any time.

"I have to—"

Before I can finish my sentence, my body convulses and I fall to the ground from the pain of the stun gun.

As I lie twitching, the shorter guard stands over me. "Prisoner will remember that he must follow no-contact protocols. If the prisoner understands, he will respond in the affirmative."

"Yes," I manage through numb lips.

The men lift me to my feet and push me down the line. The short chain between my ankles forces me to make quick, tiny steps, like a rodent trying to keep up.

We enter a wing of the prison that I've never seen before. There's a long gray corridor with doors spaced twenty feet apart. I'm walked in front of one and told to turn and face the wall. The door is unlocked behind me.

"Prisoner will turn around," says a guard.

The room is dark and small. There's a metal door at the other side. "Prisoner will enter the room," the guard tells me.

I don't know what's on the other side of that door. I'm afraid to step any closer. I stand firm.

"Prisoner will step forward," says the guard.

I feel the metal prongs of the stun gun press against the back of my neck. I'm being given a choice: walk into the room or be dragged inside.

I take a step forward and enter the empty room.

"Prisoner will stand in the center of the room," a guard tells me.

I move to the middle and get into a crouched position, bracing myself for whatever is on the other side of the door in front of me.

The door behind me is shut and locked, sealing me inside.

I crouch lower, putting myself into a sprinting position, ready to headbutt whoever walks through next. My adrenaline is pumping, and my quadriceps are starting to shake in my thighs.

There's a sound of clanking metal on the other side of the door, then the lights change to red.

Sirens start to blare throughout the prison, and a recorded voice orders all inmates to lie on the ground. I don't know if this is a riot or a fire, but I do know it's a distraction for what's going to happen next.

The door handle starts to turn, then the door suddenly bursts open. Four masked men come flooding into the room.

CHAPTER FIFTY-FOUR
TACTICAL

I let out a war cry and throw myself at the closest man. My head hits the armored plating on his chest, and I see stars. But I knock him on his ass.

Two others grab me by the arms and yank me back, suspending me in midair like a child. I swing my feet wildly, trying to make contact. The man I knocked to the ground gets to his feet and yells at me.

"Theo! Stop!"

I recognize the voice. It's Gerald Voigt's.

I don't stop fighting. I have no idea what his intentions are.

"Jessica got your message! We're here to get you out." He throws a backpack to my feet. "Put this on."

The men holding me release my arms and let my body drop. After I stop putting up a fight, one of them uses a key to unlock my restraints.

"What's going on?" I ask.

"No time. Put the armor on," says Gerald.

I strip off my prison uniform and climb into the black jumpsuit from the bag and start slipping on the armored vest. The other men put the boots on my feet and lace them up.

A mask and helmet are placed on my head, and I'm ushered through the door they entered, escorted amid an armored phalanx. We reach a stairwell and race up three floors. Each time I stumble, a steady hand props me back to my feet.

Another armed man is waiting at the top of the stairs. He pushes open a door, and the cool night wind blows through, touching the exposed parts of my face.

I forgot what the world smells like. I stop for a second, only to be shoved along.

Outside, there's a Black Hawk helicopter with its rotors spinning. A hand pushes my head down, and I'm guided through the aircraft's side door. The other men climb inside, and a moment later we're aloft.

Out the helicopter's window, flashing lights illuminate the prison grounds as alarm bells continue to chime. I take off my helmet, and Gerald hands me an intercom headset so I can hear him over the noise of the helicopter.

"Like I said, we got your message," Gerald tells me over the comms. "We didn't know where you had been transferred until then. We'd also got intel that said a hit had been put out on your life. When we contacted the warden of the facility and asked for protective custody, he said he had no record of you being there. We were able to get a judge to give us an emergency court order to remand you to FBI custody."

The adrenaline starts to fade, and I feel my heart rate go back to normal. "I figured I was about to be killed."

"You were right," says Gerald. "We have an intercepted phone call from the warden to one of the leaders of the Aryan Nation. They were gonna put you in general population in the morning. You would have been dead by afternoon."

I nod.

"Heywood wanted you dead."

I nod again. "I'll explain why."

"We'll debrief you at headquarters. I don't know if these microphones are monitored." Gerald glances at the cockpit, letting me know he doesn't trust the men running the retrieval not to tell others what we discuss. "I'd also like to know how you were able to send us an email with your location from the most secure supermax prison on the planet."

When we're in a secure place, I'll show him the markings I clawed into my arm: x9x.us/escape

One of my greatest fears is having all my weapons and secret tools taken away from me.

But my greatest fear of all is losing contact with the outside world.

Before I set out to catch N2, the serial killer nurse, I created several safeguards in case I found myself in difficult situations. One of them was a computer system that would allow me to make contact with anyone I wanted to reach, even when I couldn't access a computer myself.

The secret was to get someone else to send the message for me. While none of my captors would ever do this willingly, they might do it unwittingly. Especially if I used their curiosity against them. In this case it would be their desire to understand the message I'd written, a seemingly innocuous URL for a website.

If I were your prisoner and you found out that I'd scratched a mysterious URL on my arm, wouldn't you want to know where it led?

x9x.us is a website I set up on a server that records every single network request sent to it and the location of who sent it. When you go there, all you see is a standard "Coming soon" placeholder, but behind the scenes it'll perform different functions depending upon what instruction follows the slash mark.

x9x.us/attack90 will launch a denial-of-service attack against whoever accessed the URL ninety minutes after they try to access it.

x9x.us/911 will look up the address of the sender and have a robotic voice make a call to the local 911 dispatch.

x9x.us/files will load a script onto the host computer and quietly upload its entire hard drive to the server.

x9x.us/escape sent an email to a short list of people that included the location from which the request was sent and a message from me saying that I might be in trouble.

I don't know if I have the nurse, the warden, or one of the guards to thank, but someone let their curiosity get the better of them and, despite the no-contact containment order, went to x9x.us/escape and unwittingly sent my rescue message to the outside world.

It's a foolproof method as long as nobody knows it exists. When I thought of it, I realized how clever it was because even I couldn't resist the urge to look up a mysterious URL like x9x.us/secret.

Our helicopter lands at Allegheny County Airport, and we hurry across the tarmac to a waiting FBI jet. When I board the plane, a familiar pair of green eyes looks up from a laptop, and I'm greeted by a sly smile. There are others on the plane, so our reactions are subdued, but I'm fairly certain the feeling is mutual between Jessica and me, because we can't stop looking at each other.

PART SEVEN

MENTALIST

CHAPTER FIFTY-FIVE
DOWNLOAD

Theo is sitting across from Gerald and me, explaining what led to his revelation about Heywood. We keep catching each other's glances, and I know Gerald has noticed. Does he think there's something more there? *Is* there something more?

Like the other men in my life, Theo is a broken soul. But unlike anyone I've ever known, Theo draws strength from it. It's almost as if tragedy and misfortune serve as a kind of catalyst. Left on his own, he'd be studying his ponds while the world faded away.

My fascination with him began the moment he went back to help the wounded IDR agent in Myanmar. No matter how dark a person Theo sees himself as, no matter the violent things he's done, he never hesitates to perform a selfless act if it'll make the world a better place. Maybe it's rooted in self-loathing or a need to be loved, but it doesn't matter. What's important is what kind of person it makes him.

The man in front of me is a far cry from the gaunt prisoner I found in Myanmar, even though he's just spent additional weeks incarcerated here. There's a glow, a vitality about him.

He has purpose.

While he was in custody, I missed his observations and his curiously relevant non sequiturs. And I selfishly wondered whether he thought about me as much as I thought about him—which I did every waking moment, as I looked into all aspects of Heywood's story, trying to find the deceit so I could prove that they'd put the wrong man away and freed a monster.

I thought I'd understood the depths of Heywood's deception until I saw how he'd masterfully twisted and turned his own narrative to one that made people who should revile him hail him as a hero.

Originally, I thought Heywood wanted a pardon for his crimes, but what he really sought was a complete rewriting of history.

Employment records mysteriously surfaced, showing that Heywood, a.k.a. Michael Hopkins, was a CIA operative in the late 1990s who was assigned to deep-cover missions inside some of the millennium doomsday cults that were springing up overseas as the year 2000 approached. I've seen this done by intelligence and police agencies in the opposite direction to help plant an undercover agent within an organization or for witness relocation: fabricating prison records, employment documentation, and other details. Here it was being used to make a bad guy look good because he had something they wanted.

His job, the redacted documents claimed, was to infiltrate cults that sought technological weapons and to stay undercover, reporting to the CIA if any of them posed a major threat.

The Red Chain cult and the Void were precisely the kinds of things he was assigned to stop. Even his own incarceration was a deep-cover operation to get the most dangerous cults in the world to confide in him.

But Heywood would have the last laugh, or so the bullshit narrative he wants us to believe claims, as what he was *really* doing was using these cults' and anarchists' collective energy for a project they didn't understand: Lifeline, the public name for his neural network for curing disease.

It's a story filled with holes and unanswered questions, but it's convenient fiction for those who want to avoid making moral judgments.

As Heywood's narrative evolves and the evil he's done is forgotten, who knows what he could do next? The officials who were compromised into giving him what he wanted are already experiencing a form of Stockholm syndrome.

I watched an NIH director practically attack Theo for questioning Heywood's claims. She was an intelligent woman and a critical thinker, but Heywood understood how to turn her into an ally.

Theo takes a sip from a water bottle and collects his thoughts. I notice that he keeps gripping the cushion of the chair, running his fingers across the material. This is probably the first time in forever that he's sat on anything that wasn't metal or hard plastic.

He puts the bottle down. "I kept asking myself, why did he want me out of the way? For some reason, he was afraid I could see into his head and understand what he was really up to. Which I couldn't. Not until he put me in the one place where I had the chance to think about that a *lot*.

"Heywood assumes that everyone is like him, just not as smart. With all his talk about brain damage and the inability to feel compassion, he's really providing a convenient excuse for anyone who knows what he's done. What he didn't understand is that my sense of compassion is why I couldn't think like he did. The only way to see the world as he does was to pretend I had no compassion. What could I accomplish without that little impediment?

"The reality is that a lot of the biggest advances we've made in medical science have come from acts that were immoral, even at the time. From Nazi endurance experiments to medical studies that take advantage of vulnerable parts of our society, big advances can happen when you put your morality to the side."

"This is not new information," says Gerald. "We're all familiar with the dark side of Heywood's methods, regardless of how successful they may be. What are you trying to tell us?"

"What I'm saying is that Lifeline, or Jessica, or whatever he's calling it now, isn't what he says it is."

"You mean it doesn't work?" asks Gerald. "Wheeler and her team seem to be pretty convinced."

"I think it works to some degree. Give it ten thousand medical journals and it will show you novel ways to treat a disease or how to apply a technique better. We've already been doing this with supercomputers and sophisticated AI. Heywood just stole a bunch of computer access to crunch a hundred times more data than anybody else has on this subject. But give the NIH, OpenAI, Calico, or IBM that amount of computational resources, and they'd come up with similar results. See, right now, Wheeler and her team are probably thrilled with all the possible treatment avenues that Lifeline is showing them, but she's also realizing the biggest roadblock: it'll be years before they can *test* any of them. They won't know if a potential treatment has a hundred percent chance of success or a one in a thousand chance. When they bring the first treatment to human trials, it'll be the treatment they think has the best chance of passing, and they'll be so heavily invested in their new version of Lifeline, nobody'll be willing to question whether they've bet it all on bullshit."

"I looked into the miracle cases," I tell Theo. "Everyone claims they were healed. Experts say Heywood's treatments worked. As I said before, I even checked if he was calling his shots after the fact, looking for spontaneous remissions and then claiming them as successes."

"That's because he knew that's the first thing people would look for. Heywood is too smart for that. He found treatments that do help, but he's been lying about how he actually found the ones that worked."

"Okay, how?" asks Gerald.

"The miracle-cure patients weren't the first ones he tested these treatments on. Nor was the Chernobyl group. Those were the cases in which he tested the most promising therapies. What Heywood's hiding is that he tested *all* his results from Lifeline, including therapies that killed people and displaced more effective treatments. He presented us with only the ones that worked and hid all the deadly test cases."

"Who, Theo? Who are these test cases?" Gerald asks.

"Everyone. Or near about. Hundreds of millions of people. What Heywood is hiding is how he learned which treatments worked. It wasn't Lifeline. It was his willingness to sacrifice tens of thousands of people in the largest secret medical research project ever, by changing up prescriptions without anyone knowing." Theo turns to me. "Remember the list of companies that he'd acquired? The ones that Warden Weir invested in? One of them went right under our radar because they got bought up by a Chinese conglomerate: Autopharmix. They made medical equipment that automated medication formulation. What we didn't appreciate is that Autopharmix was acquired for its software—the code that tells the machines how much of a dose or what ingredient to put into a pill or a solution. Having bought the company, Heywood controlled the software and installed back doors, which means the machines could be overridden to change doses or substitute compounds. Many of those machines were used in factories where medications are manufactured. Because they're produced in batches, with individual doses given batch numbers, Heywood could monitor which hospitals or pharmacies they went to. He was able to mess with the prescriptions of millions of people."

Gerald is shaking his head. "We would have noticed something like that."

"Would you? The same prescription software's used throughout China, South America, and parts of Europe. All he had to do was test a tiny fraction of people and measure outcomes. He could do that by tracking patient IDs as they were used to generate prescriptions or through the software the physicians used."

The implications of what Theo is saying are dawning on me. Dad's medications are prepared in the clinic by a machine that the pharmacist types instructions into and then lets do the rest. I've given him pills without questioning if they were the right ones. His condition got worse for a while. Was this the natural course of the disease, or was he part of Heywood's secret testing? The thought makes my blood boil, and—if true—it would enrage millions of people around the world. It was one thing for us to believe Heywood hacked pharma software to suggest new treatments that all worked. It's another to think that his cures came at the cost of tens of thousands of people dying.

"Okay, I'm not saying I completely buy it," says Gerald. "But if I did, how would we manage to convince half the government that Heywood's lying?"

"The data centers," replies Theo. "Heywood wasn't breaking into them to retrieve the rest of his neural network data. He was covering the tracks of his massive experiment."

"What do you mean?" I ask.

"I think he had to cover up for Autopharmix . . . or rather, the software. He built back doors into all those medication manufacturing machines, which would leave digital footprints. He sent in his teams to cover them up."

"He used the Voids just for that?" asks Gerald.

"The Voids were also a convenient excuse to erase whatever other data he needed to," Theo replies.

"All right. So how do we proceed?" I ask.

"I have some thoughts. But this comes down to you, Jessica. We're going to need a miracle of our own."

CHAPTER FIFTY-SIX
RAW DATA

"How's it look?" I ask Theo as I make sure my blonde wig doesn't look like a wig.

We're sitting inside an SUV down the street from CenterOps, the Manhattan data center that we learned Heywood's team broke into disguised as fire department officials.

"Great. May I?" He tucks a loose strand of hair over my ear. "The glasses look good. You're probably an outlier on the attractiveness scale of New York City Fire Department inspectors."

"Have you seen some of the guys who fight fires?" I reply.

"Um, point taken. I guess I was grading on a different scale."

"Let's check in with Gerald." I put my phone on speaker and place it on the dashboard.

"What's up?"

"We're about to go in," I reply.

"Okay. But remember, since we don't have a warrant, this is on you. If anything happens, it's your asses, not mine."

I think he's overdoing it with the "asses" comment, an uncharacteristic swear for Gerald, but the point is made. "We understand. Get in. Get out. Get caught, we're screwed. Theo, you okay with that? This would ruin your FBI protective custody."

"I know what I'm getting into. Get the data on the IMT device and get out," he replies.

"Okay, we're set. We'll let you know when we're out and on our way back to DC."

"Be smart, Blackwood."

I click off and slip the phone back into my pocket. "You sure you're good, Theo? The protective custody arrangement is only effective if you don't get caught."

"I'm good. Let's go find the other server."

We let Gerald know two hours earlier that we'd located a backup server at CenterOps that recorded all incoming and outgoing traffic to the servers that Heywood pulled. If we can get hold of it, then we might be able to figure out where all that data went.

We exit the SUV and walk to the entrance of the data center. Theo is casual and doesn't show any sign of anxiety. He hasn't had my training, but I can assume from his own experience that he's had plenty of practice pretending to be someone else. The blue blazer fits him well, but his physique underneath looks like he's really meant for climbing cliffs and hiking through uneven terrain. He's the kind of handsome that's dangerous because he doesn't realize he's good-looking. I can only imagine the thoughts some of his female students had when he was teaching, or some of the male ones who were so inclined.

Theo holds open the glass door to the lobby, and we step inside. An armed guard is standing at the front desk. He looks like a former cop . . . for a reason: CenterOps takes their security very seriously.

I show him my fake FDNY badge. "We're doing inspections for Void-related damage."

"We just had you guys in here," he says, looking from the ID to my face.

"We only take the assignments. We don't make them." I hand him a card listing the Manhattan Department of Homeland Security office. "Call them."

"No need. Let me get you an escort." He picks up a phone and dials a number, punching at the keys like he's gouging someone's eyes out.

I glance over at Theo to see if this "escort" thing is an inconvenience. He's either playing it cool or doesn't seem to be bothered. I'm still trying to learn how to read the man.

A short-haired woman dressed in slacks and a CenterOps polo shirt greets us at the door. "I'm Becca. I'll be your escort."

"Thanks, Becca. I'm Dana, and this is Steven. We need to check some of the alarm systems and do a spot electrical check in your server room," I tell her.

"All right. Follow me." She uses a key card on her lanyard to let us inside the metal door. "We can start with the server room. It's this way."

She takes us down a floor on the elevator. "How have you guys been doing since the event?" she asks Theo.

"Trying to pick up the pieces. Trying to understand why some things are in pieces and some aren't," he replies.

"This way," she says after the doors open. We follow her to another set of doors; she uses her key card to unlock it. "Where do you want to look?"

Theo surveys the cavernous interior and the endless rows of server cabinets. "Let's start with a spot at random. I want to measure voltage values."

"All our power is carefully controlled," she replies, almost taking offense at the suggestion that they might have slightly variable current.

I nod, pretending to understand.

"I believe you," says Theo. He holds up what looks like a voltage meter. "I just have to convince this. Let's start here."

Theo chooses a cabinet on the outer edge of the server center. Becca uses her key card to open its back hatch.

"Explain to me what you're about to do before you do it, okay?" She pats a server rack. "These babies are my responsibility."

"I'm going to connect the thingamajig to the whatsit and see if the pretty numbers move," Theo replies with a smile.

"Smart-ass," she says with a grin of her own. "I bet you two have lots of fun."

"A regular barrel of monkeys." Theo connects a plastic clip to a power cord—which is my cue to get ready. "Have those fire suppressors been checked since the Void?" he asks.

She glances up at the overhead pipes. I use the opportunity to slide the USB device into a port in the back of the server. I'm done before she even finishes looking where Theo pointed.

"There? I believe so," she tells him.

"You probably want to have the pressure checked. Some people have had problems with leaks because the reed switches were exceptionally prone to damage from the EMPs."

"Yeah. We need to keep all that pressure," she replies.

I have no idea if what Theo said is true or not, but she seems to think it makes sense. Theo can be quite convincing with his bullshit.

He checks his device. "We're good."

"Are my power curves smooth enough for you?" asks Becca.

"I've seen better, but they'll do," he replies.

"Oh, you have, have you? I'll take that as an insult."

"Okay, fine. They're the smoothest," Theo says with a smile.

"Right answer."

Hold up . . . have I been witnessing some kind of nerd flirting and didn't realize it? "Do we need to check the sensors?" I ask.

"I think we're good," says Theo.

"Let me show you guys the way out. I'll also give you my contact information in case you need another inspection or anything else," Becca says.

I'm fairly certain that was directed entirely at Theo, or rather, Steven, the nerdy fire inspector with the square jaw. I wait until we're out of the building before commenting on it.

Across the street, a man pushing a shopping cart loaded with garbage bags stops and looks at us for a moment, then continues on. He was there when we entered.

Theo looks past my shoulder and mutters, "Oh shit."

There's a sound of a blaring siren and the flash of blue lights as two all-black SUVs pull up on either side of our vehicle, blocking us in. Doors open, and footsteps rush up behind us.

"Hands in the air!" says a woman's voice.

"By whose authority?" I shout.

"IDR," says Director Vivian Kieren. "You're under arrest for felony data theft."

I turn around to face Kieren and the six men flanking her with their guns pointed at Theo and me. We both refuse to raise our hands. Kieren directs her men to apprehend us.

"Take a step closer and this isn't going to end pretty," I growl.

"This is going to end however I like. Search him," she says, pointing to Theo.

Two men grab him, slam his head into the hood of the car, then cuff him behind his back.

I wince, wanting to jump in and stop it, but I know I have to wait for the right moment.

Kieren's men go through Theo's pockets and his bag, dumping everything onto the hood.

One of them holds up the device he used to check the power levels. "Got it," he calls out.

Kieren walks over to inspect the apparatus. "Okay. Bag the IMT. Cuff her, too, and let's bring them in."

"This is a mistake," I explain as they handcuff me. "I'm a federal agent in the course of an investigation."

"You don't know when to shut up, do you, bitch?" she says to my face. As her men hold me, she grabs me by the throat. Her nails claw into my skin. "You're done. *So* done."

I smile back at her, thinking ahead to when I get my payback.

CHAPTER FIFTY-SEVEN
LIFELINE

The nameless guard tells me to stand facing the wall of my cell. I do as I'm told with my hands above my head and allow them to put restraints on me, plus a hood to keep me disoriented.

It's exactly as Theo described, only more demoralizing, even though I know my situation isn't as hopeless as his was.

The last time I was at IDR containment, I was a visitor who knew where the facility was and who was operating it. I also didn't have to wear a hood as I was escorted through the intentionally confusing labyrinth. Knowing that the internal layout is designed to make detainees psychologically vulnerable doesn't make me feel any less exposed.

I'm walked into a small room and sat down on a chair with my hands shackled to a counter in front of a mirrored window.

The last time I saw this room, it was from the other side. Now I'm the inmate waiting to find out who's come to talk to me.

In the four days I've been here, there's been no communication from the outside. Theo is confined somewhere else in the facility, and Gerald has been radio silent since our capture by Vivian Kieren. Now I'm in her private prison.

The lights flicker on the other side, and my visitor is revealed to me. It's him.

Michael Heywood.

He sits silently, studying me. I knew this moment would come, but I had no idea how he'd handle himself. Apparently, neither did he. I remain silent, letting the rage in my face speak for me.

"I thought I'd say something clever about how the last time we spoke inside a prison the roles were reversed. But that seemed too obvious. Yet I just said it." He shakes his head. "You understand why I had to make a machine to talk to you, Jessica? I can never find the right words." He nervously bites the edge of his thumbnail. "I'm sorry. I never saw this coming. When Vivian told me that she'd apprehended you, I decided I had to intervene."

"Intervene?" I speak for the first time. "Is that what this is? An intervention?"

He smiles. "Of sorts. If she had her way, the IDR would use one of her judges to place an indefinite containment order on you. Instead of the temporary one we have now."

"I'm sure the FBI has other thoughts," I reply.

"Unfortunately, no. I think the word they used was *rogue*. I understand that they told Vivian you're *her* problem." A smile forms on the edges of his mouth, and he lowers his voice. "I'll let you in on a little secret: that makes you *my* problem." He clears his throat. "In case you haven't figured it out, I call the shots here." He raises his voice. "No need to whisper, by the way. The microphones are off. The cameras aren't on. I could say anything I wanted to you. Anything, Jessica. If I were a lesser man, I could *do* anything I want."

"I can't think of a lesser man than you."

His face contorts for a moment before he regains his composure. "That's one of the things I admire about you. Here you are in the last place you ever thought you'd be, under the complete control of the man you presently despise more than any other, and you still have your humor."

"Presently?"

"There's hope. I think you might see me differently in time."

"I think I'd rather go back to my cell."

"You don't have to do that. We could come to an arrangement. Nothing untoward, I assure you."

"Obviously. Not just because you're the biggest asshole on the planet, but because you just dropped the word *untoward* into a conversation that was rather rapey."

His face twitches. I've done this to him before. He wasn't expecting it here, though, while he pictured himself in complete control of me.

"I don't think you understand your situation. You're in a jail that I have the only key to."

"Is the key supposed to be your dick?"

He slams his fist on the metal counter, rattling the window.

A guard comes rushing in through the door behind me. Heywood jumps to his feet and yells at the man. "I said stay the fuck out of here!"

The guard retreats and shuts the door behind him. Heywood sits back down and runs his fingers through his hair. "Well, at the very least, I think that demonstrates who's in control here."

"Do you think you look like someone in control?" I ask, intentionally provoking him again.

He sits back and stares at me with his arms crossed. Then his eyes suddenly light up. "I see now. You're still under the impression that your friends in the FBI will be coming for you. You're in a state of denial."

"No, Heywood. It's what I know. A visitor's pass and a bad temper don't mean that you're running this facility," I explain. "No matter what you offered them, they're never going to give you that much power. They're not that stupid."

"Agree to disagree on the last point. As far as my power, there's what I've been given and what I've taken. Vivian Kieren works for me, whether she wants to admit it or not. One of my talents is finding people's vulnerabilities. For her it was her need for credibility. I chose to feed her intelligence that I hacked from the computer networks of our enemies and gradually built up enough trust that she'd gladly use her wide-ranging and poorly understood legal powers for my purposes."

"IDR were the ones who broke into the data center in Manhattan during the Void."

He nods. "Very good."

"That's why they were in Seoul. They weren't looking for Theo; they'd just broken into that facility."

Heywood grins. "Correct. A little late, though."

I decide to test how comfortable he feels in his safe space. "Theo was right."

"Right? About what?"

"You needed someone to cover your tracks because of the pharmaceutical machines you tampered with."

Heywood falls quiet for a moment. "I'm not sure what he was implying."

"Autopharmix? That's the company you used to mess with prescriptions and find out all the combinations Lifeline generated that didn't work. The ones that killed people."

"I'm afraid Dr. Cray may have been reaching on that one," says Heywood. "I don't know what you're talking about."

"You never had a controlling stake in Autopharmix? I saw the paperwork and the timing with the clever Bitcoin heist."

He shakes his head.

I see an opening. "If you expect me to believe you're in control, then why do you feel the need to keep lying to me?"

"I am in control, Jessica."

"So why do you act like you're afraid? As far as I can tell, I'm talking to the same scared man I saw back in that Texas police station after we caught him with the kidnapped girl he was going to murder. You were pissing yourself because you didn't think I was smart enough to catch you. But there we were. And here we are . . . and you're still scared of me. Too afraid to admit what you really are. Only now you're fixated on me. You wanted to kill me before. Now you want to fuck me."

Heywood is back on his feet, hands on the glass as he glares down at me. "Who says I still don't want to kill you?"

"It is what you're good at. How many lives did it cost to come up with Lifeline's treatments? Five hundred? A thousand? Ten thousand?"

"Twenty-two thousand," he says. "I killed twenty-two thousand people, most of whom were going to die. I gave them purpose. I gave their deaths meaning."

"Purpose? For your snake-oil machine built on top of other people's ideas?"

He smirks. "It works, Jessica."

"That's not what Theo says."

"Fuck Theo Cray. He's a pathetic burnout."

"You hate him because you know he's smarter than you."

Heywood shakes his head. "I'm glad you're finding these mind games amusing." He sighs dramatically. "One day you'll want to remember what the sun looks like, and we'll come to an arrangement."

"And Theo?"

Heywood sits back down. "Theo? Lifeline has suggested some interesting psychoactives that I want to try on him. I'm curious to see if I can make him a more malleable personality. And if they're safe enough, maybe we try them on you. But as you deduced, Lifeline is nowhere near as far along as they think. Thankfully, I have all the time in the world to work out the kinks."

I shake my head. "Wow."

"You still don't believe me?"

"I do," I reply. "I just mean, wow. I knew I'd be right. I just didn't realize by how much. Theo owes me dinner. He said I'd never get you to monologue like a cartoon villain, but I kept telling him that's exactly what you are. Who talks like this outside of a B-movie villain?"

He shakes his head sadly. "You still don't—"

"Understand my situation? Are you sure it's me who doesn't understand? Do you really think that Gerald Voigt, a man who I've stood in the line of fire for, would abandon me? That the three of us would be dumb enough to plot a search for your server, knowing that Kieren had our phones tapped? And by the way, did you see her today? Have you seen her since you told her to detain us? Or have you only heard her voice on the phone?"

His face twitches, then fits itself into a smile. "Again with the mind games."

"You know it. Let's play one more game: we both get up and walk to our respective doors and see who gets to leave and who has to stay."

Heywood's eyes narrow. He glances over his shoulder at the door, then forces another smile.

I stand, leaving my handcuffs on the counter. His eyes widen at the sight of them. He's trying to make sense of what's happening, wondering if this is a bluff.

I walk to my door, then stop and turn around. "This is killing you, isn't it? You're wondering if this perfect little prison you helped Kieren conceive might actually be your own."

He keeps that smirk on his face as he tries to retain his composure.

I turn around, face my door, and grab the handle.

And step through.

CHAPTER FIFTY-EIGHT

AFTERMATH

Kelsi the silver robot girl pushed her bicycle along the pedestrian median of the Brooklyn Bridge toward Manhattan. The setting sun made the sky glow a thousand shades of amber and the skyline look almost normal.

Tourists had returned to New York City, and her friends said the money in Times Square was good. Kelsi was looking forward to making the rest of the money she needed to take the advanced modern dance class she'd been waiting for.

This had been the roughest year of her life, not to mention the Void fucking with everyone's lives. But she regretted none of it. Sure, eating cereal twice a day when money was tight and having to listen to her roommates bang at all hours of the night was irritating. But this was what being young was about.

As she moved her bicycle around a teenager selling sodas out of a cooler he'd dragged all the way to the middle of the bridge, she caught a glimpse of a couple standing next to each other as they leaned on the railing watching the sunset.

The fading sunlight caught the woman's eyes, making them look like green fire as her dark hair blew in the breeze. The man was watching the woman out of the corner of his eye.

He looked like an actor they'd hire to play the smoking-hot professor on some television show.

The edges of their hands were touching and their bodies were close, but Kelsi couldn't tell if they were lovers or best friends.

The thought made her smile. She let them be, then pushed her bike toward the city and what lay ahead.

ABOUT THE AUTHOR

Andrew Mayne is the *Wall Street Journal* and Amazon Charts bestselling author of *The Girl Beneath the Sea* and *Black Coral* in his Underwater Investigation Unit series; *The Naturalist, Looking Glass, Murder Theory,* and *Dark Pattern* in his Naturalist series; *Angel Killer,* "Fire in the Sky," *Name of the Devil,* and the Edgar Award–nominated *Black Fall* in his Jessica Blackwood series; and the Station Breaker novels. The star of Discovery Channel's Shark Week special "Andrew Mayne: Ghost Diver" and A&E's *Don't Trust Andrew Mayne,* he is also a magician who started his first world tour as an illusionist when he was a teenager and went on to work behind the scenes for Penn & Teller, David Blaine, and David Copperfield. Ranked as the fifth-bestselling independent author of the year by Amazon UK, he currently works with OpenAI on applied artificial intelligence. For more on him and his work, visit www.andrewmayne.com.